DO NOT REMOVE
CARDS FROM POCKET

THE SEA SCAPE

By the same author

Ann of Cambray
Gifts of the Queen
Hawks of Sedgemont
The Diary of Isobelle
Tregaran
The Legacy of Tregaran
Command of the King

THE
SEA SCAPE

Mary Lide

St. Martin's Press

New York

Library of Congress Cataloging-in-Publication Data
Lide, Mary.
    The sea scape / Mary Lide.
        p.   cm.
    ISBN 0-312-07799-8
    I. Title.
PR6062.I32S43   1992
823'.914—dc20   92-7070
                                                               CIP

Allen County Public Library
Ft. Wayne, Indiana

First published in Great Britain as *The Homecoming* by HarperCollins Publishers.

First U.S. Edition: August 1992
10 9 8 7 6 5 4 3 2 1

THE SEA SCAPE

CHAPTER 1

My first memory is of rain and storm, perhaps fittingly so since they were to become symbolic of my life. The year was 1886; I must have been all of four years old, old enough to look over the kitchen half-door, old enough to remember how the door suddenly swung to and fro on its rusty hasp as if the wind had slammed at it. Old enough to remember the contrast: one moment sunlight patched on the whitewashed wall, the next darkness, noise, violence. I don't ever recall rain like that before although in normal times where I lived we were drowned in it; the moor was bogged with it, walls and roofs and people mildewed with it. But perhaps that summer had been especially dry. They say at the end of the last century the west of England underwent a climate change, and on Bodmin Moor there was a drought, withering even the marsh grass brown and driving vipers out, looking for damp.

I pushed the door open and hung over it, watching the rain waterfall off the barn roof. The stable yard was awash, dust and straw and muck frothing in waves. Overhead the sky spread black; great clouds raced past, curled white, and the moors beyond were shrouded in mist. After the heat of the kitchen the coldness hit sudden as spray and the crack of lightning was like Farmer Penwith's riding whip.

Somehow I was standing outside, bare toes firmly planted

5

in the ooze, head thrown back, water sluicing over it, hair plastered to my skull, eyes blind. I laughed. When the wind tossed the elm trees by the gate I shook myself to imitate them. When the thunder rolled, I stamped my feet; when the rains beat I opened my mouth to drink them in. And laughed again.

Then my Mam was after me, fingers pinching my underarm as she struggled against the wind. It snatched at her hessian pinafore, snagged her skirts on the broken fence. 'What be you thinking of, Guinevere Ellis?' she cried. 'Just look at you.' She thrust me back, slammed the door shut again, her face puckered up into a frown. 'And look at my clean floor when I've but now finished a-washing it.'

She pointed at my feet where the mud was running in brown streaks. 'What am I to make of you? Great girt gel, and never thinks on all the extra work. Should have left you behind, and there's a fact.'

My Mam's name was Gladys Ellis. She was short and plump, round like a hen, always on the go, darting henlike from one thing to the next on small neat feet with her neck stretched out. Her hair, which was glossy black and rolled in a bun, had come loose and ruffled round her face feather-like, and her small black eyes snapped. Two red spots flared on either cheek, a sign that she was angry or upset, and she pursed her mouth down like she did when the milk turned sour. I was small and slight and fair, not like her in appearance at all, and now I looked like a drowned rat.

She took a broom and began to swish fresh water where I stood. 'Baking day too,' she said, as if talking to herself. 'And any moment now Farmer Penwith wanting of his tea. And him letting you stay on because I begged 'un to, tho' by rights he could refuse, no place here fer a child he said. Then where we'd be, I'd like to know? In the poor house most like, all thanks to you.'

She swished again. The bristles were rough and left red marks along my skin, but I wouldn't cry. I remained motionless as she had taught me to, no word of complaint, lips

6

pursed like her own. But I do remember thinking, even then, that the anger wasn't fair, if that's the word, was too strong, as if it wasn't directed at me at all but since I was there I had to take the brunt, as if whatever fault there was, without meaning to, I was the cause.

She seized my hand and jerked me closer to the fire. The too-large dress went over my head, splattering wet upon the coals. They hissed like a cat and the heat rushed out. 'And how get them clothes clean and dry afore Evensong,' she cried, less angry now, just venting words. 'You've ruined 'em. Watch out, my gel. God'll punish you fer wickedness.'

I cowered in buttoned-up liberty bodice and grey under-drawers, my hair drying in gold spikes, sure the fire was hotter than Farmer Penwith's fires of hell, sure she meant to thrust me in.

'Mend yer manners,' she cried at me then, 'you'm nothing but encumbrance.'

That was the summer when I found out what 'storm' was. And what I was, an encumbrance.

My Mam and I lived on Penwith Farm far away from anywhere. She was the maid of all work. The farm was an old place, set athwart a valley off Bodmin Moor, sagging into ruin, although once it must have been prosperous. The lower fields had been hedged with stone and wind breaks planted of fir and ash. Now mostly it had reverted to furze and peat like the moors which stretched it seemed for ever to the east of it. My Mam was busy morning to night with a variety of chores, from feeding hens and geese to baking and cleaning. I never knew how she did it all. And I never knew how we came there or where we had come from and my Mam wouldn't speak of that.

When I grew older and tried to ask she'd cut me short.

'Curiosity kills the cat,' she'd snap. 'Let the past lie. 'Tain't worth the trouble of digging up.' But sometimes at night, I'd wake up in the room we shared and watch her when she thought I slept. She'd bend down under the bed and drag out an old tin box. It was battered and worn but she kept it locked with a key she hung round the bedpost. She'd kneel there, half hidden by the headboard, the candle casting monstrous shadows. There would be the sound of clicks, of rustling papers, of money clinking.

'Let the past lie,' she'd repeat after a while with a heavy sigh, and twist the key viciously in the lock. "Twon't change none.' She'd take up a brush and begin to tug vigorously at her hair until it crackled. 'Fine old family, the Penwiths, even if they'm come down in the world. And Penwith Farm be a fine old place all right, nothing wrong with ut. Good Delabole slate roof, that cost a pretty penny and a second parlour tho' he don't use it none. And walls of granite. They say them stones was taken from under Hawstead Tor; his father dragged 'em here in oxen carts. Part of them old heathen circles up there, I'll be bound, he'm mean enough to take anything fer free even if 'twere Devil-cursed.'

The 'he' she meant was Farmer Penwith. She'd muse a while then as if remembering; as if contrasting something, the meanness of her employer perhaps, with someone else. I never dared ask who. Then she'd sigh again. 'Only needs a woman's touch,' she'd say, pointing with the handle of her brush at the flaking paint, the stained walls where the rain blew in, 'and I could give it 'un.'

Farmer Penwith was a widower, too young to want to live alone, too old to be caught easily, although my Mam had her eye on him. He was a strange man, religious in his fashion although of what denomination I never could make out, one Sunday Methodist, the next Church of England. Twice a week he conducted Evensong at home, which we attended meekly, every Wednesday and Friday night, while I tried not to squirm and he read long passages from the Bible. I don't know if it was in his nature to be mean, or if poverty and disappointment had forced it on him, but he seldom spoke, worked his land in a disorganized sort of way as if failure were built into it, and issued orders off-handedly, expecting to be disobeyed.

'Coat's got a rip in ut,' he'd say, with a strange sidelong

8

look, his blue eyes curdling white like a nervous horse, or 'Hens bain't laying right.'

That look used to frighten me but my Mam knew how to deal with it. She'd stand at the table kneading bread, or rolling out the pastry crust. 'Best pasty maker this side of Bodmin,' she'd say, 'that's my work. But I'll do the mending, or egg collecting, if you wants, although it should cost extra.' And when after a while he'd slink out, protectively, as if I had protested, ''Neath the dirt he bain't so bad, even tho' he don't say much. I prefer a quiet man meself, better than a blabber mouth. And wedded to the land, that's fer sure, no traipsing off to sea fer the likes of him.'

She would cross her arms as if hugging herself. 'Visions of grandeur,' she said, 'that's his fault; hunting all day on his horse with lords and such, as he did once. Or so he boasts. Can't seem to get the knack of tilling fields, thinks it's beneath him. Take yesterday. He should've bought that load of sand, from up Padstow way too and cheap. I told 'un 'twas good fer sour soil, turns it sweet I said. But no, he wouldn't listen. Can't spare the cash, he says. Could've if he wanted to, but there, that's his business. Gets what he can out of us instead, we'm his right hand, he says. Right hands do all the work, get none of the thanks, I says. We'm bargain price, that's why he keeps us on.'

The laugh she'd give was bitter. ''Twas his first wife that ruined him. Best thing in his life when she died. Second best when he hired me.'

She'd slap the dough against a wooden slab as if she were pounding flesh. The two red spots glowed. ''Cept he'm that slow he don't know it yet. 'Bout time he did.'

The day he did find out was the day I learned a second thing about myself.

I must have been more than thirteen then, growing into young girlhood. I had spent the afternoon swinging on the barnyard gate waiting for the herds to go by, black bullocks lumbering along, dust-covered from the trek up from the lowland farms. Since most of his land was moor, in summer

Farmer Penwith let the grazing rights to other farmers. From May until autumn cattle and sheep roamed wild, peppering the landscape black and white, their presence somehow comforting. Farmer Penwith himself worked his own valley fields with casual help, a man or two at harvest time, a lad from the local orphanage for the sheep. That year he had hired a boy called Cy, a foundling from up near Blisland. His real name was Cyril, a posh name for an orphan. And he was a hopeless sort of lad, 'gormless', my Mam called him, none too bright in the head and awkward. But he was strong and broad, and worked hard, although it was a mystery how he got to be so big after years of being underfed. I suppose he could have been called handsome with his fresh complexion and great round eyes. To me they always looked perpetually surprised as if startled by what fate had done to him. At this time he was about eighteen, just beginning to grow a beard, and albeit slow was quick to jump when my Mam asked him. In fact she used to smile and say he had a liking for her, an idea new to me, and perhaps surprising to him. But I had noticed he would willingly do things for her, whatever she asked, and almost imperceptively I suppose she had come to depend on him.

Now I found her sitting on the kitchen steps, her cheeks flushed. It was washing day. Damp clothes flapped upon a line and linen was drying on the furze bushes. She was wearing her usual grey skirt with the hessian apron tied in a knot in front and she was laughing. I had never heard her laugh like that before, openly I mean, without restraint, and as I approached she put her fingers to her lips, her shoulders shaking.

Further down the yard, Cyril was slowly inching round the dung heaps. At first I couldn't make out what he was doing. He was bunched up as if he were carrying something, then he would stop and bob and bounce in one spot as if afraid to move, before cautiously venturing on again. It was only gradually that I realized he was holding, or trying to hold, a goose. He had it gripped under his arm, its feet held down in one hand, its neck in the other. The front of the goose bulged like a pillow, rigid with offence, and every so often its beak would snake out and peck him hard, making him yelp.

'Bless the boy,' my Mam said. She wiped the tears from her eyes. ''Twill be the death of 'un. Asked 'un to drive the geese down to the stream and blamed if he ain't trying to carry 'em.'

She got up in her quick way, as if on springs, as if even sitting still for a moment was too slow for her. She ran down the path and caught at Cyril's arm. Her head came barely to his shoulder, and when he twisted his to gaze down at her, his perplexed expression looked so gooselike she laughed again. 'Come on now, Cy,' I heard her say, ''tain't the end of the world. Let's get them old geese caught some easier way.'

She forced his arm loose. He bent stiffly and set the bird on the ground so she could wave her apron at it. 'Shoo,' she said, and as the goose began to waddle off, 'there, Cy, 'tis easy when you've got the knack.'

She smiled at him, untied the apron and gave it him to flap, but he stood there gawking at her, open-mouthed. Her hair had come unpinned and was tumbling down her back, her skirts were blowing. I thought with a queer feeling in my heart, 'My Mam, why she's beautiful.' And then, 'She's young.'

There was a click behind my back, the latch of the gate on which I had been swinging. I didn't turn round but I knew Farmer Penwith had come through and was staring at my mother just as Cy was doing. He didn't say a word then, while Cy and my mother alternately shooed and flapped at the geese, even Cy beginning to laugh and tugging at the apron strings, but later that night when we were sitting at our tea he suddenly shoved his plate aside with his food half-eaten. He wiped his mouth with the back of his hand and ran a finger inside his collarless shirt where the sweat glistened. His black hair, which curled in patches where it was cut crooked, stood on end like a brush. 'Pack yer things,' he told Cy, 'by first light 'ee'm off my land.'

Cyril never said a word. He was sitting in his usual place, tucked back behind the grandfather clock where he couldn't be seen, eating fast so Farmer Penwith wouldn't notice. He stopped chewing, a crust hanging halfway out of his mouth, so like a cow with a wisp of grass that it set me laughing.

'Bain't no joke.' Farmer Penwith's gaze swivelled to me, his pale eyes bulging. I slid down in my seat but my Mam was ready for him. She had been standing to cut the bread, holding the loaf close to her chest and cutting inward to hide the thickness of the slices. Now she put the bread down and stuck the knife in it. 'No call fer that,' she said. 'Because Cy did me a favour no point in taking meanness out on 'un. He ain't done harm.'

'Nor won't.' Farmer Penwith pulled his plate towards him and began to scoop up the gravy fast, using his knife. 'Nor won't,' he repeated, 'didn't hire 'un to do woman's work.'

'And what work's that?' she countered. 'More like the whole of it. But we'll let that pass. If he goes who's to help with the barley mow, or the tatty crop or the summer stock? You'll not find anyone else this late. And 'tis little enough you pays as 'tis.'

Farmer Penwith reared up at that, his neck stiff. He began to splutter, his mouth opening and closing without making sense. My Mam went back to slicing bread while we waited for him to catch his breath. Or rather my Mam and I did; Cyril was already stuffing himself as if convinced this was his last meal on earth and he should make the most of it.

With an effort Farmer Penwith controlled himself. 'Don't need any half-witted chap swaggering on my farm,' he shouted, his voice changing, becoming more 'posh'. 'Nor woman interfering.' He jabbed with his fork. 'Leave him be,' he said. 'Make your choice, or I don't answer for the consequences.'

'Cy's more than a lad,' she retorted, matching him, giving

12

as good as she got. 'He'm growing to be a man, if you've noticed. All he needs is a bit of common sense. A woman behind 'un'd give 'un that, and good luck to both.'

Her expression was bland. 'As fer me,' she said, 'you knows my worth. Halve my work and double my wages first if you wants fer me to stop.'

Her head suddenly poked forward in its birdlike way; she seemed to fluff out all her feathers. 'So do you choose,' she said. 'Else when Cy leaves I leave with 'un.'

Even Cy sat up at that, and gawked some more. His startled expression grew almost frightened. I might have laughed at him myself but I was also frightened. My Mam paid us no heed. Her mouth had tightened, a sign that she was serious, and she stared at Farmer Penwith as if throwing him a challenge.

Farmer Penwith became flustered. He picked up his knife and pretended to scrape crumbs with the blade, arranging them in lines. He looked at Cy, looked at my Mam, looked at me, torn with indecision. Then he swallowed hard, the Adam's apple in his thin neck protruding.

'If he goes and you'll bide,' he said, reverting back to his Cornish voice, 'I'll give *she* half of what he gets.' Again the gesture with his fork. 'Time yer daughter did a good day's work,' he hurried on, 'she'm old enough to earn her keep. Years of eating me out of house and home, time she paid me back.' And as if to cut short any argument, 'Bed and board and a tanner a day, that's my best offer.'

My heart began to pound in my chest as if the air had rushed out. My first thought was, he can't mean that. He's only speaking rough to pay me out for laughing. The second, he hasn't reckoned with my Mam. But my Mam said nothing. With a sinking feeling I recognized her expression. She had that same look when she jingled money in her box.

'Start tomorrow morn,' Farmer Penwith went on, hurrying now as if having decided he wanted to have it settled, yet speaking in an off-hand way as if the offer was not new but was part of an on-going conversation. 'In the east side field, clear out the spar, there's a job worth doing.'

Spar was white quartz with which the moorland fields were riddled. It had to be raked off, picked out by hand to be used for packing hedges. I'd seen other children bent double in the dirt, collecting the stones, and pitied them. Perhaps, I still thought, Farmer Penwith is joking.

But Farmer Penwith never joked. "Twill do she good,' he said, still looking at me sidelong. 'She'm sharp as a tack as 'tis, sharper than that big oaf by a long chalk.' A last jerk of the fork, a contemptuous glance at Cy as if to say, 'What do 'ee see in him?'

Cyril had gone back to looking blank as if he didn't understand, as if what was being said had no bearing on him, as if it wasn't his future they were discussing. Or mine. My Mam sat down abruptly. 'Almost end of term,' she said to me, talking fast as she did when she was thinking aloud, 'and you've already missed more school than not. In a week or two you'll be out, running wild all summer long.' And then, more sharply, 'Sit up, don't slouch. You be strong as an ox. When all's said and done, better have a job and stick to it than laze about. If he makes it worth yer while.'

She turned back to Farmer Penwith. 'There've been other work afore,' she said. 'What about the gleaning of the harvest fields last year? She never earned a penny fer that. Naught neither for all t'other things, sloe and bramble picking and such, why, Mister, 'tis you what owes her plenty.'

She spread her hands out on the table. 'If I agree,' she said, and now her voice was bland again, 'and 'tain't certain, mind, five shillings flat, all found fer she. And I stay on as housekeeper.'

She was looking at Farmer Penwith, a strange smile on her face. It was a smile I had not seen before, although I have since, the triumphant smile a woman gives when she holds the upper hand. Then it made me shiver. For as well as challenge there was allure, the playing of one thing off against the next, the playing of one man against a rival. I felt cold. Suddenly the table top had taken on a new dimension, had become a battle ground having nothing to do with Cy or me. 'It isn't us my Mam's fighting for,' I thought. 'It's something of her own she wants and she's using us to get it. I'm as expendable as Cyril is.' And that was the second thing I learnt.

Farmer Penwith seemed to collapse into himself like a burst bladder. 'Have it yer own way then,' he said in a sulky voice. 'When he leaves I hire she at whatever price you sets. And you gets what you wants. Can't say fairer than that, tho' you drives a hard bargain.'

At that my Mam's shoulders slackened. The hand that pushed back her hair was trembling. 'Come now, John,' she said, the first time she'd ever called him by his given name, 'we ain't proud. 'Tis still dirt cheap. But do you see it from my side. A woman's got to stand up fer herself in this cruel world, no one else to do it otherwise. I promise you one thing, tho', you won't regret it.' And she flashed him a smile of such open brilliance he was momentarily dazzled.

I was too. If it had been any other time or circumstance I might have been proud of her. And afterwards I could understand what a risk she took, for herself I mean, bartering her own hopes. Then, I was heartbroken. I didn't wait to see the end, I already knew the conclusion. Pushing back my chair I ran from the room. It was not even that I minded leaving school so much, the truth was I'd never liked it although I'd have liked the learning part if I could have been free to concentrate. Nor did I object to farm work as such. But only on the poorest farms among the poorest sort did girls work in the fields like men. I suppose if I'd been asked I'd have admitted I'd never really thought of doing anything else, and certainly not so soon. But being traded for, bought off, for some other purpose, that was what I resented. And so I thought Cy should have done had he had any sense. But my Mam was playing for high stakes this time, and it seemed she'd won.

Next morning Cyril was packed and gone before day-break. I never saw him again. At first I wondered about him, if he had grasped at all what my Mam had done to him, but soon there was no time for thinking. I too was up at dawn, dressed in men's cut-down clothes, milking cows, swilling pigs, feeding hens, doing all the work my Mam had done. Then it was off in the fields with Farmer Penwith watching every move I made, digging peat, sorting stones, cutting furze, raking taties in the wet until I thought my spine would crack, all a farm hand's work as best I could, although for pride I would have dropped rather than show I couldn't.

I never found out how much I earned; my Mam took care of that. 'Savings,' she said. She put the money in her box along with her own wages. But she did get me a room of my own, above hers, under the eaves, with a quick way out down a bent drain pipe. 'You'm a woman now,' she said, as if that made up for loss of childhood. And if sometimes now, when her indoor chores were done, my Mam spread an oilcloth on the kitchen table, and sat in the second parlour in a new dress, sipping a glass of mulberry wine, the ruffles of new curtains spread about her feet; or in the night I heard voices in her room, and if sometimes, mid week, Farmer Penwith washed and changed his shirt, and afterwards at Evensong read about sin and the need of penitence, those too were things to ponder on.

That second parlour was a refinement, proof that once the Penwiths must have been rich. It was dominated by a photograph of that first wife, looking smug, in a satin dress and long black curls, but after my Mam took to sitting there, she disappeared. Normally the room was opened only twice a year, at Easter and Christmas time, when Farmer Penwith, dressed in his best, would take his supper there like a gentleman. He'd sit bolt upright in his black serge suit and white shirt and polished leather boots he was proud of, perched on a gilt chair with a velvet seat, hat on lap, as if in church. For a treat, my Mam used to serve him a plate of pink wafer biscuits, and pour his tea into a china cup, part of a service, thin and delicate, handpainted with pink roses, a far cry from the everyday pewter mugs. When not in use the room was dark. Light slanted in lines through the faded curtains where they were worn in holes. Everything smelt of damp. My Mam polished the furniture with beeswax once a week, and this mixture of mould and wax was like a chapel smell, cold, yet familiar. When my Mam was out and I was sure Farmer Penwith was still busy in the fields or barn, I got into the habit of going in that room. I used to steal inside, close the door, and sit there in the dark, pretending.

I'm not sure what I pretended, and I can't explain why I felt the need, or what I accomplished. Perhaps it was getting my own back at my Mam; perhaps it was nature's way of protest, perhaps an unspoken cry for help. Or perhaps like Farmer Penwith I felt the need to find some link with finer things over and above the grinding round of a life I had come to hate. And perhaps like him I would have sunk into bitter acceptance had not I found some unexpected pleasure there, that gave me reason for existence. (And, incidentally, was the cause of my learning a third thing about myself, which changed my life. Although it was not altogether true as later I was to discover.)

I must first explain that against the fireplace was a cabinet where the china service sat. The lower shelves were lined with books, most of them dry texts dealing with farming. One day, I must have been almost sixteen then, I unlocked the glass door and idly took out a different volume. I felt I had unlocked a door to paradise.

The book was heavy, leather-bound, its pages yellowing too with damp, but I still remember the feeling of excitement. There were black line pictures in that book, drawings of strange far off things. Ships sailed off under impossible skies, vast palmy harbours waited to hold them. Huge beasts with smoking jaws and stretched-out talons advanced out of the pages, a man in a fur cap strode on a lonely beach. As for

17

the story: the printing was curved and small, the lettering old-fashioned and funny, but by sounding out the words aloud I grasped their meaning. In this way I learned to read as I had not learned at school. And by transference to write, although I never learned to speak. I mean I knew what the words meant, but not how to pronounce them. In any event, each book became for me the life I lacked, brought new adventure, gave me something to look forward to, gave new dimension to this parched and sterile world I lived in.

I learned to remove a volume in such a way that it left no gap, afterwards secreting it under the mattress of my bed so I could read late into the night by candlelight, waiting all day for that evening pleasure. And so I continued with my second, secret life, my antidote to back-breaking labour, until one June evening Farmer Penwith returned too soon, and caught me at it.

I had grown careless I suppose, had not taken sufficient precaution and left the door ajar, something of that sort. He banged it open and stood there on the threshold, arms on either side of the frame. 'What be 'ee thinking of?' he shouted, just as my Mam had done.

I was kneeling by the cabinet and he startled me. I jumped up, dropping the book I had been choosing and knocking a cup from the shelf. He crossed the room in a bound, his boots leaving tracks of mud, glared at me before bending down to retrieve the cup.

'My grandmam's,' he said in that strange, hard voice I'd heard once before, quite unlike his usual one with its Cornish accent.

He turned the cup round and round, examining it for cracks, almost fondling it. 'Not a piece smashed in a hundred years,' he said. Then, angrily, 'So who told you to use her things, as if you were the mistress of my house? Who gave you leave to take my books, although I suppose you can't read 'em!'

Something about his scorn pricked my pride. 'I can,' I said. 'I taught myself. Better that than let 'em rot.'

18

He stood above me, looking sideways with his pale blue eyes. Then suddenly he seemed to change, his full lips curling at the edges as if he didn't want them to and yet couldn't stop. 'Don't 'ee look so fierce,' he said in a soothing kind of way, reverting back to normal. 'I won't harm 'ee none. And we won't let on to yer Mam that we found 'ee here. Or what 'ee've been doing.'

Again the grimace, not smile so much as leer. I didn't like it, nor the way he stretched out his hand to catch my arm and turn my face towards the light. There was no reason to be afraid, yet I was and I tried to push him off. 'Hold up,' he said. 'You'm filly skittish. No need fer 'ee to worry your pretty head. Pretty as a picture now you'm growed, with hair like gold. And look at them green eyes.

'Cat eyes,' he said. 'And I bet 'eem like a cat, all claws and purrs.'

Close to, his face was seamed with lines, an old man's face, but his hair was dark, not a speck of grey, and his chin was covered with black stubble. And the hand that held me was fine-wristed under the dirt, long, slender-fingered, horseman's hands, not a farmer's.

Then he gave a grunt, released his hold, stood back, lifting his feet as if aware of the mud he'd tracked in. 'What be I thinking,' he said. ''Tain't so. Ee'm nothing but a fatherless brat, and no fine airs will hide it. Sin is sin.'

And he bent down and hissed in my ear, 'A bastard brat. Remember that. Now git.'

I ran. And that was the third thing I learned about myself, although like the second it was hedged with other things equally disturbing.

I had another place I used for hiding, for all my Mam scolded. It was on Hawstead Tor, and there I went, still trembling with shock. I climbed up to the topmost rock, propped my head on my hands and gazed out, waiting for the pounding of my heart to stop, waiting for the dirt of his words to slough off.

From my vantage point the farmhouse was reduced to

insignificance; it crouched on the east side of the tor like a frightened leveret. Level with my gaze a lone buzzard soared, its mewing cry in sympathy; in front of me the moors extended in a great expanse of space, an openness without fixed horizon. I thought 'tain't so, or if 'tis, what do it matter who I am. The hurt remained and burned.

I have not spoken of those moors before, for at first I used to fear them. People since have said how beautiful they are; Julian once likened them to an ocean. For me as a child they had always seemed cold and grey and threatening, until I learned to know them and used them to retrieve a sense of balance within myself, a sense of harmony. From the time I began to work, I roamed them, spending all my free time there, such as I had. Wild as a fox, I crisscrossed every path and track about the tor, every bog and stream, although like a fox I never ventured beyond that landmark of stones, pricked out my own territory within a certain radius. And perhaps just as a fox is doomed to risk when he ventures from his wilderness so I too was marked for harm when I in turn left my own environment.

This particular evening, the sky was so clear I could almost make out the whole of the Cornish peninsula. Further east, the higher peaks of Brown Willy and Roughtor formed a natural barricade, a great wall of stone, bleak and uncompromising. To the west the mist grey of furze and grass blended into granite hills that stretched like a backbone, narrowing towards Land's End. Southwards, dips in those hills marked the start of the valleys, or combes as they were called, fertile little gullies where villages huddled on the sunny slopes out of the wind. But it was northwards that my interest was most caught, northwards where the sweep of open land rose to a crown, and then plunged down towards the Bristol Channel.

That evening, the coast seemed so close I could almost smell the salt, hear the slush of the waves. The shadow of the cliffs was perceptible and the blue glint of the sea, caught between, was like the glint of an eye beneath half-closed lids, an elusive blue thread glittering in the westering sun. That glimpse of sea had always fascinated me. Often I'd asked my Mam about that coast, had she been there, what was it like, but she'd always shuddered. 'Ugly as sin,' she'd said, 'wet and cold. What do you want to know that stuff fer? Sea bain't meant fer men, it be meant fer fishes.' And when I questioned further, how did she know unless she'd seen it herself, 'Hold yer tongue,' she'd said, 'you'm too curious fer yer own good.'

Now that sense of curiosity washed over me, the sort of excitement I'd felt when I'd looked at Farmer Penwith's books. If I were a bastard who was my father? Was he the one who'd 'traipsed' off to sea, the one my Mam sighed over? Was that why she'd left him? Or had he left her and me? Where was he now? One day, I thought, when I'm grown, I'll go and find him for myself. I'll go to that sea and take a boat like in those story books and watch its great sails spread. I'll travel through the world to where he is, and stand before him. 'Here I am,' I'll tell him. The wind that always blows upon the moors whistled round me in melancholy yearning.

I was so lost in dreaming that I never noticed what was happening there before me until a cry brought reality back with a jerk. And so ended dreaming.

CHAPTER 2

𝒥 leaned over my perch. From where I sat or rather lay, the granite face was sheer, a drop of perhaps a hundred feet to an open scree. Below this, under a straggle of lower rocks, a grey horse was cropping grass. Its saddle, a lady's saddle, had slipped askew; foam covered its sides and as it moved it tossed its head nervously, the reins dangling. It was not a horse I recognized, belonged to no one that I knew, too fine a creature to have come from one of our few neighbours. I had the queerest notion it had been conjured up, one moment here, one moment gone, as like to vanish again as not, when I heard a second cry.

Forgetting my own troubles, I scrambled down, sliding on the scree, my ill-fitting boots slipping upon the rocks, their hob-nails sparking, to find the horse's owner sitting up and looking about her.

She was young, not much older than I was, her green skirt spread around her like bright bog grass, her green feathered bonnet dangling. Beneath the tangle of brown curled hair her eyes flashed, dark blue, hawk eyes with the pupil outlined. I had never seen anyone so exquisite. Or so angry. She would have stamped her foot if she hadn't taken off her boot so that I could see the swollen ankle.

'Where've you come from?' she cried, her voice high and imperious. 'Well, since you're here, don't stand and stare, go bring me back my horse. And quick about it.'

22

I had never heard anyone speak like that either, not even Farmer Penwith, with the sort of loudness people use to impress others with their importance.

I ignored the tone, went to the base of the tor where small springs seep from the granite, tore off a corner of my shirt and brought it dripping to her. As wordlessly she took it and began to wrap it round her foot, wincing a little at its gritty coldness. Never a word of thanks she said, but I didn't expect any.

Only then did I turn my attention to the horse. By this time I had learned enough about horses to harness them, but this creature was a far cry from Farmer Penwith's old 'goonhilly', or moorland pony; this was a gentleman's mount, full of fire, tall and spritely. Each time I tried to approach, it would snort and turn, and when I made a grab for the bridle, it reared, thrashing with its forelegs.

Its rider watched me with a malicious smile. 'I thought farm maids knew all about horses,' she said. 'You're frightening it. Tie back your hair, it's blowing so: here, use this string. And tuck in your shirt so the ends don't flap.'

I had forgotten how dishevelled I must look, and blushed at the reminder. I took the string which she broke off from her riding hat, bound my hair up, tied the ends of the too-big shirt into a knot and tightened the cord that held the breeches. Either she was right or the horse became used to me; at the next attempt I succeeded in catching hold of the reins although it tried to shake me off, grinding its head in the ground and then throwing it up in the air. I held on for dear life, frightened now myself if I let go it would toss me like chaff. And gradually, coaxing it, eventually venturing out a hand to stroke, I brought it up short enough so it was under control. It was a beautiful beast, its grey coat gleaming under the mud and foam, its great dark eyes full of wary intelligence. 'Woa, there, old lad,' I said, talking to it as I did Farmer Penwith's pony, 'you'm in some pickle. But we need yer help.'

Close to, it was bigger than I thought, its shadow looming

large, and the efforts to hold it had made me out of breath. But again the rider showed no gratitude, and without warning raised her whip and brought the lash down hard on the animal's flanks. 'There,' she said, panting a little herself, 'that'll teach it a lesson.'

The horse whinnied in protest, reared back, once more lashing with its forefeet and jerking me off balance. But I stubbornly held on. She watched while a second time I quietened it, then beckoning to me to bring it close, again raised her whip. 'No,' I heard myself say, angry now in turn. 'Bain't right to hit a creature fer what's not its fault. Why did you ride him into a lather? This part of the moor's bog-riddled. And who ever saddled him to gall his back, he'm cut to bits.' And turning to the horse, devoting all my attention to it, I began to struggle with the buckles to free the girth.

''Tisn't customed to a woman's saddle, there's a fact,' I told her bluntly when I'd finished. ''Tisn't customed to women. To my mind, 'tis a man's horse, used to men. So who do he belong to?'

'Mind your own business,' she snapped, then added pettishly, 'Probably it thinks you're a stable boy yourself, you look and smell like one.'

She sat back, stretched her foot gingerly, began to draw on her boot. Then, as if the thought had just entered her mind, 'How'm I to get home? If you're so clever tell me that. I can't walk and I'm afraid to ride. Suppose it runs away with me again.'

Her voice trembled, broke. Her eyes filled with moisture which beaded on the lashes. 'There'll be such trouble if I'm late.' She began to sob, a faint, pathetic noise almost like that buzzard's mew, meanwhile peeping at me when she thought I wasn't looking. 'I'm not allowed to go on the moors alone.'

A good thing too, I thought. I busied myself with removing the saddle before I bothered to reply, then responded to her unasked question with one of my own. 'Where's home?'

I said abruptly, straightening up, 'How far away? And if it bain't allowed why did you come here in the first place?'

'I didn't mean to,' she countered eagerly. 'Alright, I admit the horse's not mine. I only borrowed him. How was I to know he'd be so fresh I couldn't handle him? Miracle I stayed on so long, miracle I didn't break my neck.' She frowned at that, then smiled, cheering up at this next thought. 'So you'll have to lead him. It's not far, look.'

A third time she raised her whip and pointed northwards, north towards that line of blue where my thoughts had recently been centred. She didn't know it, but she had just given me the excuse that I'd wanted, an opportunity that otherwise I'd not have known.

Her 'You'll have to lead him' was a statement, not a query. I didn't like being ordered. And I knew she was not telling all the truth so perhaps she lied about the distance. I hesitated. She noticed it. 'I'll pay you well,' she went on, coaxing now, 'look, a whole sovereign.'

She reached into her pocket, brought out a purse, opened it. The round gold coin gleamed beckoningly in the bright evening sun. I'd never seen so much money at one time and the temptation was great. 'My father's Sir Robert Polleven,' she added, stressing the title, 'and I'm Miss Ruth Polleven,' as if repetition of the name were itself an inducement. 'And you know where I live, I'm sure, Polleven Manor.'

She spoke proud as a peacock: with an arrogant toss of her head. I had no idea who Sir Robert was or where Polleven Manor, had never heard of either, but the sun was still high in the sky, one of those June evenings when day seems never to end. I had nothing else to do. I also admit the thought of that sovereign was tempting, even if her home was on the other side of Bodmin. And to go northwards seemed like a God-given opportunity. So when I had helped her on, cupping my hands for her to mount, we started forward, I walking by the horse's side, reins still tightly grasped. She rode bareback, astride, her green skirt spread for the mud to dry, her bad foot dangling. At times she bumped unsteadily for the track was rough, but she was a good enough rider to hang on and the horse went easier once the saddle had been removed. ('Just hide it under the gorse,' she'd said, with a careless shrug. 'It'll be safe enough; I'll send a groom for it later.')

She spoke more reasonably now. For once she had gained her way Miss Ruth Polleven talked in an animated fashion, new to me, and although I understood only one word in ten, her flashing smile, her shining hair, even the green glossiness of her velvet skirt were all meant to charm. She reminded me of some precious doll, set apart to be admired. *Curiosity kills the cat.* I knew instinctively that she was fickle, unreliable as a moorland bog; like my mother, capable of treachery. Yet I was fascinated, the difference between our lot in life, the contrast in looks, dress, behaviour like a goad to my previous unhappiness.

Once we were fairly clear of Hawstead Tor – not easy, she had come in on the western side, the dangerous side, where the bogs are deep enough to swallow horse and rider – we turned north. She pointed out the direction, I found the track; between us we made good time, I silent by her side while she chatted. We might have been old friends for before we had come down off the moors I had heard all about Polleven Manor – a manor, not a farm, she was particular about that, her father was a gentleman not a farmer. And the house was old, the original building was Saxon, dating back before the Norman conquest – she'd looked at me curiously when she said that as if not certain I'd know the difference. 'Just like Penwith Farm,' I thought, not without a touch of irony but I kept that to myself.

I heard too about her family: father, mother, older brother, all dotingly fond of her, about her plans now she had left school, about her friends, the parties that were planned for her homecoming – if she had any idea what work a farm boy did, of the comparison between my world and hers, she showed no sign of it, but I admit I did. And I admit too, to a touch of – envy, perhaps, that she should have so much and I so little.

We had already come a fair distance off the moor, along a narrow tree-lined lane when I heard a church bell chime. The high stone hedges on either side boxed us in so the tower was hidden, but the sound was clear. 'Almost there,' Miss Ruth Polleven said happily. She dug her heels into the horse's side, making him dance nervously. 'I'll be on time.'

I hesitated, calculating. From the length of the shadows between the trees, from the gradual lowering of the sun I could tell the long summer day was almost done. Soon twilight would be upon us. I had had no idea how far the 'north' was and there would be no time to go on to the coast. As it was, before I got back to Hawstead Tor night would have come, and our farm was a fair stretch down from that. Nor had I taken careful note of the last part of our route, and dreaded finding the way back in the dark. Besides, I was growing tired. We had come several miles by now, easy for her, riding. But she never thought of that, simply beckoned to me to continue.

The lane sloped down steeply, widening out behind the church which was set in from the road. We had obviously followed a back way for between us and the village proper was a stretch of fenced land, part of the church grave-yard into which we passed through a wide wicker gate. The graveyard was edged with yews that filtered out the luminous light into long pale shadows. In places the grass was long, wet with dew that was already beginning to fall, but around the old headstones there was the sweet smell of fresh-cut hay and wild mint, intensified by that dampness. White moths fluttered around the stones; in the slanting light their wings shone iridescent. We moved softly here, the horse's grey sides gleaming, its tail brushing against the lichen-covered monuments which leaned haphazardly. One of them caught my eye, a marble of strange oval shape, the date perhaps some half-century earlier, names from some shipwreck, strange to find so far inland.

'That's my family's, too,' she said, noticing I'd paused to look. 'The ship belonged to the Pollevens. My grandfather alone was saved, he put up the monument to the poor drowned sailors.'

She smiled at this proof of her family's worth or, perhaps, at my ignorance. 'There's a bridge,' she now said, pointing with her whip beyond the church, 'up to it, the river's tidal. Once ships came up this far. The real sea's down yonder another mile or so, at St Marvell.'

And once more she stretched with her whip towards some distant point, further on where the line of blue had always beckoned. For the second time that day I felt what I had only sensed before, the real presence of that sea, a living, moving force, reaching out, surrounding us, even here in the heart of the country.

We had come to the village now; on our right the main part of the church was outlined against the sky, golden bright, as if on fire. On our left the village street ambled past a line of thatched cottages, all shut up for the night, doors and windows closed. Facing us, on either side of a wrought-iron gate, high walls ran obliquely into the distance, a wall such as surrounds some great estate, made of brick, not of stone, built by 'foreigners'. And there, on top of the gate pillars, two creatures, granite-carved, kept guard, their claws raised in medieval menace.

'They're the Polleven dragons,' Miss Ruth boasted. 'Said to protect us. That's our motto do you see, no one does us harm if the Polleven dragons keep watch.' And for a moment she too sounded menacing herself.

It was very quiet, no sound except the cawing of rooks about the tower. We crossed the open road without being seen and came to the gate. It was locked, but on the other side an overgrown drive led away between high bushes. 'Reach for the key,' she said. 'There, on that stone ledge. Now use it.'

She waited, letting the horse crop grass, while I struggled with the lock which was rusty with disuse. When I had succeeded in opening it, she jerked up the horse's head, and passed through the gap. 'Good,' she said, not turning round, 'no one comes here much so I'm safe. Close it up and hide the key.'

And with that she disappeared down the drive at that same fast walk, again no word of thanks, no goodbye, no sovereign! Key in hand, I was left staring after her, to find my own way back as best I could.

I didn't think of the money first, although when I did, I was angry. What I did think of was the house, the size of it, the splendour that must be hidden behind such a wall, that must lie at the end of such a drive. And the welcome that awaited her. Picturing that welcome I was tempted. I wanted, just for a moment, to be part of it, to share, even vicariously, in her family warmth, to witness, from a distance, her homecoming, in short to know what it felt like to be a daughter, loved and wanted.

Curiosity again got the better of me. When I relocked the gate and put the key back in its place, I remained on the inside.

The sun was almost gone: it was still twilight, that long lingering dusk which makes England's summer the perfect cover. A moment's work and I had crossed the grassy drive and scrambled under the bushes, although I suspect I could have gone openly down the path, there seemed little chance of meeting anyone.

The bushes were more like trees, vast thickets of rhodo-dendrons. Their smell was very strong in that quiet place, as if their flowers had newly fallen and lay in layers underneath those thick branches. Strands of brambles tore at my skin. I was used to them but the nettle patches stung harder. In the distance I heard an animal's startled slither. Then the bushes ended abruptly, the drive petered out into an old cobbled stone yard. I parted the branches cautiously, came out of the shadows to find the house before me.

Standing as it did in the open it came as a shock after the closeness of the undergrowth, the last rays of the sun reflecting off the windows, a tall, noble building faced with Pentewan stone, again not the usual granite. Pentewan was a village on the south coast, miles away – think of the cost of such construction! The stones were known for their soft colours, apricot and cream and gold and the glow of sunset set them flaming. A long flight of steps ran up to where the front door stood open. Below the house, a winding drive, the main one, curled through a park-like enclosure dotted with trees where fat cattle grazed, brown and glossy, different from our stocky black breed. The park itself sloped gradually down towards the river, the same I supposed that she had pointed out. It curved here in a great smooth loop to enclose the park, edged with rushes where a small boat was moored. In normal times that boat alone would have held my attention, the first I'd ever seen, as would have the trees, the satin-smooth water, the slow, leisured pace of the current, like one of those pictures in Farmer Penwith's books. Now I had only eyes for the scene on the steps.

Miss Polleven was already sitting at the top, where a wide porch ran from the front door to the open windows. She was swinging her feet, her green skirt spread. If her ankle still pained her she showed no sign of it, and equally there was no sign of the horse. She was talking animatedly, twirling her green bonnet by its ribbons; from her gestures I imagined she was describing a placid ride through the park. Two older persons confronted her, or rather perhaps she confronted them, for she was doing the talking, they the listening.

The tall, grey-haired man to her right laughed and waved a deprecating hand. That must be her father, I thought, Sir Robert Polleven who 'dotes' on his daughter. And the lady in the soft blue dress who bent to kiss her cheek would be the mother, mild as milk. A servant came to the open door, bowed, said something, disappeared, summoning them to some meal I suppose, for which Miss Ruth now would not be late. She rose, they climbed the steps, all still laughing. That laughter haunted me. I thought, in a moment they'll be gone, inside out of sight. I'll never see any of them again, and she'll forget she ever saw me.

I suppose I was so intent I ventured out too far. Turning now to make my way back I faced a sheer dense thicket which hid the path I'd come along, the shiny green leaves intertwined like tentacles. Panicked, I began to force my way through when a hand reached out to grab my shoulder. 'What's the hurry?' a voice said. 'You've barely arrived.'

The voice was Ruth Polleven's, or rather the intonation was, a masculine version of it. But it had a ripple of something else which I did not recognize although in later days I did, a teasing quality, an amused acceptance of things different. Then it made me start round, defences up, as I've seen wild animals do when they're cornered.

The young man who was standing there must have recognized that too. He let go, backed slowly off, hands held out in mock submission. I was looking at an older, masculine version of Ruth Polleven, same hair, same dark blue eyes. Except in him the eyes were heavy-lidded, set further apart, and when he moved it was with that straight-backed stiffness that I came to know marks a military man. Oh God, I thought, beginning to panic again, it's the brother, the brother who also dotes on her. And here I am, like a thief spying out his land.

'Hold fast,' he was saying, eyeing me, his voice having that familiar sardonic tone. 'Perhaps you'd care to explain what you're doing.'

And when I didn't immediately reply, more brusquely, a command, 'What do you want? I've been watching you, you know, watching us, so don't try lies.'

His hand came out again, more forceful now, and grabbed my shirt. I have said like the boots it was too large and in my efforts to escape the buttons must have parted. Now as he gripped and I pulled the material slid away. Before I could gather the stuff close about my chest where the buds of nipples were beginning to form, I saw a look of surprise cross his face, surprise, and something else, which sent me further into panic. 'Let go,' I cried, "tisn't nothing wrong.' And as he continued to stare, 'Well then, only something that's mine.'

Of all the things I could have said that surely was the most stupid.

'Yours?' The grip hadn't slackened but the amusement was back in the voice. He held me pinned against the bushes like a fly. Or like a fish. Like one of the trout that dangled from his rods which I now noticed propped against the hedge where presumably he had just leaned them. And his clothes, now I had time to look at them, were the informal ones of a fisherman, open-necked shirt, Norfolk jacket, gaiters and boots. A young man, not much more than a boy himself, without a care in the world, bent on sport, oblivious of anyone else's feeling. A sovereign would mean nothing to him. Nor promises, nor hurt.

'What I'm owed.' I amended my statement, but still insisted. 'What she offered me.'

And remembering too late the 'trouble' she'd be in if she were found out, could have bit my tongue. *'Tis a man's horse.* I thought, it must be his. And then, irrelevantly, I wonder how much he'd mind if he knew she 'borrowed' it.

'What's yours,' he was repeating almost contemptuously, 'what you're owed. Come, that's a tall order. Is the "she" my sister by chance? How could she "owe" you anything?'

There was such contempt in the way he said 'you' it made me want to crawl. Yet I wouldn't.

'I don't lie,' I said, drawing myself up as tall as I could although I barely reached to his shoulder. "Twas a mistake. But let's forget I ever said it.'

'We could ask her.' He pounced on that word, quick as a whip. For a moment a flicker of a smile lit up his eyes, then they were hooded again. 'We could call her back. She's probably still within earshot.'

He was toying with me, I felt, not really meaning anything he said, certainly not listening to me, and certainly having no intention of involving his sister. For he never raised his voice, nor did he move out into the open, simply stood there like a piece of rock waiting to see what I'd do next. A young man enjoying an unexpected sport, baiting it, seeing how far it'd jump before it broke.

I broke first. 'Leave me be,' I cried, "tain't nothing to you. You're safe in your world, and I've naught. But it meant a lot to me . . .'

I began to stammer then, incoherent nothings, such as wanting to see the house, just wanting to look at it, wanting to get away from the moors for a time, things of that kind, all the while still trying to wriggle free, clasping the shirt front close, my hair flying loose from the bonnet strings.

I didn't know I had raised my voice but I must have done. His father's shout in reply startled us both.

'Is that one of those village brats?' Sir Robert was asking. He had come to the terrace end and was peering out. Some ray of light from an inside room caught his face, exaggerating the lines around mouth and nose, making him severe, harsh; the eyebrows met. Suddenly I could see why the daughter might be scared of him. 'They've become a bloody nuisance,' he said. 'Drag him out, let's look at him. What's the tale this time?'

'It's not a boy, sir,' the young man said. His tone changed, I thought, became deferential. Perhaps he was frightened of his father too. 'It's a girl. From the moors. And she's asking for my sister.'

'Suppose she think's Ruth a softer touch.' The father snorted. 'A load of rubbish. Up to no good, the lot of them. Looking for something to steal. Or in the family way, whining for help. Drive the beggar off.'

Ruth and her mother had also stopped, alerted I suppose by Sir Robert's shouts. Now they too turned round and approached, mother and daughter, arm in arm, the picture of domestic bliss. The mother was delicate, fragile, fair, like a piece of Penwith china. The daughter's darkness set her off, made her seem all the more fragile. And seeing her

33

close up with her husband and children, it became obvious who the children took after. Although Sir Robert's hair was silver all three had those same piercing eyes. How ever to explain what I was or what I thought – 'twould be impossible. I closed my lips together in a line, tightened my thin shoulderblades. Let Miss Ruth Polleven do the explaining instead. She owed me that at least.

'Who is it, Julian?' Miss Ruth asked, her voice at its highest. She leaned forward beside her father, gathering up her green skirt with one hand. 'Never seen the boy in my life,' she said, 'and if he says so, he's lying.'

She turned away with a shrug, again taking hold of her mother's arm. The two ladies moved on, heads close together. Yet for a moment I had glimpsed a flicker of feeling on the older lady's face, a hint of sympathy. The father meanwhile had smiled sarcastically, as if to say 'I told you so', the family smile that hid coldness and scorn. I thought, I could tell the truth, I could prove she lies, show them where the saddle is. But why should I, to make myself as petty as she is to claim a coin she's withheld out of spite. Let them think what they want to.

'There you are,' Sir Robert said. 'No use to coddle them. Given an inch they take a mile, slippery as eels. Go on, drive her off, I say. What are you waiting for?'

He had picked up a whip, Miss Ruth's I suppose, and was tapping it on the balustrade as if he'd like to use it. And for a moment his gaze fixed on his son as if he expected Julian Polleven to agree. Then abruptly he spun on his heel and strolled after his womenfolk. I thought, I've been beaten before for less, and braced myself.

Julian Polleven and I were left alone in the gathering dusk, I stubbornly unrepentant, he indecisive. For a moment I had the strongest feeling that he was actually disappointed, as if somehow he had been let down. Then he said, 'My father's bark is worse than his bite, he won't harm you. And I won't harm you either. Just tell the truth if you can for once. What brought you here? Was it something she said, did, offered

34

you? Something you wanted? What did you mean about the house? What did . . . ?'

His questions fell like rain to be shrugged off. I pursed my lips just like my Mam. He could ask until Kingdom Come, wild horses wouldn't drag an answer out. Let him think what he would, it was all the same to me.

After a while he turned his back, gathered up his fishing lines, and strode off towards the rear of the house and the stables, leaving me free to dive headfirst into the bushes, scraping myself and tearing my clothes. I did not care. All I wanted was to put distance between myself and that house, between myself and him. That look of disappointment, although not my fault, stayed with me stronger than any blow.

I made no attempt now at secrecy, but I don't remember much of my progress back to the road, how I unlocked the gate with shaking fingers and traversed the churchyard where dusk was gathering in pockets like mist. I do remember the bats that came swooping out in twos and threes from the church turrets. And I did pause once more by that oval monument, shaped to resemble a boat's stern, with its sad list of names. 'Drowned', it said. How came her grandfather to be spared; who among those drowned had risked life to save his, that in his pride he could pay for it with a marble headstone? 'What's the reason,' I thought, 'that them that have shall have more?' And almost rebelliously, 'I told the truth. And to be fair, out of decency like, I let him think I didn't. Why did she, who's got so much, have to lie to protect herself? And why was she believed?'

That was the thought that galled. But I knew the answer: because she is a rich man's daughter, that's why, because it pays to believe her. Because she has a father, mother, brother who care for her, whose world revolves around her presence. I had long known life was not fair to encumbrances, that bastard brats have no recourse. For the first time ever the meaning struck home in the starkest terms, that even in such a small event as this, I was expendable.

Feeling sorry for oneself is no excuse. Wearily I got to my feet which by now were sorely blistered, retied the laces of my boots, prepared for the long hike back. That I would get a beating for sure when I returned was only one more misfortune. I let myself out of the wicker gate, set my pace resolutely forward, began the haul uphill.

'Not so fast,' a voice said from the hedge. There was a stir, a stamp of hooves. A dark shadow detached itself from a second larger one, with a great rustling. 'Now where are you off to?'

Julian Polleven was leaning against a gate post, his horse's bridle looped over one arm while the horse itself, a bay this time, stood patiently beside him. He looked as if he were prepared to wait all night, and I thought, almost inconsequentially, he must have gone straight to the stable, harnessed up, ridden fast to be here before me.

He didn't wait for an answer, came forward, his long legs easily keeping pace with mine, the horse trotting as easily behind with stirrup irons flapping. 'If it's home to the moors,' he said as if to himself, 'that's a fair distance. It seems to me if I'd walked once that far in a night, I'd not refuse a ride.'

I didn't say anything, went stubbornly on. 'Don't want no favours from you,' I told myself, 'don't want no favours from anyone. I'll manage by myself.'

'And if someone found out that I'd rescued his horse, why it would be only natural to expect some help in return.'

At my look: 'I know when a horse's been ridden,' he said, 'you can't hide saddle galls. Or whip marks.' And then, more softly, 'And I know when my sister's lying.

'Don't know why she does it,' he went on still in the same conversational way, 'just to bedevil us, I suppose. I've spent half my life covering for her lies.' He gave a shrug. 'Just because she wasn't born a boy,' he said, 'or wasn't born first, who knows. But that grey's a hard ride even for a man. Bought him to take with me when I leave with my regiment. She fell off, didn't she? And you led her home.'

36

I thought he was grinning in the semi-dark. 'Can't imagine how your skinny arms grabbed up the reins,' he said. 'If he tossed me off, by God, I'd leave well enough alone.'

'She hurt her foot,' I said.

'Ah,' he said. 'Well, that's one excuse. So now you've found your tongue, let's mount up.'

He swung himself up into the saddle, held out his hand. 'It would be a privilege, Miss,' he said, 'to return a kindness.'

I couldn't help smiling myself, feeling the dimples break out although I tried to hide them. 'There, that's better too,' he said, 'less of Oliver Twist.'

I didn't understand that either, but took his hand and let him hoist me up in front of him. 'Rocking-horse smooth,' he told me, gathering up the reins, 'a real dobbin. Not like my grey. She was a fool to ride him, you a fool to help her. Now come clean and tell the whole story.'

His arms were easy about my waist, his breath cool on my cheek. Through the thinness of the old shirt I could feel the shape of his body close to mine. It suddenly became important to give a correct answer, not necessarily an answer that he would want but one that was honest.

''Twasn't just the money,' I said, 'although it mattered. Nor because she promised it. Nor because she asked, no, needed me, or so I thought. But I was curious. Never had seen such a horse before, never seen her like neither. And I wanted to go where she lived to find out what a real family is like.'

I stopped, appalled. That was not what I meant to talk about, it had slipped out almost without my noticing. But he didn't seem shocked. 'And did you?' he asked.

I took a breath, let it out slowly. The house, I could speak about his house, question him about it. But his sister, mother, father, what could I ask him about them, where would I start?

He must have guessed what I was thinking. 'Families are as you get them,' he said, not joking now, 'like people. You put up with their peculiarities as they do yours. But if you asked me I'd say I was the misfit at Polleven Manor, although my father won't admit it and my mother's afraid to. Ruth should have been me, she'd have made a better heir. And that's why I'm leaving,' he added more cheerfully. 'At least I've got a way out for a while, although soldiering wouldn't have been my first choice. And you, where's home for you?'

When I told him, 'Penwith,' he repeated, 'Penwith Farm at the foot of Hawstead Tor? Strange old place, strange old owner, full of hell fire and brimstone and self-righteous as a preacher. You can't mean there.'

It was his turn to break off embarrassed when I said, 'That's it. My mother is the housekeeper.'

'The devil she is.'

He rode on in silence. I could almost feel his frown. 'I beg your pardon then,' he said after a while, 'but who are you?'

I turned round and faced him squarely. 'Oh,' I said, with what was to be an imitation of his sister's shrug, in a voice that was meant to be detached and nonchalant, 'I'm the farm hand. Just call me Jenny No Name.'

And to my horror, all the pent-up emotions of the day came gushing out and I burst into tears.

Like a sensible man he ignored my weakness, reined the horse back and continued to talk in a rational way about the weather, about the lack of rain, about farming in general, to give me time to compose myself, asking gravely what crops we grew at Penwith as if it were of prime interest.

'Here,' he said at last. He pushed a handkerchief towards me. 'Stop crying. It can't be that bad. Just tell me one thing.' He sounded puzzled. 'Is what you wanted to find out anything to do at all with my sister?' And to my shame I shook my head and cried again.

We rode forward once more, I still snuffling, trying to hold the handkerchief so my hands wouldn't be seen, for after all this talk of farming and farm girls, I was embarrassed by them. 'Don't fidget,' he said after a while, 'else we'll both be tipped off. Leave your blisters alone. Blisters aren't a disgrace. And don't worry. Things have a way of righting themselves given time. They won't look so black in the morning.'

We continued at a steady pace without speaking. Then, 'You must be joking about one thing though,' he said, when I had stopped shaking. 'You're much too young to be a farm hand. You should still be in the nursery with nursemaids.'

It was my turn to smile. 'Never had no nursery where I come from,' I told him with a laugh. 'Nor nursemaid neither. Unless it be milk maid, and I'm that. Jack-of-all trades, master of none, that's my work.'

'A hard life up on the moors,' he said, unexpectedly sympathetic. 'Better here. Soil's not so acid for one thing, and the climate's better. You're open to all the winds.'

I thought, for a soldier you know a lot about farming, but I was too shy to say so. 'The Pollevens come of good farm stock,' he was continuing, as if he guessed what I was thinking, 'just grown a bit long in the nose since they got a title. My sister, she'd like to have us live off air, it's more refined. When I come back from overseas I'll turn Polleven into a farm again, with or without her permission.'

He said, 'Seriously, how old are you?'

When I told him, 'That's still too young,' he said, 'you look as if you should be in school.'

'That's easy to say, but hard fer moor folk,' I said. 'Too long a walk at the best of times, impossible in winter. And there's always some reason or other to keep you at home. Teachers don't like you. They think farm children are stupid. And I was a misfit too, because of living at Penwith.' I took another breath. ''Course that's not to say I don't hold with reading and such. Penwith's got a mess of books, enough to keep you busy fer years.'

'And you read them,' he persisted, 'you can read?'

At any other time I might have been offended, but the memory of Farmer Penwith's reddened face swung across my vision. I heard his bullying threats. 'I used to, until he stopped me,' I said, and once more set my lips firmly in line.

He didn't ask me to explain, but perhaps he guessed who I meant for he said, 'First heard about Farmer Penwith when I was out hunting as a boy. He was a legend. Best breeder of horses this side of Launceston, best jumpers on the moors. Until he took to gambling. Married a rich woman, they said, for her money. Gambled it away and then didn't she lead him a life. Drove him to drink and women . . .'

He coughed and stopped talking as if aware of indiscretion. 'The day she died,' he went on after a while, 'they say he drank himself blind, harnessed up his favourite horse and smashed it at a hedge. Almost killed himself. Retreated then to hide his guilt, speaking like a peasant, living like one . . .'

I bridled. 'Well,' I said, 'my Mam and me, we're the peasants he lives with.'

'God,' he said, contrite, 'I've offended you. I didn't mean it the way it sounds. I . . .'

He stopped himself once more, said, 'Damn,' then pulled at my shoulder so I was again facing him. 'Look,' he said softly, 'I don't care about these things. Listening to my sister and father you might think otherwise, but it's not how I'm made. I'm not just saying that to make excuses. I'm an officer, right, one of the so called "ruling classes". The backbone of the army is made up of ordinary men; they're the ones to rely upon, they see you through. If you want I could give you a hundred examples, they've saved my skin a score of times. I really meant it when I said you have to take people as they are, not how or where the world's put them.'

I thought, even to being illegitimate, but I didn't say it.

He tapped his boots once more on the horse's side, we scrambled up the last part of the track and came up on the moor. The wind was blowing here, fresh and sweet. After the heat of the valley it felt right, and the full moon hung so low that every leaf and grass was outlined in silver. Ahead of us the jagged mass of Hawstead Tor loomed against the skyline, looking unfamiliar from this angle, mirror-changed in the moonlight.

The horse surged forward, we moved into a floating stride, hardly touching the ground, feather-light. His arms were tight about me; I felt our breathing quicken, settle into a rhythmic beat, and I thought, oh God, 'tis over before 'tis scarcely begun.

We came to a halt at the far side of the tor, as near to Penwith Farm as made no difference but behind the shelter of a stand of firs so no one would see us unless they were out looking. 'You'll be alright?' he asked, for the first time a trace of anxiety showing. 'He won't hurt you?' in a way that afterwards made me wonder what else he'd heard of Farmer Penwith and the lives we led. No one had ever been anxious about me before; no one had worried about hurt. And I had thought him incapable of feeling!

He dismounted, then put out his arms to lift me but I slid down under them. 'Thank you kindly,' I said with a bob of a curtsey, 'I'm that obliged. But I'll find my own way home from here, alone.'

'The devil you will.' He sounded amused. 'And if it should be I'm riding up on the tor another evening, you'll be too proud to speak, I dare say.'

I was already beginning to run, the shirt tails flapping. 'Tomorrow, for instance,' he was shouting. I didn't reply. All I could think of was the way our hearts had beaten as one, all I could remember was what Farmer Penwith had called me. At a safe distance I couldn't stop myself from turning to watch him disappear back the way we'd come. And it seemed to me that at the crest of the tor he too turned in the saddle and waved as if he guessed I'd be watching.

And that is how Julian Polleven brought me home that first night so I could fall in love with him.

CHAPTER 3

didn't know what love was then of course, a feeling so far removed from my experience that it took time for me to understand or accept the impossibility of it. All I do know is that I returned to Penwith Farm too full of wonder to be afraid of anything. And I bore with the next morning's cuffing for being late, the nagging, the preaching, as if something was wound about my skin to protect me from harm. Not all my Mam's nagging could stop excitement bubbling up; all day it simmered beneath the surface, like a kettle just off the hob.

The weather continued fine and I spent from sun-up cutting hay in the lowland fields. We used scythes, or rather Farmer Penwith did and the handful of men he'd hired specially. They moved in a row, sweating in the heat, the blades swishing through the grass with a curious hissing. Each swathe tipped sideways in a wave; the feathered tops fell like foam. Clouds of grasshoppers sprang before us on springs, the air was filled with rustlings as small creatures, rabbits and such, bolted for safety. From time to time a shot rang out when one of the men took aim.

I shut my ears to that sound, turned away, continued walking behind the men to bind up the shocks, the scent of grass with its under-tinge of fern heady as wine. My task was to lean the bales to form a stack as was the custom in our parts. The cut edges scratched, the sap oozed, wisps of fronds and Queen Anne's Lace caught in my hair. By the day's end I was sunburnt and tired, yet I scarcely noticed. We ate tea out of doors among the shocks, the men sitting grumpily by themselves with their own haversacks, Farmer Penwith's scanty hospitality proverbial. My Mam bustled importantly with a large urn, playing farmer's wife, pretending stale bread and watery jam was substitute for the customary fresh-baked splits with butter and cream. She's changed too, my Mam, I thought, at least in this. She's not the woman who'd slip Cy a double portion on the sly or cut bread extra thick. She's grown mean like he is. A sudden urge to confide in her ebbed away. The habit of reserve which I'd acquired held firm; I kept to myself as I usually did, leaning back against a hedge, legs stretched out like one of the men, eyes closed against the sun, careful not to look at her or anyone, careful not to appear different. More than ever Farmer Penwith's words seemed strangely threatening. As soon as I could I excused myself, pleading weariness. 'I'm off to bed,' I said. But first I went to the barnyard to wash, mindful of Miss Ruth's sneers; ducking my head beneath the pump like a boy, then carrying jugs up to my room so my Mam wouldn't notice.

The water was cold, icy from the well. In winter it ran peat brown but in early summer still tasted soft, almost too soft to give lather. I used it to rinse my hair, fluffing it out in finespun spikes, added lavender to lave face and breasts, put on my Sunday dress, a faded blue gown, grown too short but the best I had. Then without noise I slid back down the pipe, away to the tor, running free as a bird, like a gambler staking all on this one chance.

Unwilling to wear those ugly boots, I went barefoot, although, mindful of snakes at that time of year, I'd have preferred to be shod. I climbed Hawstead Tor, my toes gripping at the cracks. Until I reached the top it never occurred to me that Julian wouldn't be there, so certain sure I was. The first unexpected vacant rocks, the spread of empty moor, the empty grey-blue horizon, were almost like another blow. Disappointment fell like a weight. Then I heard him say, 'Ssh', as if to keep me quiet. He was sitting to one side, pointing to the open scree where a fox was padding, its red coat burnished copper. As we watched it slid into the bracken, its brush high like a beacon, paused for a moment to scent the air, then disappeared.

'My father'd be glad to know its whereabouts,' Julian said cheerfully, 'but I shan't tell him. Although when I was a boy I used to enjoy hunting like your Farmer Penwith.'

He coughed, changed the subject. But I didn't care. Whatever fears I'd had of Farmer Penwith were lost up here. And I suspected he was talking as he had last night, to hide something.

'Don't like killing,' he said, 'there's a confession for a soldier. But some things you have to fight for. A fox's not done harm.'

'Walked the last part, up the scree,' he was continuing, 'or rather scrambled. That's a stiffish climb. Left my horse tethered down yonder.' He nodded to the back part of the tor where his sister had fallen. 'Thought it better,' he said.

He never explained exactly why, but I guessed that was what he was hiding. So he wouldn't be recognized. So Sir Robert Polleven's son wouldn't be caught with a farm girl. So he wouldn't be embarrassed. But I was wrong about that too.

He was dressed in rough walking clothes, but booted like a horseman. That would make climbing difficult. Over one shoulder he carried a leather pouch like a gamekeeper's bag, which he now opened and drew out a paper parcel. 'Brought you these,' he said, almost too casually, 'some old favourites.'

Inside were books, slim volumes of old rubbed leather with his initials stamped upon the covers. I leafed through them covetously, then pushed them back. 'Can't take 'em,' I said, 'but thank you all the same.'

'Why not?' The question was casual too but I had begun

to know his style; underneath he was waiting intently for an answer.

I didn't know what to say: that I had no time for reading, that I didn't want to be beholden, both equally true. Or that I didn't want to take anything that linked us further, not exactly true because I did.

These ideas conflicted, swirled in my mind like leaves, fragmented and disorganized, subtle ideas. I was not used to subtleties, I had no words to express them.

He took the books up and set them in a neat pile on the rocks. 'I wish you would,' he said, as if he meant it. 'Something to remember me by.'

He looked at me, looked away out over the countryside. 'I've explained before,' he said, 'I'm here on leave. It's hard to speak of soldiering on a day like this, harder to speak of leaving, and I've only a week or two left. But I was thinking. If it doesn't bother you, if it doesn't cause difficulty,' he was picking his words with care, frowning a little with concentration, I felt, not talking now to please me, but to convince himself, 'if, in short, you don't object, I'd like to spend the time with you, if you'll permit it.'

I'd never known such politeness; no one had ever asked me if I 'objected' to anything before; no one had asked my 'permission'. The very idea was disturbing.

He continued to stare out over the open moor. Then he laughed, a short, almost curt, laugh. 'I'm not sure I could explain why,' he said, 'in a way you'd understand. I'm not sure I should have asked. I almost didn't come. I waited down there on the moors, like an idiot. Forgive me. I've no right.'

He got up. 'I'd better go,' he said.

I thought, 'If he leaves I'll not see him again, 'twill be lost, all the might-have-beens, or may-bes, all the possibilities.' I said, ''Tisn't me that's bothered; 'tisn't me you makes difficulties for. Just look at us; there's some difference between us, sure enough, like beer leavings and wine. But if 'tis embarrassment you're thinking of, I'm the one to embarrass you.'

The words came out easily, a flood of words. 'Oh, I know what maids warn about gentlemen, how they claim they likes to talk and then later, why 'tis another tale. But I don't think you're like that, you treats a person proper. And I bain't like that neither, no matter what you hears of Penwith Farm.'

He was listening in his intent way. It made him seem so vulnerable that I suddenly smiled at him. 'For what 'tis worth,' I said, 'I'll take a risk. And I'll look at your books, tho' I'm no dab hand at reading and 'twill be hard work. And I'll gladly keep you company if that be what you want. But fer both our sakes we'll make it secret, that'll be best fer both.'

He smiled too at that as if relieved, sat back as if a load was off his mind. 'Fairly spoken,' he said. 'There, I know that much about you, you speak your mind. But if we are to be friends, I need your real name. You know mine, I think, what's yours?'

When I told him he smiled again, that brilliant familiar smile that made my breath stop. 'I like it,' he said, 'Guinevere of the long tresses,' and he opened the books and there on the fly leaf wrote it in, *Guinevere*, with the date, *June 1899*. And that was the day I most remember, when I first became alive.

We met often after that, every evening for the next week, while the hay-making gave me an excuse to retire early, and my Mam and Farmer Penwith were too busy about their own affairs. I suppose it sounds naive that I should imagine Julian Polleven spent those evening hours with me without some ulterior motive. And I suppose it sounds equally naive, or devious, that he could appear like that, like some god perhaps, condescendingly scattering his favours, blinding a poor simple girl, pretending he didn't recogize the dangers or the consequences. It isn't only country girls who warn of unrequited affection; the whole of English life does. Our very language is riddled with it; our literature, from the 'Lass of Richmond Hill' to *Tess of the d'Urbervilles* revolves around the theme: that young gentlemen should persuade country girls to be betrayed, seduced and left. So much for love between unequals. I was the fool to think otherwise. But God knows I needed someone I could love. And so I think in his fashion did he.

For I learned a lot about him up there on the moors, a lot in a short space of time. We just sat and talked, while the brilliant June evenings flared about us and the dew settled on the heather and hung in drops from the gorse. What did we talk about – about everything, about nothing, as people do who have suddenly found someone to talk and listen to. He certainly was not as I had first imagined him, and I suppose perhaps I wasn't either. At least he seemed to find what I said interesting and I wasn't used to that. He told me about his soldiering, not much for he was newly commissioned and was expecting a first posting overseas; about his past life, mostly away from home at school, with holidays and excursions to places I didn't know existed but which when he spoke of them came alive in the way the pictures in books had done. We often spoke of farming, for that was a shared interest; he had plans for that, how to better the native breed of cattle, how to improve the sheep. And I told him about the moors, about the birds and flowers I knew, and what I thought about things as if we had been friends for ever – about everything, about nothing, except the reason why he came or why I permitted it.

One other thing I learned, what he'd hinted at before, was his dissimilarity from his family, for all they looked alike. He never explained what caused it; I thought perhaps it was his mother's gift to him, but he seldom mentioned her. It made me aware of his loneliness, strange, that one who seemed to have so much should feel lonely, another thing we shared. But as he never questioned me further about my Mam or Penwith Farm I never spoke of them again. Who and what we were seemed truly forgotten, put aside as of no consequence as he had said they should be. They say that time has no meaning when one is in love. And it is true that the days now dragged slowly as if the hours were twice as long and conversely the evenings sped past as if they had been halved, but I think a better way to measure love is the harmony of expression, as if what you say and think comes into both minds at the same moment down to the very words you use. Perhaps we were children living in a false paradise; perhaps the old and wise would mock at us. I only know for my part I felt more secure than ever in my life. And if neither of us thought of an ending that was not out of folly, it was out of happiness.

The last evening that we met was the last of the hay-making. After that first time I tried always to arrive before he did; it was an added pleasure to sit on the rocks, like a princess on a throne waiting for a prince. But the weather was changing. We had been up earlier than usual to finish before the rains came. A southwest wind means rain in our part of the moor, and by teatime the mist had begun to slide over the tor, prelude to storm.

It felt good, that mist, after the previous heat, a true Cornish drizzle, and I liked the feel underfoot of the grass suddenly damp and springy. The hay was in, a great relief, meaning for our cattle the difference between winter starvation or survival, although only because my Mam had nagged had we continued with the work. In his lack-lustre way, Farmer Penwith would have given up and let the last field rot. My Mam was therefore in a good mood, pleased with herself, confident of her position. She had retired to the parlour with the bottle of Farmer Penwith's brandy which had replaced her usual elderberry wine. She was not likely to question where I was. Any suspicions she'd had of that first late evening must have faded. She saw no trouble from me. As for Farmer Penwith, he had avoided me as I him; that threat too seemed to have diminished. The cloak of mist and rain added to my feeling of well-being. I reached the tor as the first drops splattered, as if I had flown on wings.

Julian was waiting for me under the shelter of some lower rocks where big boulders had hollowed out a natural cave. The space was cramped, not much room for two, but he stuck his long legs out. 'I mustn't keep you long,' he said, 'you'll get wet.'

He put out a hand as if to touch my arm, withdrew it, spoke of something else. 'Do you know what they found under one of those stone circles down there?' he said. And when I shook my head, 'A flanged brooch the colour of your hair. And a great beaker with an engraved goddess, a wheat fillet around her brow.'

I didn't know what those things were and didn't like to ask. He wasn't looking at me, but I could tell he was holding something back as if he wanted to say something else. 'A harvest goddess,' he said, 'to bless the crops and multiply. And bring good luck. So perhaps you'll bring me some.

'My orders have come,' he said. 'I leave in a day or so. I don't know when I'll be back.'

His voice was bleak, uncompromising. I could feel the strain. He held his shoulders tight as if he were pulling against a plough and his gaze was fixed on some unidentifiable object on the moors below.

My happiness evaporated. Suddenly I could hear the wind moaning through the bog grass. What about us then? I wanted to say, to scream, but I didn't. It wasn't his fault, it wasn't anyone's fault. And I had been warned.

'Don't look like that,' he was saying, 'I can't bear that look. The same funny, lost, look you had when we first met. Oh God,' and now he did look at me straight, 'I've made things worse.'

Part of me wanted to say, yes, you have. You've given me some hope, a vision, and I can't go back to where I was. Part of me wanted to say, you've no right to leave, what's to become of me? But I didn't say any of those things because it wasn't fair.

'Jenny,' he was saying, 'Jenny, it may be years, I may not return, I may be killed. I can't ask you to wait.'

I took a deep breath. 'Why not?' I said.

He stopped, stared at me, his face growing pale. I said, slowly, the words forced out of me, 'From the start I said I'd not mind the risk, and I don't. And that if you think of the differences, I don't give you nothing, the advantages are all to me. I drag you down. But that don't mean I'*m* nothing. And if it so be that you care fer me, as I care fer you, that's all that counts, the caring. Naught else in the world.'

'Oh God,' he said, in a queer choked voice as if something was strangling him, 'you don't know what you're saying. You don't know how you're tempting me.'

He tried to laugh. 'A real goddess, eh, offering me a fortune.' But it wasn't funny and he knew it and he was struggling to stay calm. And I knew what he was feeling, the guilt and the desire, and didn't want him to be torn by them. That's not what loving is, I wanted to tell him, there can't be guilt to love. When he turned to face me it seemed the most natural thing in the world for my arms to come about him to try and comfort him, and for his to come about me.

We held each other like that perhaps seconds, perhaps hours, his arms so strong I thought my ribs might crack. I'd worn a shawl but it had slipped off, he was touching my hair, running his fingers through it. 'Like gossamer,' he was saying, tracing the outline of my face, as if to learn it by heart. Under his jacket I could feel the muscles as he moved towards me, a pulse was beating in his neck where the brown of his skin disappeared into the shirt collar.

I don't remember how we kissed, it doesn't matter, it seemed we had been kissing all our lives, drinking in each other, feeding each other. 'Like birds,' he said. Nor does it matter how we came to be lying in that small cave-like enclosure, with the bracken crushed beneath us and his body warm on mine. There was a moment's wonder, a moment's hesitation when I felt his hands now drawing up my skirt, feeling down my back, touching between the legs in the secret private place, a moment's hesitation when he suddenly wrenched at his own clothing, forcing the fly buttons open, peeling down the breeches. I only know that when he surged upon me I arched to meet him as if there had never been a time when we had not been joined, and whatever pain there was was forgotten in the joy of that coupling.

When we were done we still lay together, breathing in each other's breath, embracing each other, caressing. Never in my life had I known such tenderness. It washed over me like a benediction. I do remember thinking, no matter what, we've got this to remember by.

Perhaps he felt the same, for he said once, the words coming out as if he couldn't stop them, 'You're so generous, it's the giving in your nature that I marvel at. It makes me humble.' Although why he should say it, a young man, his place established, his future all before him, didn't strike me then.

'But I'll make it right,' he kept saying, 'I owe it you to be as generous.' I never thought, make what right, or how, or what is this generosity that he promises, that he owes me? Those things never crossed my mind, or if they did it was wonderingly, almost abstractly, not how they would affect me personally, certainly not what I could get out of them. And if they motivated his feelings, as I suppose they did, I would swear that it was not from a wish to safeguard himself or escape from a predicament that he might afterwards regret. We weren't talking of 'owing' and 'payment' in those terms.

I do not mean we were babes-in-the-wood, ignorant to the point of stupidity. Farm children learn early about the facts of life, and there wasn't much I hadn't heard through the bedroom walls and the floor above my Mam's room on the nights when Farmer Penwith visited her and stayed until dawn. On the other hand, I know I wasn't grasping and greedy like my Mam, and I don't think he was. It was just that somehow for both of us the caring had come uppermost and buried all those other self-seeking considerations. And that I suppose was the miracle.

We parted when it was already dark, later than I had intended. The evening had settled down to steady rain, the wind had freshened. He came with me on foot as far as we dared, left me reluctantly. 'Take care, sweetheart,' he said, pulling the shawl closer over my head while the wind whipped at my skirts. 'Tomorrow we'll talk again.'

How many girls have heard that said; how many men have made that promise? When that morrow comes then is the reckoning, then is the promise broken.

I gained the farmhouse without difficulty; well, I've said my Mam was in good mood with her brandy bottle, the fire was still lit in that second parlour; she'd be sitting easy yet a while. I meant simply to steal upstairs, climb into bed, no one the wiser. A bobbing lantern outside under the barn overhang attracted my attention and I stopped on the first landing step to peer out through the window.

The window was set deep into the thick walls, and the glass was misted. I had to kneel on the ledge and use my elbow to rub the pane clear. Needles of rain blurred the swinging light but eventually I made out Farmer Penwith's profile. He was bending over something which he had slung over the stable door, and I was puzzled until I recognized what it was: a saddle, Miss Ruth Polleven's saddle which I had hidden at her request, and forgotten since.

When I was a child and my Mam was in a temper, I used to feel a pricking along the spine. I did so now. The last thing I wanted was to confront Farmer Penwith, but I knew I had to. And when reluctantly I came again outside, drawing my soaked shawl even closer, it was as well I did, for he had placed the saddle inside the stable and was coming to find me. And in his hand he carried Julian's books.

'So you'm back,' he said, with his sidelong glance. 'I wondered when 'ee would be. Yer Mam said you were asleep in yer room, worn out with haying, but you weren't, were 'ee? And you weren't reading, leastways not my books. So whose are these, I wonder that you've left them hanging around?'

He held them out, the covers dangling. 'To Guinevere,' he read in a sneering voice. 'But these initials ain't Guinevere's.' And sharp as a whip-lash, 'But "P" do stand fer Polleven, right, the same name that's stamped on the saddle.'

He smiled. There was something dreadful about that smile, full-lipped, red under the black stubble. 'So what be you doing with a Polleven on the moors?' he asked in a low voice. 'Out in the rain to all hours?' As he had done in his parlour he reached out a hand to touch my hair. 'Wet through I shouldn't wonder,' he added, mockingly. 'Don't tell me you got that wet just crossing of the yard.'

I didn't try to defend myself, didn't ask what he was doing in my room, but I did recoil from his touch as from a snake, and he noticed. 'Hoighty toighty,' he said, 'fussy now, aren't we. Used to better things. Well, then, Missy, let me tell you something. The Penwiths were kings afore the Pollevens was spawned. And man to man I still be twice his match tho' he be half my age.'

He grinned. 'Unless it be the father that you fancies.'

He still held the books dangling, letting the rain run off them. After that first shudder of revulsion I steeled myself to make no sign as my Mam had taught me, but somehow the sight of those sodden pages, the thin paper beginning to turn to pulp, seemed to sum up all I felt. It might have been my heart he hung up for derision.

'So now, here's a difficulty,' he said, still in a semi-jocular way, 'what to tell yer Mam. Fussy, yer Mam. She'd not be that happy if I told what I knows. So perhaps we'll keep it secret, just 'twixt the two of us. That'll be the second secret that we share, perhaps it calls fer a celebration.'

He took a step towards me but I didn't retreat this time. 'Don't show anything,' I was telling myself, forcing myself not to shiver, 'don't show you care. Pretend anything as long as he don't know what you feel.'

'She'll be nodding her head off.' He was jerking his own towards the parlour. 'Dead to the world till morning, I shouldn't wonder and then so besotted to make memory like a sieve. But we'm awake, alive and well. We've time before us.'

He ran his fingers through my hair again, dragging the length out, winding it, then with a sudden vicious twist pulling me towards him so he could press his mouth on mine. I can't tell how dreadful it was, that parody of love, to have him echo what Julian had said, to have him do what Julian had just done, to have this second embrace superimposed upon the first. It made me sick. And when he drew back, panting a little, wiping his mouth on the back of his hand, I had the sudden equally dreadful impression that it was Julian himself who stood there, a Julian twenty years older, like this man a lecher and a fornicator, a destroyer of all things pure and good.

'That's more like it,' he said, his blue eyes bulging. He wiped his mouth again. The wind had picked up and the rain blew but we were still sheltered under the overhang. 'We won't say no more about those things fer the present. Just cut along to bed. Strip off them wet clothes and get under the covers. I'll be up in a while to keep 'ee warm.'

I turned as if to obey. Something about my passive acceptance must have alarmed him. He caught hold of my arm and again forced me to face him. 'But if 'ee speaks of it,' he said, and now his voice was full of menace, 'if 'ee says aught, 'tis out of the door fer mother and daughter both. I'll have the pair of you before the magistrates quick as a wink, arrested as harlots and thieves. There's the saddle to prove it.'

I knew he was capable of what he said, and he knew I knew. He let go; I went past him into the rain. I crossed the yard, opened the door, passed the parlour where my mother was snoring in the velvet chair that she had sold herself to have, climbed the stairs. But I didn't go to my room. I went into hers.

I knew I was safe for a moment there, the last place he would come, and I took the candle, lit it and reached for the box under the bed.

It was still there, heavier than it looked, and the key was still hanging on its hook. When I opened it and removed

55

the layers of papers that covered the contents the shine of silver underneath reminded me of the gold coin which Ruth Polleven had offered as a bribe. I didn't stay to count it, that money my Mam had secreted away miser-like, but sorted it through in piles until I had picked out what I thought I had earned, what was truly mine, what I was 'owed'.

In a corner of the box I found a little leather purse which I took to put the wages in that my Mam had bartered me for. As I tried to close the box, stuffing the old papers back in, a name leapt at me from the headlines: St Marvell, the village near Polleven Manor, the village by the sea. I didn't stay to read what was written about it, but I took the name as an omen. And the decision to go to Polleven Manor became fixed firmly in my head.

I stowed the box away, closed the door behind me, climbed up to the attic. Still in the same numbed fashion, without haste, I changed into my work clothes, rolled a few articles into a bag, lifted the window. For a second the candle guttered into a void; the flame caught at the shafts of rain, the elm trees dipped and swayed.

Then I was down the pipe and safe away, not once looking round, as if something in me had snapped, some rope perhaps that had held me tethered longer than it should have done and in snapping had freed me of all regret.

Although I've said I knew the region of Hawstead Tor well, the darkness made progress difficult; rain lashed at me and the wind tore at my clothes. It was not a night to be out-of-doors, and I made slow work at first. But it never occurred to me to turn back; I never even thought of it, held my mind blank, simply concentrated on the step ahead. Step by slow and careful step, that's what kept me going, just plodding on, head bent before the storm, like one of those moorland ponies that move doggedly until they drop, going by instinct, aware of the bog patches before I came to them, avoiding the wet crevices where a slip means disaster, my mind fixed like a compass on one place, where Julian was. Fate was kind. I came unscathed out on the northern slope just before dawn and began to wind along that back road towards Polleven Church.

I rested then for a while under the hedge where he had waited for me. Nothing new in that; I'd learned how to curl up like a hedgehog, finding shelter under tree roots. When day was fully come, a watery day with streaks of cloud and wind still veering from the west, threatening more rain, I shook myself awake, tidied my hair with a bit of comb, turned up the collar of my coat. I didn't go into the churchyard, skirted it, crossed the open road and followed the western wall to the bridge.

The tide was in, the current frothing brown, bits of twigs and branches swirling under the old arches. I hung over them for a while, munching on a loaf I'd bought, watching the swirl of the downward current, not thinking of anything, still not allowing myself to think. Then when I judged the time right I followed the path along the banks until I came to the main gate of Polleven Manor. Only there did I hesitate.

If I had come this way instinctively, if I had found my way to Polleven like a homing pigeon, it had not been with real forethought. I had had no 'plan' in mind. I do not think I even considered seriously Julian Polleven's promise of the night before, nor what it meant, even less what it could mean if I chose to make it so. In fact the whole of yesterday seemed sunk in some deep pit; there was no way to haul it back to life. Nor had I considered how my actions might be construed, or misconstrued, or how Julian might react to them. I had been impervious to all nuance, or rather had gone past it into some further place where nothing could touch. In later years they called such numbness shock. Then I only knew that I was calm, yes, calm, not at all like the last time I had come there, not intimidated nor envious. And that it seemed wrong to disappear without a word, to ignore Julian, as wrong as if he did the like to me. And that in seeing him, all would come right, whatever that meant, would count as 'repayment of promises', if those words had any significance.

So I approached the park gates deliberately and it was perhaps this air of decision that forced the keeper's wife to let me pass. For I paid her no attention when she asked what I wanted, simply pushed at the iron gates she was holding and went through. Even in the rain the main driveway curved in a white line across the green of the grass, although the river was almost hidden and the cattle had disappeared for shelter under the trees. And at the drive's end the great spread of the house reared above the wet and damp, a rich man's residence, his challenge to the poor and needy of the world.

I walked down that gravel path without constraint. And when I came up to the steps I didn't go round to the back to the servants' entrance, but climbed them and stood under the front porch to ring the front door bell.

They say sometimes when people have had a hurt they don't notice grief or pain at first, they keep walking or talking and going about their ordinary lives as in a trance, as if nothing had happened to them, until suddenly, the breath is squeezed out of them, as by a giant's grip.

It was not until the door opened that I felt the pain.

CHAPTER 4

I suppose to the maid who answered I must have looked deranged, hair plastered to my skull, old coat and breeches hanging in wet folds, boots mud-caked. I never thought of that. 'I'm come for Julian Polleven,' I said, 'tell him 'tis Guinevere.'

She gaped at me, hand to mouth. Well, I didn't fault her. I might have done the same if a tramp had dared set foot at Penwith. Or if a witch had materialized off Hawstead Tor and come haunting on All Soul's Eve. 'Bless my soul,' she whispered, backing in fright, 'oh sweet Jesus deliver us.' And catching breath, she let out a howl that would have scared the devil himself.

It was Ruth Polleven who heard her and came to the doorway first. She was dressed in a morning dress, all frills and lace, with gold trinkets round her neck and dainty velvet slippers on her little feet. The contrast between us this time was even more marked, but it didn't bother me. 'You remember me,' I told her and she couldn't deny it, the shock of recognition had leapt into her eyes. 'And I remember you. Don't take on so, I'm not here to ask favours, albeit I did you one. I want fer to see your brother, 'tis me he'll be expecting of. So ask him out, I'll just wait here till he comes.'

And not waiting for an answer I squatted down beside the stair rail, feet stretched out as if I were sitting against a hedge.

59

Ruth Polleven's face paled.

'You're mad,' she cried in her imperious way. And when I didn't move, in a voice like her father's, 'Julian, Mr Polleven to you, isn't here. He's out.'

The maid behind her nodded in agreement. 'Gone,' she piped, peeping out behind her mistress's skirts as if she thought I might bite.

'Then give him a message,' I said. 'Tell him Guinevere was asking fer him. Say she'll bide at St Marvell tonight. Tell him as he do remember his promise of yester'een, so she remembers hers.'

'Whatever can you mean?' Miss Polleven's voice rose a notch. 'Last night was his last night here. He spent it here with us. So he can't have made you any promises. And there's certainly nothing that you can have promised him.'

I looked at her fixedly until she dropped her gaze. 'I did you a service once,' I repeated. 'I rubbed my feet raw for you. Well, that's nothing. But yer brother's done you as much, many times, he told me so. He deserves better of you. So do you give him that message, mind; 'twill mean the world to him.'

If Ruth Polleven truly thought me mad she could have shown some pity. Or if she had any pity in her nature now would have been the time to show it. 'Out, gone, left, all one and the same,' she cried, mouthing the words as if I were stupid. 'Can't you understand? He's no longer here. He's already on a train bound for London, to rejoin his regiment.'

She took a step forward, her eyes flashing. 'Don't ever come here again,' she cried. 'I wish I'd never showed you how. I wish I'd never met you to bring trouble upon us, now I know what you are, a bastard and a whore, living as you and your mother do with that dreadful farmer. And that's what I told my brother. It was my duty to. So what could he see in you, what could he ever promise? You must be crazy even to imagine it.'

And she slammed the door.

60

I didn't care what she called me, and I didn't believe that Julian would leave. 'I'm not like that,' he'd said. But what had I first told him? 'I know what gentlemen are.' I began to hammer at the door but no one answered. I beat on it until my knuckles bled. And then a great shudder shook me, as if I had been dreaming and had been shaken roughly awake. And I thought, suppose she is speaking the truth for once. She may well have told him those things to scare him off; even if he says he doesn't mind, he'd mind them, any man would. And suppose it's true he has left; from the start he made no secret about having to. And suppose last night he knew he would go this morning. Like a snake's venom the thoughts curled round my heart, I couldn't stop them. Suppose last night he was lying about another meeting. Lying is a family failing, suppose it's in him. Suppose he was always lying and meant nothing that he said.

I turned round and went down the steps. Like an old woman my backbone seemed to have crumbled, but I forced myself to walk on, not even looking round when the door slammed a second time and there was a spurt of gravel as someone ran after me.

It was the little maid. The rain was ruining her black dress and her white cap had slipped askew. 'Here,' she cried. She held out a coin, wrapped in a piece of paper. 'It's his address so you'll know where he's at. Had to copy it out meself when his trunks were took to the station.'

I ignored the piece of silver although she urged it on me, kept the paper, stuffing it in my pocket as a talisman. The sound of that 'Gone, left' was like a drum.

To this day I don't know how much Miss Polleven had twisted the truth about her brother's departure, or about what she had told him. Either way I knew she'd never give him any message and even if he were still here he'd never find me. Nor can I explain what made her so hard, or what prompted her maid to sympathy. And perhaps none of that mattered. What mattered was that, gone or not, for me Julian was lost. And there was no going back on that. He was as

61

lost to me as my childhood home, as my past, as everything else I'd known.

When I was a little girl my mother used to say, 'Let the past lie'. That's what I had to learn, to bury it, push it out of sight. I veered across the park towards the river where the little sailing boat still bobbed on the current, his boat probably, one he wouldn't be using for a while. I could float downstream in that boat, out into that unknown bay. A wave could take us under, drown us and it wouldn't matter either. But I wouldn't untie that boat. What had happened had to be faced, had to be taken up, shaken, and dealt with. Put into place and forgotten as perhaps my mother once had done. I had to accept the probability that I'd never see Julian Polleven again, nor return to Penwith Farm.

Some sturdiness of character now stood me in good stead, some survival instinct which I had inherited from my mother. Like her I was a survivor, although I wished I were dead.

I continued along the river bank, breasting through the bushes, the rain still falling, the path churned to mud. When presently I came again to the main road, almost without thinking I took the right-hand fork, towards St Marvell and the coast.

The rain had almost stopped when I came to the edge of the village that bears that name, and since I was to know it well I suppose I should describe it. The day I first arrived I noticed little; the narrow, crooked streets, the twisted alleyways, the maze of paths that tunnelled between and under houses like rabbits' burrows meant nothing to me. Later when I did notice, it was that warren closeness that I found overwhelming, that tight-knit existence so different from the moors. I never missed the moors so much as there in that crowded village.

That first afternoon it was nearly four o'clock when I stood at the top of the hill that crooked down towards the sea. I remember the time, I heard the church clock strike, and it reminded me of something in another life, the sound of the evening bell when I had come home with Ruth Polleven. But the Polleven name had to be forgotten, buried, like Penwith Farm. There was nothing for me left in either place.

The streets were slicked with wet, slippery slick, my hob-nails caught on the cobble stones. On either side, a bare handshake apart, the cottage doors were shut. It might have been December instead of June; even the flowers in the little front gardens were blackened with damp. But at the street end where the lane met with several others, a square flared out, beyond which was an inner harbour with its line of tethered boats. Beyond them was an outer harbour, and beyond again, the open sea.

All that expanse after confinement was like a breath of air to cramped lungs. I couldn't help running out along the jetty, the wind catching at my hair and clothes, the salt spray stinging. I found myself teetering over a heaving swell, a grey mass that stretched to the world's rim. Spumes of foam rose up and fell, the cliffs were white with froth. A great beating began inside of me, a shaking as when a tree is cut at its bole. I stretched out my arms, threw back my head, and let water sluice over me.

Either the coldness brought me back to earth, or sober practicality. I retraced my steps, sat on a bench by the inner pier, and made myself concentrate, the sensible side of my nature coming to the fore, again my mother's gift. First I pulled from my pocket the paper with Julian's address. I could just make out the writing blurred now by the constant wetting – Julian Polleven, of the . . . Dragoon Guards. I shredded the paper, let the wind take the pieces and blow them into the harbour. Next I took out the purse of coins that had come from my Mam's box, emptied the money on the seat beside me, stacking it in piles. From the bottom of the purse two crumbled pieces of cardboard fluttered to the ground. I bent down, picked them up from the puddles, dried them with my shirt sleeve. They weren't cardboard, but two faded photographs at which I stared.

There weren't any photographs at Penwith Farm except that of the dead first wife. From the cracked and yellowing surface these old likenesses stared back, waiting to be recognized.

One was of a youngish man, tall, angular, with a shock of fair hair. He was dressed in a dark woollen jersey, a fisherman's jersey, and held a cap, a captain's cap, awkwardly in both hands. His expression was awkward too, as if he felt shy to be caught not wearing his cap, as if he were embarrassed at revealing himself. That awkwardness made me like him, and the solemn look he had as if he wanted to burst out laughing, and the lock of hair that dangled over one eye seemingly waiting to be pushed aside.

The second photograph was of a child, hard to tell if boy or girl for it was dressed in the frilled petticoats that all small children used to wear. But the legs were sturdy, boy's legs, spread apart and the boots were planted firmly as if meant for running. And the look was rather like the man's, except more truculent.

I would have thrust these back into my pocket when a thought paralysed me. Why should they have been hidden away like this, unless my Mam had some reason for secrecy? I snatched them up, held them for a long moment to the light, for the sun was just beginning now to emerge under the dark edge of clouds, and an occasional beam caught the wet cobble stones and made them gleam. I had the strangest feeling as if I had done this long ago, as if I knew both man and boy and had suddenly remembered who they were.

The rush of recollection throbbed on the edge of discovery, subsided, leaving a hollow almost like a loss. When I turned the photographs over the backs were blank, no clue of who or what they meant. But it seemed to me, sitting there in my steaming clothes with the water still dripping off, that somehow fate had given me a family back.

'If it be 'eem going to sit there all day,' a voice broke in, an old man's voice, 'I wish 'ee'd give some space.'

An old man was standing looking out, a fisherman I guessed, for he was wearing a fisherman's jersey, and he was dragging a length of netting. If he took in the piles of coins he was too polite, or clever, to mention them but he must have seen them, for his eyes flickered just for a moment. When I had shifted my belongings he sat down beside me with an audible sigh of displeasure, took up a needle and began to weave, pushing the curved end in and out between the tarry strands of net, muttering to himself. He was not exactly friendly, I thought, discouraged, but since he was the first person that I'd met I asked him shyly if he'd ever heard of a Captain Ellis.

'Cap'n, cap'n.' His muttering grew louder. 'No cap'ns here, and never heard of no Ellis. This be a fishing port, Missy, no great place.' He nodded towards the line of boats which creaked and strained on their mooring ropes. 'Good Padstow luggers,' he said, 'best pilchard boats in the world. None do deny it. But didn't stop 'em sinking in the storm of 'eighty-five.'

He laid aside his netting, fixed me with his sharp black eyes. 'Great pilchard shoal,' he said. 'Biggest I ever seed. Comed in with the tide, bubbling like beer it were, thousands on thousands of tons. We was all out and ready, and didn't us start to haul when the sky darkened. Call this a storm.' Again he shook his head. 'A cat's paw. We hung on, tho' there were those who cut and made a run fer home. Didn't matter none, those who was caught was caught and done fer, those who was saved was saved. God does the choosing, there's a truth.' And he eyed me with the same sharp look.

He picked up his needle, began his weaving; in and out the curved end flew. 'Once the harbour here were packed with boats,' he said, 'thick with 'em, like sardines jammed in head to tail; 'ee walked over water when the fleet was in. That winter we lost the best part of our ships and crew and cap'ns, maid, so don't 'ee ask fer one. Half the women in the village widowed, chilrun orphaned, don't do to ask fer no one in St Marvell. 'Ee be asking fer grief.'

He noticed the two photographs I was holding. 'Be that the man?' He reached over, took them; too disappointed to argue, I let him. He peered at them, holding them up to the light as I'd done, the cracked texture suddenly frail against the broad, work-hardened fingers, his thumb as large as two of mine.

'Never heard the name Ellis,' he said, putting them down, 'and don't know the little tacker, they all do look alike. But I'd wager 'ee a tanner that's Ben Trevarisk's picture. Had that way of looking at 'ee under his hair.'

'Where does he live?' I interrupted breathlessly. 'Does he have a wife and family?'

He looked at me again with that shrewd, far-off glance that all men who live by the sea have. 'Did,' he said. 'Did live up there yonder on the cliff path, the cottage with the porch. As fer family,' he coughed, as if to change the subject, 'don't remember none. 'Cept there's a son still living in the same house.'

The look was different now, not kinder, but knowing, as if he knew something I didn't know, and wasn't going to tell me. He didn't say, 'I warned 'ee,' but he was thinking it. 'Go up yonder and ask,' he said, after a while, 'the son'd remember his father. He were only a boy in 'eighty-five when Ben Trevarisk drowned.'

And he picked up his needle and went back to his mending, but I sensed his disapproval. And his own suspicion was like a shield to protect himself and his village from intrusion of the past.

And that was how I lost a lover, and found and lost a father all in a single day.

I left the old man to sole occupancy of the bench, shouldered my bundle, and started up the path. The houses here were equally jammed together under the cliff, half burrowed out of it, so that the roofs were set back into rock. Each one stood up a storey with a flight of wooden steps like a ladder leading to the door, the underpart seemingly used for storage for there were sails and ropes and traps stacked haphazardly under the steps, and nets were spread over the rails. Ben Trevarisk's cottage was mid-way up, identical to the others, except for the front overhang with its little slate roof and a narrow seat at one side. I couldn't help comparing it with the last front porch I'd stood under, and remembering the welcome I'd got.

There was no knocker or bell, the door was shut tight, so when I had tried banging on it, I stood back and called. There was a shushing sort of sound inside, then a scuffling. The door grated open, letting out a smell of fish. The man in the photograph stood looking at me, the same fair hair falling over his forehead, the same awkward frown. 'So what do 'ee want?' the look said, but he didn't say anything, just stood looking me up and down. And when I finally blurted out, 'I'm wanting Ben Trevarisk's son,', 'Here I be,' he said, standing straighter, 'what's it to 'ee?'

I should have been more tactful; I should have ventured cautiously. I still wasn't sure of the relationship, if his father and my Mam had been married, I mean. But when I blurted out, 'I think he's my father too. My Mam's Gladys Ellis and I'm Jenny,', 'God damn 'ee fer a liar,' he said in return, 'she and her Mam be dead.'

And he glared at me, challenging me to deny it. By then the shuffling had grown louder, the door pushed wide, a handful of boys hung round the edges, some with the same shock of fair hair. There was a little girl though, with green eyes and hair like floss, the image of me, and he saw me looking at her. Reluctantly he dragged the children aside. 'Alright,' he said, in a grudging sort of way, 'don't deny father and she was once man and wife. If you be Jenny that makes us kin. But she weren't no mother to me.' He hesitated. 'Better step inside,' he said, standing back, 'no need to shout it to the world.'

And when I had crossed the threshold and he had slammed

the door shut, 'Don't think to make yerself at home,' he said, blunt as a spade, 'there bain't room fer that.'

'Who be she, thun?' A woman was standing close to the fireplace, a wooden spoon in her hand. She straightened up, arms akimbo, feet bare. She was still young, once must have been pretty, was pretty still in a slatternly way, her hair screwed tight, her dress dirty. But who was I to judge, I must have looked worse, as she was quick to point out. 'She's a tramp,' she said, in a singsong sort of tone, her accent thick. She too looked me up and down. 'How do you know who'm 'tis, just on her say so. Some fool you be, Ben Trevarisk, atter what them did to 'ee.'

I recovered my voice. 'Don't want no shelter,' I said proudly, 'nor to ask fer anything. If there's an inn I can pay my way. But I've come looking fer my father, and that's no wrong, although to tell truth I never knowed who he was afore today. I'm from off the moors, up near Hawstead Tor. And my Mam, Gladys Ellis, bain't dead . . .'

'She is to me,' he said.

He retreated to the fire, the children straggled after him. The whole family huddled together as if confronting a ghost. The room was larger than I'd have thought, narrow and long, the walls of rock, the small front window set back several feet, the whole grey-white with smoke.

The smell of fish grew stronger, a burning smell, and with a curse Ben Trevarisk pulled a pot off the fire, letting the contents tip. I remained in the entrance, a stranger whom no one wished to welcome, an outsider no one would let in.

Then the man seemed to sag. 'So you'm little Jenny,' he said. 'I should have knowed 'ee, damn me, but you've growed.' He pulled out a stool and sat down as if his legs had buckled. He held his head between his hands like a man bereft. I think he was crying although no sound came, only his shoulders heaved.

His wife busied herself with the children who clustered round her, wide-eyed. She served the contents of the pot, dishing out the fish stew angrily in dollops and then putting the remainder back on the fire as if afraid I'd ask for some. The children perched themselves on stools round the table and shovelled the food in, from time to time stopping, spoons in hand, as if to watch what happened next. No one paid any attention to the father, and his wife, exasperated, seized a bowl, served herself and sat down with her back to him, as if to say, 'Do as you want, I wash my hands of you.'

'Brother,' I said. I stopped, the word coming strangely to my lips. 'Brother, if it be so, you do me wrong to think I've comed to beg. And whatever wrong my Mam did, fer it seems you thinks it of her, don't hold me part of yer grudge. I swear I never knew naught till now, all else was before my remembering. But I'd dearly like to hear you speak of our father, if it's not too hard on you.'

He straightened up at that, wiped his eyes with his fist, began to talk in a singsong way, as people do reciting an old sad tale. 'Ben Trevarisk was me father. A proper man. I still remember how as a nipper I used to go out in his boat, learned me trade off him. The day of the storm he wouldn't take me, sensed some danger perhaps, there, 'tis hard to accept, but he was like that, quiet, see, thinking of others, never of hisself. The boat wasn't his, he worked it fer its owners, well, if 'ee don't know the pilchard trade 'tis a complicated business. He stood to gain a percentage of the catch. 'Twas to his advantage to stay out hauling as long as he could. But the wind were fierce. Not only he were drowned but many like him, all them who didn't have the right to cut and run. They was all fishing fer a percentage, see, and they didn't want to forfeit none.'

His voice broke, steadied. 'The wind blew off shore three days, it hammered on this house. Tiles off, chimneys down, boats splintered at their moorings. Never seen waves so high, the whole square was flooded. And when the tide turned and the sea dropped, the wreckage floated in. Never found him, nor half the men, but the boats we did. 'Twasn't the storm that staved most in. Rotten gear, see, company

69

boats, never did look atter 'em. He'd have had a chance with a decent boat, he could've rid out any storm. Best sailor ever I did know, ask anyone.'

He spoke as if this had happened a day ago, as if every day since he had relived it. Tears streamed down his face. I felt my heart contract. 'Don't,' I said, 'don't.' I went up to his chair. I wanted to put my arms round him.

Pity angered him. He lurched up, his expression truculent. Suddenly the small boy of the photo stood there. 'So now 'ee knows how Ben Trevarisk died,' he said. 'Hope 'ee'm satisfied. Trot on back to yer Mam. Gladys Ellis'll keep 'ee safe and sound.'

Mention of that name seemed to enrage him. His fists doubled. He took a step towards me; I thought he was going to strike; I retreated rapidly putting distance between us. It was his wife who picked up the tale, though she did so between mouthfuls, still not turning round.

'Went off too did Gladys Ellis, well, Gladys Trevarisk. Ellis were her maiden name. She comed from inland some place, never did like the sea. She stood at the chapel door with her two children when the service fer the drowned sailors started, wouldn't come in. "Bury them corpses if you want," she said. "Tain't all of 'em. The sea's got the rest. The sea's got my man. Won't render 'un back till doomsday come. But it shan't have nothing else."

'She took her son, him sitting there, the second Ben Trevarisk, and pushed him inside the chapel. "Take'un," she said. "Fishing be in his blood. I can't stop 'un. But if I give him up then he's no longer mine. Had me heart once," she said, "what's left to give?"

'Off she went, taking her little maid with her, and that was that. Never seed her again. Left her son to drag hisself up, best he could. Never cared no more fer him. So if 'ee be Jenny Trevarisk,' at that she did turn, as fierce suddenly as her husband, ''tis a name not to mention, not in this house leastways. 'You've had it lucky, Jenny Trevarisk, no one abandoned 'ee.'

70

And all that old grief, that old bitterness, spilled out and made a barrier between us that could never be bridged.

There was nothing I could do, nothing I could say to right the wrong done to him, not even a recital of my own wrongs. What had almost crushed me had maimed my brother as surely as if my mother had slashed at him with an axe. And why she had left one child, her firstborn son, her heart strings, why she had left at all, was as lost as her husband was, the husband I think now she must have adored. And why she changed her name, pretending, if she did, not to be a widow and not to have a legitimate child, or at least to allow that interpretation, that too I can't fathom. Except I read once that there are wild creatures who, when caught in a trap, will gnaw their own legs off. And there are humans as wild, who when they are hurt tear at their own flesh to dig the hurt out. It was all of a piece with my mother's character, she was a victim of it, and we, her children, were victims too. And the pity of it was, the sadness, if only the first Ben Trevarisk hadn't drowned, none of it would have happened; my brother would have been like the father he so resembled, and my mother would have remained a happy wife, not driven to destroy what she loved so she could continue to live.

I never did mention my Mam's name again in that house, although sometimes when he was in a more cheerful mood my brother would speak of the period before his father's death when we must have all been happy in our little family circle. And that was the real reason I was persuaded to stay on, to glean those titbits, to catch snatches, glimpses of a time I didn't remember and he didn't want to remember because it meant so much to him. And out of the bits and pieces a picture emerged of a boy child who once had been loved and wanted, and of a girl child who had been her brother's favourite. And like a wall of glass that barrier of bitterness prevented us from ever finding ourselves again.

The actual reason I did stay that first night was because of the children, and the wife. Having said her piece the wife lapsed into silence; her husband sat down again in silence; the children, too frightened to speak, finished their soup in silence. I still waited in the corner, and as the seconds dragged into minutes I became aware of how tired and cold I was, how hungry, until I thought I must fall where I stood. It was the little girl with the green eyes who reminded us of manners and showed true hospitality.

She slid around the edge of the table and came up to me, bowl in hand. 'If you'm Aunt Jenny,' she said, in her little singsong voice, like a bird piping, 'you'm needing some'at to eat.'

She pushed her bowl into my hand, forcing my fingers round it. 'Go on, thun,' she said, 'I've had enough.'

She was about seven, younger than her father'd been when he was orphaned, old enough to feel if not to understand. Her face was pinched as if with cold, a line of doubt worried at her forehead, her smile was anxious, eager, shy. I dropped my bundle, went down on my knees to hold her, the bowl of fish stew tipping until she had the foresight to take it back. Over her head I could see her father and mother exchanging glances. Then the wife said, 'Well, if 'tis so, 'tis so. But don't seem right that she pay fer a bed in some inn, when fer the same price us could give her one.'

She stood up, began to stack the bowls, making a to-do of scraping them though there wasn't much left. 'She'm welcome to sleep,' she said off-handedly, 'she can share with Emma, they'm getting on like a house on fire already. Just fer a day or two. 'Twill be cleaner than the inn, that's fer sure, and she can eat with us. Just as long as she knows we bain't so mighty as to offer it fer free. And she bain't too stuck up to muck in with us.'

She always spoke of me like that, 'she', and my brother never called me anything. But to the children I was soon Aunt Jenny. I accepted the grudging offer of hospitality, made do with bread and cheese scrapings that first night when the fish stew was finished, slept in a corner of a back room on a truckle bed with my niece. My brother and his wife – her name ironically was Charity – disappeared up a ladder with the boys to an upstairs loft. I lay on my side, listening to Emma's soft breathing, her hair spread like thistledown. Despite the pervasive smell of fish that I never became used to, she herself had that child smell of warm milk and honey, and the lashes over her closed eyes brushed cheeks whose skin was cream. Outside the shut window, hidden by a piece of tattered netting, the creaking of the boats and the louder creak of stays and masts kept me awake. Above that noise, the sound of the sea was constant, and as long as I lived in the village I was never far from it, like a continual muttering. Now I could hear the suck of it on the stones, and the dash of it against the harbour wall. Thoughts of its grey expanse surged into my dreams; I fell asleep thinking of ships with their sails spread. And it seemed to me that my poor dead father came looking for me, that young man with the embarrassed smile and shy eyes who cared for others and whose death cut off caring in my mother. 'Where be my girl, thun?' he said. He stooped down from a great height, tossed me up, caught me against his shoulder. I could feel the roughness of his fisherman's jersey against my cheek, and the blisters on his palms where he worked the oars and ropes. His hair was stiff and smelled of salt, and he was smiling. 'Little Ben and me brought 'ee some'at,' he said, 'found it caught in the nets. 'Some'at 'ee'll like. Listen.'

He felt in his pocket, pulled out a shell. It was large and pointed, still damp, with the smell of the sea strong about it. He held it to my ear, cupping his big hand round mine to steady it. Deep inside the pink lustred interior a surging began. ''Tis the ocean,' he said, 'comed all the way from the Pacific to please 'ee. Listen again.'

And it seemed to me that the sound of the sea echoed out of that shell, and lapped around me as I slept, and the salt of the waves was like tears on my cheeks. And when

I woke in that cramped back room with Charity clanking a pail of water and the stir of the village shutting round on all sides, I did not know whether I was remembering dream or memory.

CHAPTER 5

In the end I stayed several months with my brother's family, hedged in by that village closeness, grudgingly endured by Charity, painfully acknowledged by Ben. Only with my nephews and niece did I have any real rapport. And perhaps that was better. Like a foreigner in a foreign land I could learn language and customs more easily from children than from their elders. Deliberately, painfully, I tried to obliterate Julian, not even allowing him entrance to my thoughts. Like my mother before me I suppose, I tried to tear grief out. She was wrong about that. People, memories, don't disappear because of willing them to. The past doesn't stop just because it's the past.

Any attempt I made to come to terms with the villagers met with failure. Although I was always conscious of them, they kept me at a distance. They must have known who I was, the scandal of my Mam's leaving impossible to forget, and I called myself by my real name, although Jenny Trevarisk sounded strange after so many years of Ellis. But no one ever mentioned it. Like the old man I'd first met, they pretended ignorance. They nodded good morning, perhaps, and then when I had passed, put heads together, tongues going clickety clack. I felt the whispers spread between those coupled houses; like treads of mist they circled, twined and interlaced, obscuring the real facts, embroidering new ones. At first I didn't mind. I had the children as my playmates and the whole of the sea shore as playground. It was only later with more immediate needs that I realized how much of an outcast I had become, in a place so inbred that another village three miles off seemed further than a continent.

The children laughed at my fancies. ''Tis a blessing they houses be so close,' my older nephews said. They grinned, at nine and ten too knowing for their years. 'When there's whisky to be hid, or there's some'at wrong, them revenue officers can't find out where 'tis. Every house's joined, see. You can knock on the walls to signal, then slip from door to door. The customs come in one way, you'm gone t'other, easy as pie. And every house's got a "hole", meant fer hiding things.'

When the fire was out they showed me theirs, under the hearth stone, big enough for a cask or two, hollowed out of the rock. 'Used a lot in the old times,' they boasted with a wink, 'when there was brandy smuggling, or wrecking. Don't do much of that now of course, but it might come in useful one day.' They laughed at my expression, hands in pockets of their torn trousers, like little men.

Stifled by cottage life, by the smells of fish, the dirt, the confusion, as often as I could I played with the children out-of-doors, if it can be called play that is, for it was also work. Every morning, rain or fine, we were expected to leave the house: no one went to school not even the older lads. And as on a farm, so here I discovered there was rhythm to village life, based on the going out of the fleet and its return.

Most days the boats sailed with the tide before dawn. When they came back the village swarmed to meet them, old men, women, children crowding on the quay, the too-young and too-old to watch and comment, the rest to help, tying up the boats and sorting the day's catch. This press of humanity was something I wasn't used to; in a year at Penwith Farm I could count on one hand the people I'd met.

The confusion of that moment when the fleet returned reminded me of the frenzy when pigs are fed, or when bullocks are gathered in after the summer's grazing: what a shouting and a bellowing, what a milling herd! Boys my nephews' age leapt to hold the boats, hauling on the mooring lines until their knuckles cracked. Men dragged off the bulk of the catch, using panniers, or square wooden boxes called 'gurries'. If the tide was out, as sometimes happened, the boats were drawn up on the beach and pony carts were used instead, the poor ponies struggling through the sand, their drivers pulling at them, the children tickling their legs with whips.

I hated when the fish came in. Bodies shining, tails flapping, I'd never seen anything so alive. Then in an instant all that glitter gone, all that sheen and freshness stiffened to stone. I'd seen dead animals on the farm of course, rabbits, sheep, cows: nothing seemed so bad to me as that stiff rigidity, that sudden squelching of light.

Little Emma felt the same. She hid her head. I stroked the delicate strands of curls and wondered what the future held for her. It was clear that, like my brother, my older nephews had fishing in their blood, were only waiting for their father to take them out to sea, were longing to be taught how to empty lobster pots and bait hooks, and drag in nets. They knew instinctively when their father's boat, the 'Dolphin', returned, and after it was moored they'd jump on board to sort the fish, flipping the edible into casks, throwing the useless overboard for the waiting sea birds. These gulls swooped and screamed, seeming to know too when to expect the fleet, circling the bay in flocks.

On good days there were lobsters for the city markets, black and gleaming with their threatening claws; sometimes crabs scuttled with their frightening sideways walk; once a giant ray got tangled in the net, its pointed barbs admired by the boys, from a safe distance! And when all these things had been carried off, the residue was gathered up for our own use: the broken fish, the odds and ends, the bits the boys could snatch from the passing gurries – 'cabing', such theft was called.

77

The main catch was taken either to individual store rooms beneath the cottages, or to general curing cellars known as 'palaces'. I never went there. That was the women's own domain; there they worked in frantic haste to process the fish prior to sending it away. Some of them sold pilchards, hawked them round the countryside, 'jousters' was their name, and they'd scream at each other as they bent over the fish, packing it into baskets they wore on their backs with long straps for balance tied about their heads. I kept clear of them as well, with their strange speech and uncouth gestures; they were jealous of their work, zealously guarded their right to pick and choose; if challenged, boasting of one of their kind who had once been to 'Lunnun, to see t'Queen'.

I learned that pilchards were the staple provision, although the big runs came in the autumn. Pilchards were a kind of herring, full of bones. At nights the sound of their bursting air bladders filled the cottage with squeaks and groans. Most teatimes we had pilchards boiled over the furze fire, or fried, or baked in the oven as a pasty or pie, 'star gazy pie' with the fishes' tails and heads left sticking up so the eyes stared out. Our lamps were lit by pilchard oil; it was pilchard oil that oozed from the barrels in the under-crofts and caused the stench, pilchard oil that seeped down the cliff path into the harbour, staining the walls. It was pilchard oil that got in our well, turning the water so fishy that, by comparison, even moorland bogs tasted sweet.

I think Ben couldn't bring himself to take his boys out on the 'Dolphin', for all they pleaded. "'Tain't my boat,' he'd say, shaking his head when they asked. 'When I buy me own that'll be the day.' But there were many days when he never went out himself, but stayed by the fire and brooded.

I guessed he worked on one of those company boats that the old man had mentioned but I never liked to question him. As the likelihood of his ever obtaining a boat obviously receded further every year, this fact contributed greatly to his gloom, making his poverty all the more crippling.

For he was poor, my brother. I'd thought we'd lived rough at Penwith, but that was luxury compared with him. Married young, having five young children, a slatternly wife, Ben never stood a chance. Most of what he earned he spent in drink, unable to keep away from the local inn. Every night he went there, returning late, often drunk and randy, to spend next day in tears and gloom, overcome with guilt. In many ways I thought he resembled Farmer Penwith, and I often pitied him. Sometimes I even pitied Charity. But she could have kept the house clean, I thought, she could have washed the children and their clothes. I was hard on her. The poverty and drinking and guilt were too much for her, they pushed her under. But when sometimes she raked me with a baleful look I sensed her hate. It wasn't all for her husband's sake, part was for her own. Although she must have known how poor I was, by comparison I must have seemed rich. Each week when I paid her for my keep she both accepted and resented it. Perhaps she remembered her own girlhood, perhaps she envied me mine. Those looks, those sullen reproachful looks stopped me trying to be friends, although I longed for one. Nothing I could do was right, not even helping in the house, not even keeping the little ones amused (for she let them out too, to roam the quay, with a shrug as if to say, they'm old enough, the two younger boys barely able to toddle and only Emma to watch over them).

I got into the habit of taking all three with me, keeping out of her way too, avoiding her. And as time went on and there were reasons of my own to keep to myself, I was careful never to be alone with her, wary of her malice and her caustic tongue.

Most days the children and I went on the beach, scrambling over the harbour wall. The beach lay at the foot of the headland under cliffs which here fell in sheer slabs of slate. When the tide was in the sea beat round the edge of the rocks, a line of white, and a stream of bubbles showed the drift of the currents with the shifting wind. When the tide was out the rocks were uncovered. Deep pools appeared, lined with seaweed, under which all manner of creatures lurked. Between the rocks were stretches of golden sand, sifted fine from the pounding of the surf, and littered with the flotsam and jetsam of the Atlantic ocean.

We never came home empty handed. Along with the other village children we vied for booty, carried spars of wood twice our size, gathered broken nets and lobster pots, empty bottles, pieces of rigging. Like gleaners in the fields we harvested the sea, often lingering until the tide turned so we could catch shrimps as they came in through the rocky channels, using caps or skirts as nets. Bending over one of those deep narrow chasms was as back-breaking as weeding fields, feet braced upon the shell-studded sides, arms plunged in up to elbows. Yet I didn't mind. I never thought of swimming, I didn't know how to and neither did the children, but the coolness of that water, satin soft, the soft green weed, the translucent bodies of the shrimps floating past, the green light that shone through them, all seemed too delicate for that rough coast, seemed breath-stopping.

Having made our catch, having admired the tapering bodies, the fine antennae, Emma and I would have let the shrimps go, but my nephews scooped them up for selling, too valuable for our own eating. We did eat the shells we picked, knocking them off the rocks with smaller pebbles, winkles and mussels and such, which only hunger drove me to tolerate.

Sometimes we went up on the headland when the sea was blue like sapphire and even the waves seemed stilled. We'd hang over the edge, a hundred feet high, and look down into the painted water, almost to the bottom, where purple strands of weed curled and writhed like snakes. Out to sea boats looked smaller than models, but they were actually big, not the usual boats from the village, from further off.

The boys knew all about them. 'Drifters, see,' they said. They pointed out the nets slung like a curtain over the sterns, dipping deep into the ocean, indiscriminately taking up all kinds of fish, fishing the waters clean. And they'd point out the origin of these 'foreign' boats: 'Yarmouth,' they'd say, or 'Lowestoft, on t'east of England.' They'd scowl, imitating their father. 'Drifted a long way to steal from we.'

They'd try to explain the village's way of fishing, the traditional way using shallow nets, 'seining', mainly for pilchards, and how the drifter boats fished deeper, striking down to the bottom, scooping up everything within sight. And they would get angry, speaking of quarrels between these 'up country' boats and the local crews, how in season the strangers worked all week long, even on Sundays, not stopping as Cornish fishers did. And they'd tell how once the pilchards used to show up like great dark patches on the surface, millions and millions in one shoal, so many that the lower layers died before they could be lifted. And they'd take me to the little stone hut where the lookout, or 'huer', kept watch for that one massive shoal that would make the village prosperous.

'P'rhaps this year,' they'd say. And they'd clamber on the walls, pointing westward where the pilchards came from. 'Hevva, a shoal, hevva,' they'd shout until the cliff tops rang, and taking up branches of furze wrapped in Emma's apron against the prickles they'd make signals as the huers used to do to the waiting fleet.

They didn't explain what I was already beginning to sense: the fear that pilchard fishing was done for, that those great shoals were a thing of the past, and that the drifter boats with their deeper nets were ruining traditional Cornish fishing.

I'd look at their thin legs and arms, at Emma's anxious face; I'd think of my brother's misery, and I'd curse the fate that showed such little pity to men whose lives were hard enough. And I'd think then too what would become of me, and what I should do in the months ahead, and despite all my resolves I would remember Julian and curse the day I'd met him. Love is like that I suppose, easily turned to hate. But it wasn't really hate I felt for him, it was only the anxiety. For things weren't right with me, I could feel it. And although I had no name for it, the uneasiness sat heavily. There's one thing an unwed girl fears most, more than being left that is, and now I feared it would happen to me.

All these conflicting emotions churned. Sometimes I felt that they had me caught, like that pilchard shoal. But perhaps the sea was also in my blood. For even when I most despaired, and there were nights when despair laid its black hand on me, I never tired of the ocean in all its moods and colours. One day it would be cornflower blue to make the spirit sing, to make me think of skylarks and the gorse and heather patches; the next it would be grey like smoke, full of mystery and omens. Sometimes where it met the sky the line between was so sharp I believed I was looking at the world's end; sometimes the meeting blended into misted space enclosing the village in a bowl, where I swam, again fish-like, waiting to be trapped. I began to feel about St Marvell as I did about the moors, knowing it well in one tiny quarter that is, cautious of the rest. If by the summer's end I was able to share the villagers' worries whether the pilchard shoals would come again full force, by then those general anxieties blended with my own concerns. My resources were almost depleted, I needed work; I dreaded asking for it, for fear the fisher women would refuse. But all these paled by comparison with that other trouble that I had, although I hid it too, terrified someone should suspect, not willing to admit it to myself.

By then Charity had already begun to hint that I should move on. 'Can't feed she fer naught,' she'd say. I presumed she'd rummaged through my clothes to find what little money I had left. (I had no other hiding place, and again presumed she searched when I was out.) But perhaps I misjudge her. She may well have calculated from what the old seaman had told her first. 'So much cash,' he'd have said, 'the whole seat took up with it.' (Although he too never acknowledged seeing me, passed me by without comment.) Or she may well have been guessing, shrewd enough to guess most things, even those she shouldn't, even those that shouldn't be mentioned, even those bound to cause harm.

Charity however had only hinted at my leaving, not anxious to lose my weekly contribution before she had to. It was late August before something occurred to make that hint a certainty. And it was Emma who brought it about.

Little Emma, with the extraordinary eyes and the puzzled look, who, like her grandfather, had a heart of gold, who could do no harm to anyone. That she never meant to goes without saying. She too was victim of a way of life that loaded children with responsibility, turned them into imitation grown-ups too soon.

The day had been cold, harbinger of autumn, a dragging sort of day through which I had moved listlessly, certain now of coming trouble, uncertain how to deal with it. Although the tide had been far out, the water was too cold for lingering on the beach. The boys and I had come back, our arms filled with driftwood, and they were stacking it under the steps for the fire when Charity came to the door. Her sallow face was flushed and the sharp tone she used to her sons suggested some immediate catastrophe. 'Tell she to come here,' she cried, her body quivering with indignation. I tensed with nervousness, followed her indoors, trying to imagine what had happened.

My brother was sitting in his usual place before the fire, his shoulders hunched with suffering. Emma stood in front of him. She had been blackberrying, for her sacking pinafore was purple-stained, as were her mouth and hands. She had been crying. I wanted to snatch her up and bear her off but I didn't say anything, let my sister-in-law do the talking.

She gave the child a poke. 'Speak up,' she said.

'I were up at High End,' Emma said, her voice a monotone. 'I were picking of the berries.' She stopped. I nodded encouragement. High End was the name given to the fields at the top of the village where it began its sharp descent. It was a fair distance off for a child to wander on her own, but I couldn't imagine that being the cause for all this fuss.

'I was picking 'em,' Emma said, 'and eating 'em.' She looked at her father then but her mother was implacable. 'And a man comed up to me on a horse.'

At mention of the word horse I felt my body stiffen. 'What sort of man?' I wanted to ask; my mouth was too dry to talk. Suddenly the image of Julian filled that room, transported me with hope. I saw him on his grey stallion, bending down towards the little girl. I saw his smile, I saw his eyes, I saw the outstretched hand.

Her mother poked Emma again, fingers digging through the ugly dress, cut down from someone else's. 'Go on,' she said.

She didn't look at me but I could sense the malice.

'He asked fer Jenny,' Emma said, the tears now rolling freely. 'I told him she were in the village and that she were my aunt. Told him that he were mistook, her name weren't Jenny Ellis. "She'm Jenny Trevarisk now," I said, "like me, since the marriage."'

There was a silence. I felt my heart begin to beat in slow, heavy time, I felt the dryness in my throat.

'What else did he say?' I cried. 'Did he leave a message? Did he say where he'd gone or how I could reach him?' I took a step towards Emma. 'Oh, sweetheart, speak.'

Emma's face puckered into its familiar look. She pursed her lips, for a moment reminding me of my Mam. 'He said,' she pronounced clearly, 'he said to tell 'ee he remembered, that he'd come back fer 'ee. But since he would be leaving right away again, no need fer 'ee to bother. And to wish 'ee well in yer new life; and glad that 'ee were happy. Did I do wrong?' she suddenly burst out. 'Did I do wrong to speak? The horse was some big and he looked so tall, I was that scared. But then he spoke to me nice, I didn't like to run. And he looked so kind wishing of 'ee well, I told him what I could.'

I had sunk onto a stool, my legs unsteady. I couldn't

say a word. To know that Julian had returned, even if he were already gone again, seemed of itself a gift. I didn't want to know why he hadn't come before, or where he had been all these months; even the confusion about my name didn't seem serious compared with the joy in his reappearance. It was only later that I saw it for what it was, in all its misapprehension; saw all the implication for misunderstanding and mistake, saw the consequences.

Nothing loath, Charity was the first to point them out.

'A gentleman,' she sniffed. 'Who be he then?' She shook her finger at Emma hard as if expecting the child to answer. When of course she didn't, with another sniff, 'Some fine gentleman who'll be off that quick now he thinks she's wed, tho' who would look at she twice, double-faced baggage that she is. In any case, no stopping of him now, I'll be bound, glad to be let off the hook. But whatever did he promise she, I wonder, that he comed all this way to speak of it? And whatever did her give in return? Seems to me,' she drew herself up, pronouncing judgement, 'seems to me she's bin up to things no proper maid should. I warned 'ee of it, Ben, I did. No one comes here like she, I said, wild and bedraggled yet with money to burn in her pocket, if there bain't some'at bought and hid.'

'Who was he, Jenny?' Ben said. By contrast he sounded almost gentle, ready to listen to reason, relieved perhaps, as if he was wanting to hear some good news at last. So when I told the name his anger was all the more shocking for being unexpected.

He started up, his face so dark it made the stain of Emma's blackberries pale.

'God rot 'ee fer an ingrate, Jenny Trevarisk,' he shouted, 'God rot 'ee fer the shame. Don't you have the sense you was born with? Charity were right; I should've slammed the door when you first camed, not let you in to bring disgrace.'

Pushing his daughter aside he stumped out of the cottage. We heard his sea boots clumping down the steps and along the cliff. 'There,' said Charity, 'that's some'at else she've done.'

She glared at me, for the first time talking to me straight. 'Off to the pub fer sure, that's where he'll be, swilling down the beer, and where's the money coming from, or who's to feed the little 'uns when he's drunk it all? He's a fool, Jenny Trevarisk, a girt great fool, never seeing what's beneath his nose. And so are you, thinking only of yourself, never bothering to ask. The Pollevens've bin owners of most of the St Marvell fleet since times back, no love lost on 'em. 'Twas Polleven boats that mainly sunk in the storm, 'twas Polleven boat that drowned yer Paw. You've struck yer brother to the heart, I tell 'ee straight, that a sister of his could stoop to lie with his father's murderer.

'And don't tell me you didn't lie with him,' she added virtuously. 'You had it stamped on you when you comed, a flashing of his money, pretending you wanted to hear about a father you've no respect fer. And don't tell me you bain't a carrying of the fruit of it, under that flashy dress. I ought to know when a woman's expecting, I've had enough of me own. I heard you of mornings, out in the privy where you thought you couldn't be heard. And all the time you've been here, and not once yer monthlies, that says some'at. But I'll have no whoring in my house, or worse. So take yer things and go. Or let Ben kill you hisself when he comes home, for I swear he will.'

She advanced upon me, I stumbled towards the door, Emma clinging to my knees, the little fellows bawling. When I had reached the bottom step she slung my bundle after me. She must have had it all prepared and waiting (minus the remaining cash with the exception of a few pennies).

'Go back where you comed from,' she screamed, 'nothing but trouble follows you. Evil the day that you were born, curse the day that spawned you. Curse 'ee fer a shameless harlot that don't know right from wrong. Curse your bastard brat.'

And down the street on their front steps the neighbours

heard, the women with their arms crossed, their children tucked behind them, the men pretending to light their pipes, minding their own business. They never spoke, although they must all have known what Charity said, and their belligerent stance, their fixed looks all substantiated her judgement. 'We stand with her, she's one of us, you bain't,' that's what their silence said.

When I reached the open square, I could hear my brother's voice. He had gone into the inn, his usual haunt, and was once more retelling his life story, shouting it out, crying it out in impotent fury to anyone who'd listen. The square was not exactly full, but people were gathering, a second Trevarisk scandal in the making. I stopped, aware of my headlong flight, my sister's screaming that still came faintly from above. The line of people, the narrow, crooked streets, the close-packed houses seemed to crowd upon me; more than ever I wanted to push through them; in each direction buildings blocked the way. The lack of air stifled, the knowing eyes judged; any hope I might have had of shelter, of help in my predicament, died without my asking. It didn't need the innkeeper's wife to hammer home what I already felt.

She advanced from the doorway of the inn, her black hat bobbing. She was a loud-voiced woman at the best of times, given to scolding cats and children, capable of dealing with the village drunks if she had to, her hat with its wreath of flowers a symbol of all that was respectable, spokeswoman for the community, a pillar of the chapel.

'We've been watching you, Jenny Ellis, or Trevarisk as you calls yerself, tho' we ain't spoke afore. Yer Mam left us with a curse, God pardon her, fer I don't; she wiped our dust off her shoes. She left us her son fer rearing, well, who else was there to do it except the women of the village? But never thought of that, did she, how Ben Trevarisk lived when she were gone? A burden on us, an extra mouth to feed when times was hard, an extra load. So why now should we take in her daughter when the brother turns her out? As fer yer young gentleman,' she said the word disdainfully, 'if so he be wanting to make an honest woman of 'ee then more power to him. If not, Charity speaks sense. Ben Trevarisk's a good man, a God-fearing man, even if he drinks a bit, 'twould break his heart to spare his sister's shame. If I were you, Jenny Trevarisk, I'd be off double-quick, unless you wants a worse disaster. Ben'd not take disgrace lying down. And we've no room fer paupers, nor their offspring, and that's a fact.'

There was a murmur from the crowd, of approval perhaps, or condemnation. An old fisher woman cried, 'She's nothing but bad luck,' while one of the wilder 'jousters', half-drunk herself, offered a different solace. 'Join us then, my lover, men ain't all that bad.' Like a baited bear I felt chained to a post. And as before, so now the past rose up.

I don't remember stumbling from the village, nor finding my way out on the headland. I was high on the cliff top when I came to myself. The wind blew in gusts up there and the sea was a leaden grey, sullen under sullen skies. Even daylight seemed grey. At my back the village sank behind the slate cliffs like a medieval castle, where suddenly all those twisted paths and narrow alleyways resembled castle walls, impossible to breach. Ahead, the coast stretched mile after mile in open formation, great tongues of land pointing out to sea then bending back in upon themselves. I stood upon a narrow promontory open on three sides, a spit of land high above the water where rocks were jagged black. Waves curled and broke and surged below, tearing at the cliffs.

On the point was a kind of dip, a broken circle of ditch and dyke which part of me recognized from something Julian had described as an old fort. Once it had been a refuge, a place of safety. Now I crossed the shelter of the ditch, lay face down on the springy grass at the cliff edge and felt the earth shudder as the waves crashed. Long ago this place been inhabited, people had lived here, people who had built these outer ramparts only to have them broken down. And when the enemy burst through the walls and swarmed across the ditches, had any resisted, what had become of the survivors? All lost, I thought, all drowned and gone. The oldness of the place, its loss and destruction became part of my own. Too tired to fight I thought, now I truly have nowhere else to go, no one to turn to, nothing to keep me going. A wave as deep as the waves below washed over me; a second time I grieved for loss. And within me like a stone I felt the guilt of my unborn child.

I might have lain like that for hours, I suppose, until night had fallen, bringing with it the promised storm. I might have lingered there for days, drenched with rain and spray. If eventually I would have been sucked off or swept away, I wouldn't have resisted. Out of that despair a stranger came to the rescue.

An unusual rescuer at that, a neat little person, prim and proper in her navy cloak with the white pinafore under it. Her navy hat was pinned firmly on her head, although the wind had teased her hair to curls and her cheeks were flushed with walking. 'Whatever be you thinking of?' Her voice was scolding, already set in its customary maternal fret, yet at the same time solicitous. 'You'm proper mazed with cold. The sea's coming in and there's half a gale blowing; 'twill blow you off them cliffs if we don't get a move on.'

And that was Beth Martin, my saviour and friend.

She stood at the edge of the path, not venturing out to where I was lying; already the wind was picking at her skirts and turning them into sails. For a little thing she spoke with authority, although where she had come from I couldn't imagine. I'd never seen her before although later I discovered she roamed freely from village to village often on errands to the sick and needy but in so effacing a way as to be almost invisible. Now her brisk way of speaking, the command in her voice, brought me back to sense. I sat up, wiped my eyes, tried to stand. The wind almost bowled me over.

'Get down, get down,' she mouthed at me, the words torn away in a great scud of air. And seeing I didn't understand she dropped to all fours and began to creep out to me, hanging on to tufts of grass for ballast. Frightened now myself, I copied her, inching along between the gusts, crouching into the crevices, waving to her to go back herself, she being that much smaller and slighter and so at greater risk. We met halfway, where the dip of the first dyke flattened in a wider place so that the immediate danger of being blown away was diminished. Both of us were panting, were scratched and torn. Her skirts were stained with green, her hands were bleeding, but she still had her hat jammed firmly on. What she saw in me I never asked. I saw a round brown face, the skin smooth and shining for all that she must have been close to thirty. She had round brown eyes, a snub of a nose and a mouth that was meant for smiling, although now it was drawn into a serious frown. I said the first thing that came into my head. 'What be you doing here yerself?'

'Looking for you,' she said. 'And we'd best hurry, we bain't safe yet.'

Without waiting for answer she turned and crawled back the way she'd come. I followed, dragging my bundle behind me. And when we came to the regular cliff path, which itself was unfenced and open on the seaward side, she turned off inland across a stubble field, still bent low under the wind's force, I still following. And that was how Beth Martin brought me home.

CHAPTER 6

Her house, or hut more like, was on the other side of the headland from St Marvell. The cliffs dipped down here into a sort of sandy cove, an irregular crescent bounded by high rocks on either side. A small stream came ambling down from higher ground, the whole forming a sheltered valley filled with bushes and small trees. Her cabin as it was called was situated at the upper end of this little valley, above the stream. It was made of cob, strengthened with driftwood, its roof turfed over with grass sods, set down into the earth like a fox's den. In front, attached to the main framework was a kind of lean-to shed open to the sea, with wooden slat seats on either side of the doorway, as if meant for sitting on. It was quiet and dry there, out of the wind, and Beth plumped herself down on one of the seats and began to undo her boots which were encaked with mud. When she was finished and had drawn them off and put them neatly at one side, she turned her attention to me.

'Well now,' she said, carefully unpinning her shawl and shaking it before untying her hat and removing the large hatpin, 'I've been hearing about you, Jenny Trevarisk, all summer long when them old cats had time to spare from watching you. And I've been watching of you too, tho' not like that harridan of an innkeeper. I've seen you often with yer brother's chilrun fer one thing, when you didn't see me, and you'm that good with 'em. Seems to me tain't what yer Mam did that's at fault to set 'em a-yapping, but what they thinks *you've* done, if you've done anything, that is. So now that's out of the way, suppose you tell me about yerself, if you wants to, that is. I'm not keen to pry; I'm here to lissen.'

And when I had told her, more or less as I've told it here, she nodded her head several times, stood up, looking seawards. The cabin was set high enough to give a good view over the bushes down to the entrance of the cove where the waves were already beginning to beat on the beach in spumes of spray. The wind caught them and swirled them like smoke; the surge of the water was a distant rumble, an earthquake. She watched for a while, arms stretched out, Moses at the Red Sea crossing; I almost expected her to shout, 'Stop!', like King Canute, to turn the tide back. The damp had made her pale hair curl again, her eyes gleamed.

'I live here alone,' she told me then, softly, but distinctly, 'with me brother, Jeb. He'm a sailor, off on his ship most of the time, but since we've lived here from childhood, 'tis home to him as much as me. While he'm gone there's his room free, if you fancy it.'

I started to protest, thanks, fears of giving fresh offence, explanations tumbling out. She waved them off, faced me squarely. 'My Mam weren't wed,' she said, 'I think our Paw were married, but it didn't stop she from loving him. I were born first, Jeb after, both of us love chilrun. That's what my Mam called us, love chilrun, 'tis a pleasant name, better than what they used to shout after us. And when she died, we stayed on in her house here by ourselves, I looking after Jeb until he growed. There were some money coming in at first but Jeb wouldn't have none of it. Manage by ourselves he said. And we did.

'We won't starve,' she went on, talking to let me collect myself, in that way reminding me of Julian. 'We keeps a boat down near the cove. Then there's some land fer a goat or two and a few chicken. And in the autumn when the fish run I works in the cellars, up Port Zenack way. 'Tis further off but better so, less questions asked, none the wiser. We'm free there, see, free of St Marvell gossip, 'tis like another world.'

As if guessing my thoughts she added, 'I bain't a church-going woman, never had time fer it. So I don't take to heart the preaching about sin and such. Not many hasn't sinned sometime. And I don't hold with gossip. To me 'tis more important to find out truth, not spread lies, or half lies, for the sound of it.'

The brown eyes gleamed, the soft mouth worked. 'In my time I've had my share of talk,' she said, 'perhaps it killed my Mam. It shan't kill you, not while I'm here to stop it. Don't say 'tis much I offer, don't say 'twill do much good, but if it be you needs a place 'tis here fer the asking. You and the baby both.'

She looked at me straight again, her eyes knowing, not with mean intent, but kind acceptance.

'Fer that's so too, now bain't it?' she asked. And as if laying down a burden grown too large for me, I finally admitted, 'Yes.' Yes to all she offered me, yes, to staying in her home, yes, to the coming of a child.

The relief I felt cannot be put into words. Nor the warmth of her hospitality as she now bustled about, making up the fire, reheating a rabbit stew. When I tried to tell her again that being with her, even for one night, was more, much more than I had right to hope for, 'Nonsense,' she said. She picked up a bundle of sticks from the pile beside the hearth. 'A tree is made of branches, right,' she said, holding one up. 'They fit together, trunk, branches, stems. So should womenfolk support each other, not tear each other down. But if it frets at you, imagine you're doing me a favour while Jeb's away. I'm that lonely, no one to talk to. Besides, you'd like to see yer brother's chilrun once in a while, and they need you. It'll be alright.'

She smiled at me, her mouth dimpling at the corners.

'And suppose the father turned up fer you, where else would he look?' She continued to speak in this way, of my future, of my future child, easily, naturally, a *love child*, as her own experience saw it, calculating dates, making plans as if she looked forward to it. I watched her. She wasn't beautiful, her youth was past, by the flickering fire her face looked worn, but goodness sat there like a light. I thought, life's passed her by because of other people's troubles yet surely some benign influence keeps her gentle, brings her content.

In one thing however it seemed I was wrong. She too had a man she loved, whom she 'walked out with' as she put it, who waited for her as she him. She longed to have a child herself; I think she might have envied me, if envy had any part in her. Her lack of censure, or reproach, was so different from anything I'd known, as different from Farmer Penwith's morality as chalk from cheese, that I was overwhelmed by it. I sat by the warmth, let her voice drift, followed my own thoughts, for the first time in weeks allowing myself to think of Julian without bitterness.

Where have you been, I asked him then, that you left me so long? Why have you returned to make me remember you? Suddenly poor Emma's mistake, my sister-in-law's spite, appeared in all their monstrous forms. I almost cried aloud, 'Come back, don't leave me alone. What I could bear by myself, I can't, not with this burden.'

Beth took my hand again as if she had heard me. Her own face had contracted with sympathy. 'Wishing won't change anything,' she said, almost as my mother might have done but without the cruel sarcasm. 'I know how hard 'tis. But if he came back once he'll come again, if you can but send him word.'

She closed her eyes as if in prayer, a different sort of praying too from Farmer Penwith's. She had said she was not a church-going woman but I felt the quality of it. And as we sat there, quiet-like (although outside the wind howled and the sea raged up the inlet), a kind of peace came over me, an acceptance, a sense of my own insignificance in the harmony of things. And for the first time I felt the child within me as a gift, Julian's gift, not a punishment.

That night I slept more soundly since I had left Penwith, in an upstairs loft divided into two by more driftwood and reached by a ladder at the back – whatever money had come into this house it could never have been much. True, outside the sea still crashed on the shore and a gale blew; like the bushes in this part of the coast the little cabin sank under it, bending lopsided with the wind. Everything kept surprisingly warm and dry (the mattresses down-filled, 'From our own geese,' she said, the blankets hand woven and thick), not like my brother's cottage whose stone walls leaked non-stop. And although there was the usual smell of fish it was cleaner somehow, fresher, not decayed and oozing, rather the smell of the open sea and the free creatures that live in it. I awoke again to peace, to calm seas, sunshine, the sounds of early morning. Birds sang along the stream, the damp ground released a scent of growing things, even though it was almost autumn. And it was in that quiet hour when all the rest of the world was waking that I remembered Julian's address, the address on the paper I'd thrown away and deliberately forgotten. That too was something I had suppressed, but it had been waiting there all this while to be remembered.

We rose early for, like my Mam, Beth was always busy. While I blew the fire to a blaze she bustled about, fetching bread from the larder, heating up goat's milk. She chatted constantly, about her brother, about herself, about her 'fiance' as she called him, making me understand that indeed I did her a favour by letting her talk. 'It won't be easy,' she said finally, as we still sat at the table and the sun motes danced in the open door. ''Tis some rough, and the women be rough-tongued too until you get used to 'em.' She was speaking again of Port Zenack fisheries, promising to put in a good word for me. I didn't tell her what my Mam had said, *Strong as an ox* she'd called me.

'I can but try,' I said. And that was as true of writing letters as curing fish.

A strange interlude now occurs in my life, while I waited, hoped, longed for Julian's response, and felt my child quicken within me. I wrote him almost every day, living through these letters. I didn't tell him of the child but I did explain Emma's mistake, and where I lived, in hopes he'd come and fetch me. I told him things too about my new life, simple things I thought he'd like, how much I admired Beth, finding in her a mother's model, although she was so few years older, how she taught me to knit and sew while I in turn taught her to read, or rather when I could, borrowed books to read aloud at the end of the day, thus sharing with her some of our old favourites, seen now through her eyes.

I told him also of the man with whom she was 'walking out' (although since he came by bicycle that expression was not particularly apt!). He was an older man, lived down near Truro, miles away, and once a month faithfully he'd appear, having pedalled or pushed his bike all of a Saturday. He was tall and thin with thinning hair and a long, lean face and surprisingly young eyes, a bootmaker by trade. He used to joke that only boots as good as his could have carried him that far. I described his patience and his shyness, his sly little jokes, and how he seemed not to mind me, sleeping outside in the lean-to with a heap of blankets. And I tried to explain that once, when in a fit of rebellion I'd thought, 'What does she see in him?', contrasting that patient devotion suddenly and vividly with all our young passion, the look on his face as he sat by the hearth, the answering smile on Beth's, made me sense something that I hadn't thought of before, the other side of loving, the steadfastness. That thought I did try to express, along with the yearning. And if I longed to write of my wonder in this coming birth, to share with him my hopes, to ponder what it would be like to have a child to tend and look after, would it be satisfied with me alone until

96

he came, would it ask for its father as I used to do, those also were thoughts for saving and I kept them to myself.

Nor did I tell him of my work; that was something I feared he might dislike, or might be angry that he couldn't prevent, and thus feel guilty and resentful. Yet if I lived in a dream world through letters, this daily round was reality. Every morning that autumn I went with Beth to Port Zenack, pleasant in fine weather over the cliffs, with the sea fretting below the headland; not so pleasant in the rain, or when we returned at night and had to take the long way round.

By now the pilchard season was in full swing, there was a need for women in the cellars, and for that I felt thankful. But Beth had been right, the work was hard, dirtier, more full of smells and filth than I could stomach. As when I was a child I gritted my teeth and endured.

Port Zenack was very like St Marvell, a similarly isolated community living as if it had a wall around it, even neighbouring villages strange and forbidden territory. There were the same tight-knotted lanes, the same crowded houses, the same sense of a rabbit warren. It too was first and foremost a fishing village which lived, breathed, dreamed pilchards. I never did see them boiling in a foaming mass as the old sailor had described but I often watched the seine boats go out and return with their nets only part full, to the villagers' great disappointment. Now I had become part of that milling herd which dragged panniers of fish to the 'palace', indistinguishable from the rest of the women under layers of clothes, almost shapeless with padding. (Since we worked partly in the open air we suffered from the cold.) Our nickname, 'fair maids', derived from a type of barrel, and must have been a masculine joke, for there was little 'fair' about us. Many of us scraped our hair up in large mob caps, some wore extra stuffing in the shape of horse hair belts tied round the waist, all of us covered ourselves with heavy outer aprons. We wore thick gloves to protect our hands but the salt stung through them to the bone, our fingers were red and raw with it, it blistered our cuts.

97

And nothing could keep us clean or hide the stench of fish (although Beth was particular about that, stowing the protective outer layers in a special corner, and then when we had returned home, using the front lean-to as a kind of outdoor wash room, where we sluiced ourselves carefully with water left heating on the fire).

The 'palace' where we worked was a large stone building with an open rectangular courtyard in the middle. Huge granite pillars supported the outside walls, and the floor was paved with small pebbles, a hard surface on which to stand for hours. It sloped into a kind of gutter, which led to a pit for the refuse and the oil. Our task was to take the fish as they were unloaded, wash and put them in big concrete tanks where they 'settled' for several weeks in their own brine. I was astonished by the speed and skills which the experienced workers had, turning, arranging the fish in lines, scattering them with salt, especially as at the same time everyone talked non-stop.

I worked beside Beth, copying her brisk efficiency, like her not saying much but listening (she was a good listener when she had to be, sorting out news of those in trouble for example, always ready to help). In this way I picked up many jewels of information: stories, legends, superstitions. I heard about the Rector of Morwenstow whose ghost still wanders on the headland, I heard about the Padstow Bar which had drowned so many boats. Courting, marriages, births, the women spoke freely of their own family affairs, taking no notice of me since I was under Beth's protection. I saw a different side of Cornish womenfolk here, without the rancour and derision. In fact I saw what I could have found in my brother's home, if Charity had allowed it.

I remember once they were speaking of naming a child, some fancy name that made me think of poor Cyril. They laughed at the thought. 'We do give ourselves airs,' they said, mocking themselves, 'ain't that right, Miss Beth?'

Beth, whose real name was Elspeth, nodded at me as if to agree and whispered loudly, 'What of Guinevere?' which set them off again. I smiled back. It's nice to be laughed at if you're part of the laughter, and for the first time I felt I was.

Much of their talk was more sober, repetitious of my young nephews' comments. There were arguments about the virtues of old methods of catching fish and curing it compared with the inferior, new-fangled ways; about the decline in markets although now there was a railway to take the catch 'up country'. There were fierce criticisms of 'company boats', and 'company wages', only one-third of the season's catch going to the seamen who were responsible for it. Even their own wages were ridiculously low. When the foreman tried to humour them by offering them brandy with their 'vittles' (mostly dry bread and cheese) he was shouted down. My previous fears of being met with hostility were quickly forgotten in this quicksilver community, as lively and flashing as fish in a net.

And it was there amid that idle chat that I first heard news of war, although I imagine South Africa was as distant to their thoughts as mine. Soon 'war' and 'Boers' and the 'Natal' were on everybody's lips as if familiar household words. People mentioned Ladysmith, Kimberley, Mafeking as if sieges and their relief were part of normal living. A fear took hold of me. When women spoke now, proudly for the most part, of their sons, grandsons, brothers off to the Transvaal, I immediately thought of Julian.

Almost four months had passed since that August day when he had returned to find me and ever since I had continued to send those letters to him, going regularly to the post office on my way to work. Not a word had I had in reply, nothing. I told myself, 'Tomorrow', but tomorrow never came. Now an obvious and dreadful reason for his silence presented itself.

Julian had spoken in a general way of going with his regiment overseas, nothing specific. The address I wrote to was in England. I had presumed, perhaps rightly so, that his first orders had been changed to enable him to return to Cornwall in August. But suppose now he was already in

99

Africa fighting the Boers, suppose my letters never reached him, suppose he did not answer because he couldn't. *He may be dead.* The silence, the not knowing what had happened, became unbearable.

I could have gone again to make enquiries at Polleven Manor; pride wouldn't let me, not even to ask in the village, not with my pregnancy so pronounced, not to put shame on us both. I could have begged Beth to go in my stead; she would have, but that too seemed an unfair imposition. And I don't think I would have learnt much anyway, Miss Ruth Polleven would have seen to that. Once I had even tried to question Emma more closely when Beth brought her to see me. The child was excited at our meeting, clung to me like one of those rock limpets, remembered only the grey horse, no other details. I kissed her, gave her sweets and clothes for her brothers, watched her sadly leave with equal sadness realizing that she couldn't help. There was only one other source of information that I could think of, although I dreaded using it.

Farmer Penwith would know about the Pollevens, and my mother could find out from him.

I had not been in touch with my mother since I had left the farm, and I certainly never meant to go back there again. But in these past months I had begun to think of her. That my brother had reason to hate her I did not dispute, nor that she had done me great harm. But I suppose there is a basic yearning which every daughter feels when about to become a mother herself, to see and talk to her own mother, to ask, 'Is this how it is?' And I could not put all the memories away, not all were bad. I sometimes still saw my Mam cooking in the kitchen with her rolling pin brandished as she talked about Penwith Farm; I remembered her smile as she ran towards Cy. And although I have said that perhaps the sea was in my blood, the moors were too and in many ways I missed them.

There was also a practical reason why perhaps I should make peace with my Mam again, having nothing to do with my affairs, but to do with Beth's. Her brother had returned. He appeared one November morning, or rather we heard him whistling as he came striding down the valley, his pack on his back. Beth recognized him immediately, dropped the dish she was holding, darted out of the door, her skirts flying. He bent and swooped her up, a giant young man with flaming red hair.

Everything about Jeb Martin was the opposite of his sister; where she was small and neat he was large and untidy, where she was talkative he was quiet; only in affection were they alike, both showing that special closeness that I think peculiar to orphaned children. I often thought of that now as I watched them together, she preparing the meals he liked, he doing repairs about the house at her request, both wanting to please the other. They made me regret again the estrangement with my brother, for of course I had never returned to St Marvell either since leaving it. Their closeness made me feel that I was imposing on them, that I wasn't being fair in staying on.

When Beth had said I could remain until Jeb's return, she had presumably not expected him until several months later. What brought her pleasure, as it should, brought me a difficulty. It didn't seem right that while I had his bed, he slept on a cot in the lean-to with a curtain over the opening to block the worst of the draughts. I asked Beth's advice – she wouldn't speak of it, and when I approached Jeb he was equally non-committal.

'Used to the open,' he said, 'always slept on deck if I could. The smell down under is something fierce. And you'm company for Beth.'

He smiled at me, very like his sister then. He had been chopping wood and was surrounded by a pile of slivers, the cut logs were stacked beside the doorway, the air smelled of fresh-sawn sap. 'Don't think of leaving, where would you go?'

He didn't mention the baby but I couldn't hide my condition and I knew he and Beth must have talked. I said, blushing a little for I still couldn't catch on to her way of openness, 'But 'tis your house, and you've a right to it. I'm in the way and 'twill be more so when the baby's born. At least I could find somewhere else until you leave . . .'

'Bain't thinking of leaving either,' he said. He took up the axe, hefted it a few times, laid it down. 'My ship's in dry dock a while,' he said, 'I'm not going anywhere. Except back to fishing, got a place on the Victoria company boat, the 'Mermaid', up at Port Zenack.'

It was a long speech for him. I was startled when he added, 'Time I settled down. Beth's been waiting long enough fer me to marry afore she does. Until that happens, we'll carry on as we are.'

I thought, yes, but there'll be plenty of young village girls who *will* be in a hurry when they know you're home. And although it was typical that Beth would hold back on her own pleasure for her brother's sake, again it wasn't right for me to cause her more delay. I began to see how selfish I was, relying on them both too much.

By now we had come to mid-December, the days were short, the nights brittle with frost, the ground rang hard when one put a foot on it. All the plants and bushes along the valley turned black, and the marsh grass beside the stream was coated silver. Some days the boats couldn't even leave harbour, and more and more I felt the strain of the long day's work, the long walk home. As the war news deepened, as bad news now came, for even Jeb and Beth talked of it, my anxiety grew. So I sent word to my mother.

I chose a place at Jeb's suggestion, mid-way between Penwith and Port Zenack, avoiding Polleven. I didn't mention all the other reasons for my asking to see her, said only that since it was close to Christmas it was time to make peace. Beth, who knew most of my story by now, eyed me in her thoughtful way but she didn't question me as I was afraid she might. As it was I left early one morning before Beth was awake, tiptoeing past the sleeping Jeb who by then had taken to spending the nights on a mattress before the fire. It was still grey dark out of doors, there was a sliver of moon as I picked my way up the valley knowing almost every step by heart. As I went I tried to think what to say, rehearsed a dialogue. I wasn't even sure my mother would come of course, but I thought she would. I knew her well enough to know she'd be curious, especially when I mentioned returning something 'I'd borrowed'.

And not even she could ignore the plea for help which I couldn't avoid making.

Close to the top of the valley where it came to the road there was a rustle in the undergrowth and a fox's brush showed just for a flick of russet among the silver and black grasses. I took that for an omen. It made me walk more briskly along the highway. The inn was a fair step on, but I was used to walking, and the road roamed easily up and down. Except for the cold the day was dry and Beth had lent me her cloak which was thick and warm. By the time I reached the village and saw the inn where I had suggested we meet, a mild sun was peering from a pale sky, and the ice patches had almost melted. I hesitated then, suddenly afraid, afraid of seeing my mother again, afraid of not seeing her, afraid what she might tell me. It took a while to screw my courage up to go on those last hundred paces.

The inn was an old coaching house used to break the journey between Camelford and Wadebridge. It looked its best decked out in holly for the Christmas season. With almost a start I remembered the date, Christmas Eve; that explained the bustle in and out of the doors, the number of horses tied in the stable yard. And sure enough when I passed I saw our old brown pony harnessed to a trap and so knew she'd come.

Inside, the main hall was crowded with ladies and gentlemen, dressed in their finest, some of the ladies wearing furs, many of the men in top coats and hats. They sat at little tables decorated with white cloths, the silver and plates shone. Christmas wreaths were draped across the mantelpiece, there was a Christmas tree. Men in short black coats, waiters, ran to and fro balancing trays of food; glasses clinked. I shrank back, pulling the cloak close around me, searching for my mother. She'd make herself at home there, I thought, she'd sit down with the best, think nothing of it, order a glass of her favourite brandy . . .

'Looking fer me, are you?' said a familiar voice.

Farmer Penwith came out of a corner where he must have been waiting. He was smiling, that lopsided grin that showed he didn't want to, and his eyes were wary. I noticed at once that he too was wearing his best clothes, the black suit, the tie and collar, the polished leather boots. He had a new hat and when he took it off as he now did, his dark hair had been newly cut. I caught the smell of some sort of hair oil, and his fresh-shaved jaws gleamed.

'There's no point in coming all this way to run off again,' he was saying, speaking in his 'educated voice'. It sounded even stranger after all my time with the fisher women. 'Your mother showed me your letter as of course she would, and I offered to come and fetch you myself. For you're coming back, aren't you, that's the real excuse for writing.'

He beckoned to a passing waiter, stood aside to let me follow to a table. Too bemused to resist I sat down opposite him. 'Your mother's well,' he went on, laying his hat beside him, picking up the menu. Well, I suppose he'd done this often in his extravagant youth, nothing new to him. 'She sends you greetings. She's longing to see you. Tell her to hurry home, she said.'

I knew he was not telling the truth and I think he knew I did. At each lie his eyelids fluttered a little and he'd give that strange curdled glance I remembered. I accepted the hot tea, let it stand untouched in front of me, folded my hands under the cloak, listened while he talked on glibly about the improvements to the house and farm, about how much I had been missed, about how silly I had been to run away, everything except the reason why my Mam hadn't come and he had.

104

At last when he had exhausted every topic he could think of, and he was by nature taciturn so this froth of conversation was itself indicative, he leant back in his chair, wiped his forehead and said, 'Damme, but you've still got that knowing air about you. Alright then, your Mam didn't come because I wouldn't let her. Thought you both might be off together, now you're hinting at repaying her money that you took. Carried on about that something awful she did, worse I think than learning why you'd gone . . .'

'Which you told her, no doubt,' I said, 'all, that is, except your part in it.'

He looked at me, playing with his knife and fork as I remembered he did when he was nervous. 'That's quick,' he said, 'that's sharp. Always said you had claws. Well, Miss, if the big world hasn't treated you right, perhaps 'tis because you don't treat it right yerself. No good turning your back on friends. Remember I meant well by you. If you took it wrong, was that my fault?'

I waited, saying nothing. Sooner or later he'd give me the opening I was looking for.

'Took back the saddle,' he said after a while, 'there, I did you a service. Said I found it, which was true enough, but not how it was hidden. The Pollevens aren't a grateful lot and their Miss Ruth's like to be a stuck-up old maid. Didn't see the son, but that's not surprising, as they hardly invited me in the house, kept me standing in the doorway, although once I used to entertain them often enough.'

Still I said nothing.

'Damme,' he cried again, wiping his forehead. 'But what do you want, then? Alright again, I'll tell you what I think. You've run out of the cash you stole from your Mam, and want to come crying back. And young Polleven's not come up to snuff, well, hardly could expect it, with several thousand miles between you; never did make sense to me. For my part you're welcome, as long as you remembers the conditions from the night you left.'

'And my Mam?'

105

He shrugged. 'She's a reasonable woman,' he said. That was all, but I knew what he meant.

I stood up, deliberately opening the cloak so that my swollen figure could be seen. While he gaped at it I told him I wanted nothing from him nor my mother, that I had suggested a meeting in a Christian spirit to let by-gones be by-gones, that Julian Polleven was looking after me.

He listened in turn to my lies, half lies, with a sardonic expression which when I mentioned Julian broke out into a grin. 'Damme,' he cried a third time, 'but you've got gall, maid. Gives you everything you need does he, by God, including a bun in the oven. Looks after you does he, well he'll have to work double hard then, being a prisoner since Mafeking.'

He watched me narrowly for effect. 'But if you come back with me,' he said, low-voiced, brutally frank, 'you can have everything you want. There, I've said that much, everything, even as you are, carrying another man's bastard. And your Mam won't say a word, won't dare hinder us, not if she knows what's good for her. I swear it, what more could you ask?'

'No,' I shouted, 'No,' as once I had 'yes' to Beth; no to his proposal, no to my Mam's complicity, no to Julian's imprisonment. And I jumped up, knocking over the dishes, and left him sitting at the table midst the wreckage of the finery, among all those fine people where neither of us belonged.

CHAPTER 7

n a blaze of denial I rushed from the dining room,
brushing waiters aside, startling guests. I heard a man
say, 'My gum, who's that?' Another cried, 'Steady
on', while his wife drew back her skirt as if afraid of
contamination. I didn't care. Head high, defying the world,
I stalked through the crowded hall, out the main doors, across
the pavement to the inn yard. It was the work of a moment
to untie the pony, climb into the trap; I had trotted smartly
over the cobble stones before they knew we'd gone.

Once on the highway, the pony pricked up its ears at my
remembered voice, put on unusual speed in anticipation
of home, its little hooves tip-tapping. Long before Farmer
Penwith could have recovered to pay the bill and slink
after me we were out on the Bodmin road, heading inland
towards the moors. I was halfway back to Penwith Farm
before I drew breath.

It wasn't on my own account that I wanted Farmer Penwith
to be guilty of lying. I didn't care how he insulted me, or my
mother; it was the story of Julian's imprisonment that had
to be invention, a spur-of-the-moment cruelty. Hadn't he
let slip earlier that when he'd returned the saddle Julian
had been at the manor? Desperately I searched for nuance
in every word, in my mind re-scanning every remark. One
could go crazy with such searching. Despite my bravado,
instinctively I knew Farmer Penwith wasn't that clever.

Julian's name had cropped up by chance, had not been used for deliberate reason except by myself.

I couldn't let myself think that. Because if I did then Penwith must have told the truth, and truth in this instance was worse than lie. *Some things are worth fighting for.* But not to have Julian shut up far from home, hungry, cold, perhaps wounded. The rumours of what Boer prison camps were like were already rife, if they took prisoners that is.

Instead of turning back to the coast, I urged the pony forward. And if I must put a reason to what I did next, say simply it was the need to sort falsehood from fact.

By then it was early afternoon. We had passed few people on the open road in contrast to the morning; everyone who could would have finished their travelling. Village streets however were more busy, people in and out of the local shops doing last-minute buying. A man went by carrying a goose, reminding me of Cyril; small boys cracked walnuts under a stone making the pony jump. The crisp air had reddened my cheeks, my hair was flying, the pony tossed its head as if to say, 'Hurry!' To a casual passer-by we might have seemed bound on a simple Christmas journey.

We rumbled over a cattle grid, came up on the moors. A wind was blowing, sending white clouds scudding; tattered strips of gorse bowled along the edges of the track, their yellowing prickles rattling. A few scrawny cattle picked at the grass which in this season was white and sparse; only the bogs kept their emerald. Strangely enough that openness which I had missed when I was absent from it appeared as overwhelming as those narrow, crowded villages. I felt a stranger in my own land, everything out of kilter. It was not until I saw the jagged finger of Hawstead Tor that this sense of strangeness gave way to recognition. That black outline of stones might seem intimidating; to me it was a reminder, witness to the many hours Julian and I had spent in its shadow. As long as it remained what we had felt surely must endure, despite Farmer Penwith's sneers, despite, God forbid, Julian's imprisonment.

From a distance the farm appeared small and grey under the tor, a huddle of buildings blank-eyed to the road. Seeing it now after absence I thought how solitary it looked, as if in need of company. And I wondered, almost idly, how my Mam had happened upon it, the perfect place for retreat, the perfect place for hiding.

I rode into the barnyard with a clatter, hitched the reins about the post, clambered down, my pregnancy making me awkward and clumsy. The kitchen door was closed, the windows closed, but I saw a curtain flutter. My Mam was in the second parlour, and she was watching me.

I didn't go inside but stood out in the yard, unharnessing the pony, finding a handful of grain, careful to keep the cloak wrapped around me. When presently I heard the kitchen door's familiar creak, 'Here I am,' I told my Mam, 'alone.'

She came out then and stood on the steps, the wind catching at her petticoats and black dress. She still held a glass in her hand, and when I came up close I could smell the brandy on her breath. 'I've left him to make his own way,' I told her, forestalling her questions. 'Tell him the pony strayed and someone found it and brought it back, so he can't be sure I came this far. He'll not find another pony this side of Bodmin tonight, and 'tis a fair way to walk. So we've time for speaking, if you want. If not, I'll say my piece and leave you. For I've a fair walk ahead myself.'

She was dressed in those silk clothes she had affected in recent years. Looking at them now with a more sophisticated eye I guessed they were taken from that first wife's wardrobe, and altered to size. My Mam had always been good at sewing, but never with time to teach. Never with time to share thoughts, never with time for me at all. I was always an encumbrance, something she 'should have left behind'.

She wavered on her little feet, her black curls dancing. There were threads of grey now in those curls, and her eyes had lost their fire.

'I've come back to see you,' I told her, 'well, I wrote you, hoping that we should meet. Not that I know why exactly. I'm sure my leaving must have been a shock. Although for my part there wasn't much I could have done to prevent it. I suppose you didn't think what a shock I'd have today, seeing him in your stead.'

It was her turn to be silent, her head poked out like a hen, in the way she had. Her silence didn't disturb me. 'Suppose you didn't wonder what drove me away in the first place? Or why I went on the moors looking for friendship? Time you did.'

Nervousness made me fierce. So did grief and longing. Love me, I wanted to shout.

She looked down, looked away, a little doll in her long black silk. 'I've seen Ben,' I told her. 'I know what you did to him. Well, for better or worse we've both survived without you. But I'd hoped perhaps there would have been something left between us two, some rag of affection perhaps, that'd have let you take me in now when I most need you. But I see it wouldn't work.'

She broke in then, one agonized cry. 'I can't,' she said.

She tottered forward clinging to the door to steady herself. I remembered how once she had jumped up and run down those steps blithe as a girl. 'I can't,' she repeated, 'can't, can't, can't. I've naught left to give.'

And that was truth.

Words came tumbling out now, a spate of them, like that waterfall of rain I'd first seen as a child. 'Think 'tis easy to lose all you love? For don't make any mistake, I knew once what love was. But you can't know what 'tis like not to have a man about. No one can, unless they've been there, the loneliness, the need. Well, I tell you straight, I were a married woman, never knew the like of the lusting he can give, 'twas like a drug. I couldn't go on without it. I still can't.'

And as when I was a child, the 'he' she meant was Farmer Penwith.

'And don't think it's easy to live through his hand-wringing after, the prayers and sin and guilt, like to smother him.

110

And 'tisn't easy neither to see yourself passed over, never knowing who will take his fancy next, never knowing who will be the next one, some girl from the village, even my own daughter. But I've come to terms with that. I've risked too much with him, shan't let it change anything, even if he drops me like a worn-out glove whenever he pleases. He always comes back. I'm his right hand, remember. He won't really turn me out.'

She stared at me, eyes hard, yet shamelessly naked, shamelessly pleading. 'He'll marry me in the end,' she said, boasted, surely it was drink that made her boastful. 'He's got to. He owes it me. And then, Penwith Farm'll be mine. That's what I've worked and waited for.'

She made a gesture; it took in all that lonely moor, those withered fields, the ruined buildings. And just as when her first man died she had torn his memory out, even from her own heart, so now, conversely, she clung with equal passion to a man whom she didn't love but by whom she was obsessed.

I didn't want to hear her say these things, no daughter would. I just hoped when my daughter was born she wouldn't hear so much.

I stood back and once more let my figure be seen.

'I'm having Julian's child,' I told her now, bluntly, for there was no point in denying it, and I wanted her to know. 'I'm telling you myself so there'll be no taint on it, so you'll understand for me 'tis a joy, not a curse. I'll survive that too, with or without you, so don't you fret.'

Her face crumbled, paled. She sat down on the steps as if her legs had collapsed under her, and hugged her arms across her chest, rocking to and fro. 'Dear Lord, don't say that,' she keened, 'let her be joking.'

She suddenly sprang up and came towards me, taking my arm and trying to drag me inside as if in an excess of sympathy. I think for a moment, just for a moment, she wanted to believe she could. But when I didn't move, 'Listen,' she said, as if I had jolted her sober, 'is it too late?'

At my look, 'Too late to do something about it,' she cried. 'Get rid of it.' She shook me with impatience. 'Surely you thought of that?'

I felt her arms about me, the first time I think we'd ever embraced. I felt her tears, the first I'd ever seen her shed. The more she spoke, the more I realized the differences between us, and the more I felt my heart contract at her greed and lack of sensitivity. But when I started to speak of Julian, what news of him, trying as I framed the question to hide the fear it caused, 'Oh, child,' she said, and it could have been pity in her voice. 'You don't know what you'm saying. 'Tisn't imprisonment, 'tis death.'

She mouthed words then I didn't seem to hear, 'Heir to old estate missing in action.' They might have stood out black and stark, a headline in a language I didn't understand. She went on trying to give details, trying to excuse Farmer Penwith, making apologies for him as she used when I was a child, explaining he couldn't deliberately have meant to deceive, he had left too early for this news; he was only repeating what had been reported first a few days ago – as if all this were more important then what he hadn't had time to learn about.

'Don't worry,' I heard myself repeat, 'I'll manage. And I've brought you something back, something that I shouldn't have taken.'

I pulled out the little bag with the money that I'd saved, and the two photographs.

She knew enough not to stop me, had the grace not to try again. 'Go in the trap,' she cried. 'He'll never miss it.' And when convinced I meant to walk, 'Send word then when it's due.' Her voice came weakly after, 'Rely on me; I'll come to St Marvell.'

I knew she wouldn't. She'd never go back to where she had come from any more than I could.

It was still day when I passed under Hawstead Tor, but I didn't go to the top as I had been planning. I turned my back on it too, went steadfastly forward as once I had before. And as that other time I didn't let myself think, concentrated only on putting one foot in front of the other. If somewhere in that gloaming I crossed John Penwith making his laborious way south as I went north, I didn't know it. I came off the moors into the cold of night, with snow flurries biting into the flesh and dusting the surface of the roads with ice. Head down, I went instinctively towards the only place I could count on, until as once before on a lonely journey I heard something stir in the hedge.

I had reached the turning of the road by now, one way back towards the moors, one way towards the inn, one way north towards Port Zenack. I wasn't frightened by the sound, but I stopped and wiped the snow from my eyes. It was late on Christmas Eve, all good souls should be at home in bed. Only drunkards might be abroad, sleeping off pre-Christmas cheer, or thieves, waiting for unwary travellers.

'I been keeping watch fer 'ee, Miss Jenny.' Jeb Martin's voice came booming out of the whiteness, and he advanced slowly like a shapeless bear coated with snow, his boots making large black tracks. He shook off the blanket he had worn over his shoulders and draped it over me, clasping his large hands over mine to rub them back to life, finally giving me a flask to drink from. Its contents made me splutter and I pushed it away. 'There,' he said, with something of a grin, 'don't tell on me. Beth'd have my hide if she thought I took to liquor. But it'll put some life in 'ee. You've been gone too far as 'tis.'

Another half grin. 'Went to the inn,' he said. 'Beth made me, just to make sure you were alright. Caused a proper rumpus there, didn't it just, the stable were a riot, everyone claiming his own horse and hanging on fer dear life while Farmer Penwith tried to unseat 'em. Cursed you up and down didn't he, by gum, until someone told him to shut his mouth. "Bested at yer own game, John," they said, "serve 'ee right." And that's a fact.'

I let him talk as my mother had talked, words again

flowing over me like that first rain. And I let him take my arm, and support me along the road, gradually feeling life come back to frozen feet and hands as the brandy and the extra covering warmed. But when we came to the turnoff to his sister's cabin he paused, as if embarrassed. 'Don't take it wrong now, Miss Jenny,' he said, 'but Beth and I have decided. 'Tis easier fer me to live up Port Zenack way and so I'll go there after I see you home. You're not to think you puts me out, it tain't so. I just wanted you to know.'

He didn't seem to mind that I hadn't said anything so far, or that I said nothing to him now at this new proof of kindness. Instead he fumbled in his pocket and brought out a little package. It was wrapped in ribbon, soft and smooth to the touch although the rest was rough and uneven. 'And since 'tis close enough to Christmas morning not to matter,' he said, 'I'll give you this.'

I didn't open it, stood there in the drifting snow looking at him. 'Tain't much,' he said, a little anxiety creeping into his voice, 'tain't nothing special, something I picked up on my travels, comes from the ocean floor, a type of coral. The ribbon's new tho'.' He tried a laugh. 'Bought it while I waited fer you, off a travelling pedlar. Thought you'd like the blue colour.'

I should have thanked him, I should have unwrapped that sailor's gift, an offering meant to bring pleasure as once my father's had done; I should have thought of the hours of waiting, patient in the cold. I could only say what was in my heart. 'He's dead.'

I can't describe the next weeks and months. They are dead too, let them pass. I was ill, close to death myself but that I can't remember. It must have been almost mid-March when I came back. It was as if I had been gone on some long lonely journey where I had to keep on walking, over thin veldt grass where the wind blew in sandy gusts; where the outcrops of rocks, seeming first like moorland tors, changed into grotesque shapes hiding strange grotesque animals. I seemed to be searching, searching, but never knew what for – water perhaps, perhaps shelter, perhaps someone; my not knowing added to the terror.

In lucid moments I knew it was too soon for a baby to be born, that it mustn't happen. When the birthing began I remember clinging to Beth's arm asking her to stop it. I remember her eyes as she bent over the bed, her voice gentle too as she whispered, 'My dear, 'tis as God wills.' I turned my face to the wall, endured. And when all went dark, and not even nightmares kept me company I set my mouth as my Mam did, lived on.

That March morning I heard Beth come into the room and knew who she was, knew what room I was in, I opened my eyes. She was standing at the small window unfastening the hinge. Now she threw the casement wide. The air rushed in and all the outside with it, sounds and smells and light. 'There,' she said, and there was triumph in her voice, 'hear the sea. Smell the earth. It's time fer you to wake up again, 'tis spring.'

She came towards me, her round face smiling, her arms full of fresh-starched clothes. 'Bless me, but you've returned to us,' she said. 'I'll tell Jeb. Comes every day to ask. Sitting by the hearth downstairs right now, playing with Lily.'

She paused in her chattering. 'Yer daughter,' she said. 'We called her Lily. She came early, see, like a flower, a lily flower that grows through ice.'

She laughed and wept at the same time. 'Tenacious tho', same as her mother. Wouldn't give up. And nor would we. We nursed her like a fledgling, Jeb and me. Dotes on her, Jeb does,' she said, 'a real father. Hear her laughing for him downstairs. I'll fetch her up.'

Out of some red mist I seemed to remember a thing with wizened white face and stick-like arms, its fingers hooked like bird's claws. I seemed to hear someone say, ''Tis too small to live.' I turned my head towards the stairs, and heard the rippling thread of a baby's chuckling.

Once my will had decided, I quickly recovered strength. And when the baby lay in my arms, in that empty place where my heart had been, something began to quicken into life. She was a delight, grew like the spring flower for which she had been named, with a fleece of soft fair hair and her father's eyes. Not only Jeb doted on her, so did her cousins, so did Beth and her shoe-maker. *A love child.* She was, wrapped in it, surrounded with it, both of us cocooned with it. It stifled us. We couldn't keep on like that, I thought. Life wasn't that cosy. For example, although Beth let Emma and the boys see their cousin I doubt if their father even knew there was a child and if Charity did she wouldn't have told him. Sometimes I even sensed the wistfulness behind Beth's caring, the longing for a child of her own, although she'd never admit it.

"Course I'd like children,' she said stoutly when I tried to ask. 'But not yet. I can't leave Jeb. As long as he's on shore I stay.' It seemed to me that it wasn't Jeb who kept her there; I did. And Jeb himself appeared to have relinquished all intention of going back to his ship, was happy as a fisherman, spent all his free hours with us, trudging over the cliffs at work's end, always with some gift in hand, always with time to spare for Lily, again in truth as devoted as any father. And seeing that frail little thing cupped in his enormous hands, seeing how she stretched out to bat at hair or chin, I realized how strong already was the bond between them. The day I understood how deeply I was in Jeb's debt (it appeared he supported us; Beth too had given up work – 'No time fer it,' she said – she meant my child and I had taken up her time) was the day I addressed the difficulty I had put aside and should have faced those months before: how to arrange my life so I was no longer a burden on my friends and was as independent of them as they of me.

Jeb had been fishing and was drawing the boat up on the beach, long sweeping jerks, an economy of movement. It was a small rowing boat, the one Beth kept, not of course the larger one that he worked on at Port Zenack. He had renamed it the 'Lily', the letters painted white over the blue prow. The keel sliced across the shingle, the shell crust crunched; with one quick pull he drew out the oars and undid the rowlocks. I waited until he had finished with mooring, a few turns of rope around a spike embedded in rock above the high water mark, then went down. I had been sitting on the turf edge where the stream came gushing from the undergrowth, spilling over the sand like a miniature delta mouth. Sea pinks grew there, their round tufts just beginning to bud, and watercress and wild mint. Spread along the valley the bushes were in early leaf, pale green and gold. The murmur of the stream blended with the deeper sound of the waves; above the cliffs black-backed gulls screeched and swooped, fighting over territorial space, and the sky was like a robin's egg, a cloudless blue oval.

I walked slowly, still easily tired, and Lily was growing heavy. I had her bound in a shawl across my back and her shallow breathing kept time with mine; her weight was warm and comforting.

Jeb looked up with a smile and hoisted up a string of fish. I knew the spring runs had been slow; at market prices he was holding a week's wages. 'Just give me time to clean 'em,' he said, 'Beth'll cook 'em fer your tea.'

I thought, 'He's always giving something. How can he make a decent living with two extra mouths to feed? Lily and I aren't his responsibility.'

I said, picking the words with care, for I didn't want to offend, "Tis too much, all yer kindness to us, yours and Beth's. What can Lily and I give you in return?'

He laughed at that, but his laughter was uneasy. I think he guessed I was serious. He began to stow his gear away, winding up the lines, binding oars and rowlocks for carrying back up the cove. 'And it isn't right,' I persisted, 'to take and never give. So I need your help in moving on.'

He stopped so abruptly it was as if I had thrust a knife at him. 'Bain't you happy here?' he asked. 'Bain't you at home?' When I couldn't answer, 'Then what you say be daft.'

I said, 'Think of the money you're wasting not living in your own house . . .'

'That's my business,' he broke in, fierce as a lion, 'and don't see what Beth has to do with it. She's my sister, I take care of whom I please.'

'But she'd like to marry,' I persisted. 'She can't, not while she has to look after us. And perhaps you'll be wanting to marry too; I've no call to be in either's way.'

'Don't want to marry anyone,' he said. 'Leastways,' he hesitated, biting his lip, shifting the weight of the oars, 'leastways, no one who'll have me.'

I smiled at him. He was almost twice my size, a giant of a fellow, and yet he seemed young to me, innocent. I wanted to encourage him, say, go on, try. Something held me back, some cautionary flicker.

He dropped the oars to the sand, draped the fish across them, stood looking even more ill at ease, shuffling his feet like a school boy. 'Miss Jenny,' he began, "tain't only to help you and Beth that I comes here every day. I comes for my own pleasure. There, I've said it. For what I get out of it for myself. I'm not the noble fellow you thinks me, no, I'm not.'

His face grew even more red with effort. 'What more could a man want,' he said, 'than come home and find you waiting.'

He said, 'I know I'm not much by contrast. I know 'tis too soon. But I loves you, see, I wants to marry you and give Lily a name. I'm willing to wait. Just don't leave us, give me a chance.'

His words took my breath away. I mean they were truly unexpected. He must have seen the effect. 'There now,' he said, 'I'm all sorts of fool. Don't take heed of me. I won't say no more. But when you're ready or want to speak I'm willing. That's all I ask, see, a chance.'

He leaned over and laid one large finger against the baby's cheek, a large gentle finger. 'She'm as dear to me as you are,' he said.

118

Then as if ashamed of all that talk, again a long speech for him, he shouldered his burden and strode up the beach. All sorts of impossible thoughts swirled in my mind. I heard my sister-in-law sneer, 'Who'd look at her twice.' I imagined my Mam's advice. 'Go on,' she'd urge, 'not many men'd be that stupid.' I watched my sleeping daughter. The long dark eye-lashes fanned cheeks that were healthy pink, the fine-nailed fingers clasped the edge of the shawl; as if aware of scrutiny she stirred and shifted but didn't wake. I thought, she has the right to a father, who am I to deny her one? And who has more claim, next to her real father, than a man who has cared for her since birth? And I thought of Beth, and how she had the right to happiness too for her own sake. And I thought of Jeb.

And the trouble was, the sadness was, that in spite of all the reasons why I should, I didn't love Jeb and never could.

And it was sad for me, still to feel bound to a man whom I had known for only such a short while, whom I probably would never have married anyway. And who was dead.

The sun was a haze in that blue sky, the birds cried, the incoming tide spread in golden rivulets over the sand. And the saddest thing of all was that in that spring day, amid the sense of growing, moving, living things, Julian didn't seem dead at all, had never seemed more alive.

I don't know what Jeb told his sister, perhaps she had already guessed. In fact, looking back I think she had been match-making from the start, although what she could have seen in me for her brother, I can't answer that. I knew she too would say, 'What more can you hope for?' And I couldn't argue with that.

Two days passed while I lingered, torn between ingratitude and escape. I had no money, what I had earned before Christmas long gone. And although I was strong enough to have returned to work there was the difficulty of the baby. But Jeb's confession, if that is the word, had broken the harmony of our little world and there was no way to put it back again.

Beth did not reproach me but I felt her unease like a cloud. It put constraint between us. And Jeb, afraid he had overstepped himself, kept away out of shyness, fearful of seeming to intrude. It was Beth's 'man' who finally brought perspective back.

He arrived as usual on a Saturday afternoon, hot with cycling. He had had to push his bike most of the last part, uphill, and he was tired. His blue eyes still blazed but during the recent months his long face seemed to have grown thinner. When he bent over to pull off the cuff clips that kept his trousers out of the dirt I could hear his panting. Beth heard it too. She didn't say anything, went to the spring to fetch him water. I sensed her concern. Nor did he complain but when he had eased himself down on the step, 'I be growing old,' he said, his voice blurred with fatigue. He drank, tried to laugh. 'Bain't the man who could've run up hill fer 'ee once,' he said.

He suddenly took Beth's hand. 'Been more than ten years I've waited fer 'ee,' he said. 'Must have worn a groove in the road. Ten years on they'll point and say, Mark Chote left them tracks. But time's going on fer 'ee as well, my maid. 'Twon't do to wait fer ever.'

He was a just man, what he said was just. And Beth knew it was. And so did Jeb. And most of all so did I. We were all gathered there in the lean-to. Jeb had returned that day on the pretext of having a chair to mend. He was bent over it, his hands capable and steady. I saw how they trembled just a moment when he heard those words. Beth and Mark were seated on one side of the doorway, I on the other with the baby on my lap; we might have been models posing for a rustic frieze carved out of wood. I remember there was a buzz of flies in the lilac bushes, somewhere a lark was singing. Despite the sun I felt the cold shiver of premonition.

Finally Beth stood up. She had flushed then paled as

Mark spoke, and she stammered a little, although I had never heard her at a loss for words before. 'Don't press me,' she said. 'I don't like it. I know what 'ee thinks, but 'tisn't that easy.'

Mark said, 'It could be, if they two would get on with it.'

He was smiling with his mouth as if in joke, but his eyes weren't smiling, and the lines about them were fine drawn. He had kept his coat and hat on, as if about to leave although he had just arrived. 'They two,' he repeated, 'hold the rest of us in their palms. Well, I'm growing tired of it. Come on, lad,' he spoke to Jeb, 'what's wrong with 'ee? Need me to teach 'ee a few lessons in courting?'

The bluntness broke in upon our restraint. Beth and Jeb both started to speak at once but I overrode them. 'No,' I said, 'it isn't his fault. Nor Beth's, Mr Chote. I'm the problem. Lily and me. But I've come to a decision. Jeb should come back here to live, then he and Beth can do as they please. Lily and me'll go to Port Zenack. I'll get my old job back, and someone to look after Lily.'

They started to protest, at least Jeb and Beth did, not Mark Chote. 'She'm right,' he said. He too stood up, tall and thin, stooped with working over his last, a man who had waited long enough. 'Beth, my love,' he said, 'tain't in me to make 'ee choose. But the years are slipping. I've seen 'ee with that child, like a daughter, as she is to me. But you need sons and daughters of yer own. And so do I, afore 'tis too late. She'm young and so be Jeb, we'm not. I want fer you to come with me. If you decide against it, then sad as 'tis I'll not be this way again.'

Jeb and I looked at each other, moved out of earshot. Their decision was theirs to make. And mine was mine. 'Dear friend,' I said, for so he was, the best of anyone, 'I have thought and thought of what you said, and do thank you from my heart. 'Tis more than I could hope fer, and that's the truth. But I've never lied to you about nothing, and I won't lie now. 'Tis better fer you, truly, if I go and you forget.'

121

He cried out at that. 'But I'll still see 'ee,' he said. 'You won't cut me off. You won't take Lily from me, not yet a while.' And such was his misery that I promised. Although I knew it wrong.

CHAPTER 8

*T*hat is how Lily and I came to live in Port Zenack in one of those little alleyways that I had thought so confining. It had a fancy name but everyone knew it as the Corset, and so it was; barely a foot-and-a-half wide, Jeb couldn't have come through sideways. The owner of the house where I rented a room was Widow Pendar, an older woman who had lost her husband at sea and who was willing to accept me for a widow too, a war-widow, with a child. She must have known differently, I made no secret who I was, but it seemed to please her to keep up this fiction. And in a way it pleased me, I don't know why, it just made sense somehow, that's all. (And here I should remark again how close-knit each village was, even to its tittle-tattle. St Marvell might have been a continent apart for all they cared for its scandal here. And although among their own they reserved the right to gossip to their heart's content, mostly they turned blind eyes, deaf ears, to outside gossip. And so what might have been said of me in St Marvell made little or no impression.)

The room I rented was small even by village standards, with a window overlooking the alley, inches from our neighbours. Cooking smells and arguments and children's cries drifted in and out on the air currents. There was space for a single bed, a child's cot made from a box, a washstand and not much else, but then I didn't own much more. I can't pretend that after I had settled in and sat on the bed looking at the blank wall I didn't feel lonely for the cove and cabin and the sound of Jeb's whistling. But I put that resolutely aside. And early next morning I dressed the baby in those knitted clothes that Beth had taught me how to make and, carrying her on my back like an Indian papoose, went down to the quay and took my place with the other women.

At first the foreman was adamant. 'No place fer a baby,' he said. Perhaps he was right but where else could I leave her? Although I could not argue my case the other women did. 'Don't 'ee give way to 'un,' they advised, 'stand up and tell 'un what's what.'

They made a formidable barrier, arms linked so no one could pass. 'Mean old devil,' one cried, while the rest swore at him, vowing they'd not work either, unless he gave me a chance. 'Try her out afore 'ee sacks her,' they said. 'She were a good worker afore. If the baby screams or she don't pull her weight, then 'ee've the right to get rid of her.' Each crowded round me, with suggestions how things should be managed, according to each's own preferences, some swearing that cleaning was easiest, others recommending the salting. I don't think the foreman would have budged an inch, out of prejudice, if Jeb hadn't appeared to settle matters.

He was the soul of tact. 'Tell 'ee what,' he said to the foreman, 'we'll rig up a bed, out of the way. Can't have yer work place looking like a nursery.' He winked, went off with his long stride, reappeared dragging a wooden contraption. 'What do 'ee think of that then?' he asked, nudging it forward with his foot. He had taken a gurry and found some wheels to place it on, like a dilly or go-cart boys make. Around the sides he had attached wooden slats to make a kind of hood, the whole easily lifted off and on the wheels. When he had pushed it under the inner arches, where he placed it on a stone slab off the ground, it was well out of the main bustle, and took up little space.

'Best piece of work ever I done,' he said, with his half-grin, standing back to let the women admire. 'And since 'tis fish oil that gives 'ee Cornish maids such fair skins, well then, Lily'll be well named among 'ee.'

They all laughed at that. And the foreman, intrigued in spite of himself, finally agreed to 'give ut a try'.

'Just once,' he warned. The women poked each other and laughed again. 'He'm done fer,' they whispered, 'just saving face, that's all 'tis. Go on, me handsome, 'ee've got un licked.'

I wouldn't *choose* to have a child reared like that, but when I went to work each day Lily slept or played in a cradle made by a fisherman from a fisherman's box. Freshly scrubbed, clean-padded, the dilly kept her safe and warm. I could keep my eye on her and tend her all I liked. And when she rode back and forth, propped up against a pillow (I kept everything spotless neat as Beth had shown me), to my mind she looked like a princess with her fair hair and white skin and her delicate features. And why the foreman finally capitulated, and why the women stuck up for me, I don't know, for their own children were a burden to them. Except I think there was an innate goodness and pity for someone less fortunate. And when in time Lily grew too large for her homemade pram, eventually my landlady took care of her, although for me it never was so good as those first days. And if the smell of fish was as strong as ever, at least it was an honest smell, nothing to be ashamed of.

A year had passed since I had come to St Marvell and first seen the sea. A long strange year. At its end I could not regret what had happened. Beth was married in July and went to live in Truro. Jeb had gone back to his own hut. I saw him almost every day when the boats came in, and often watched the other women watching him as he shouldered boxes of fish with ease, hoisting them over the slippery decks or trudging up the wet sand. He was always affable, a smile for everyone; I never saw him out-of-sorts, and if there was a dispute usually he was the one to settle it. I liked his way with people. And although he never said much, I liked it when he did, to the point, nothing superfluous or fancy, nothing ambiguous.

Most of all I liked the way he still doted on Lily. And so as the months passed we slid into a way of living in which little by little he regained some of the ground that he had lost. I came almost imperceptibly to depend on him, as perhaps my Mam had done with Cyril. Except I swore never to make use of anyone as she'd done. When we walked out together along the cliff of an evening or strolled on the quay on fine Sundays, Lily riding in her box, or better still perched on his shoulder, we already may have seemed a 'courting couple', expected to become man and wife, although true to his promise he never mentioned it. And given time, we might have drifted into that relationship, or rather out of inertia I might have. Something always held me back; I don't know what, some part of that pattern which made the name 'war widow' seem right, some determination perhaps to prove loyalty to a vanished dream. Or pride, which wouldn't admit even to myself that, had Julian lived, he might never have married me. But most of all it was the feeling I had about my daughter. Lily was not born for the life we led. She was marked with some special grace which, if not for me, at least for her one day would cause fortune to spread its bounty.

Again I do not defend my position. Nor can I say it was fair on Jeb; I freely admit he deserved much more. But since friendship was the best I could offer it seemed to satisfy him. And so the second summer passed. The curiosity I aroused living alone (unusual in a village where everyone was related), the story of my misfortunes, was superseded by another event, of greater importance.

A 'royal personage' was to visit the royal duchy. This was the news that obliterated every other interest. The war, the queen's health, the decline in fishing (again the season had been sluggish slow), all took second place; even royal scandal was forgotten. We became obsessed with which village would act as host, when and how the visit was to take place, who was to be received by the royal visitor. Children played at kings and queens, chopping off subjects' heads as if topping fish; words like 'Your Highness' came into common speech, practised secretly in hopes of being uttered in public. Excitement grew. 'Fancy that, to see him in the flesh,' people said – all the flesh that is, concern now expressed about the royal ability to squeeze the royal bulk through those little streets. A Highness needs room to look his best; narrowness cramps regal style. For a while the council seriously debated tearing down some of the older cottages – much to the consternation of the inhabitants. 'Bain't been near us in fifty years!' a spokesman summed up. ''Twill take fifty more till next time. Where're we to live in the meanwhile, out in the open?'

They sounded peeved. And so was I, and more than that. While villages vied with each other, while money poured out unstintingly for decoration and refurbishing, I thought how a quarter of that amount could have improved our living. Instead of painting walls, wells and privies could have been repaired, the school enlarged, another teacher hired, children chased off the streets and obliged to be educated.

'You'm talking like one of them Socialists,' Jeb teased. But I wasn't joking. I didn't mean for Lily to be deprived as I had been. I wanted life to be 'fairer' for her; I wanted her to start off equal. And if perhaps I was thinking of the Polleven family and those bitter inequalities, who would blame me? (Although I had early ascertained that, still being in mourning, they would not take part in the festivities. Well, that was their right; I couldn't fault them for that, but I was relieved that I wouldn't see them.)

St Marvell was one of the favoured villages. Hopes sank for Port Zenack, to flare again when it was announced that the royal entourage would watch fish being unloaded and processed there. Suddenly all plans centred around tidying up our village, how to make quays and fish cellars look and smell as neat and clean as possible. The quays weren't hard to manage, a good hosing down, a general removal of litter, a whitewashing of stones, but paint won't hide the smell of fish. The cellars were impossible to 'spruce up'; well then, they must be hidden.

The first proof we had of this was when workmen appeared. Hired by the company boat owners they bustled about with scaffolding. 'Proper job,' the women joked, 'make a real palace out of it.' They wiped their hands on their sides, pushed back their caps, prepared to do battle for themselves, making rude comments about workmen in general and their lack of skill, suggesting that it wasn't boxing in that was needed but tearing down. When their suggestions were ignored they pelted the men with fish, a time-honoured custom. The barricades went up nevertheless. And when they were in place we realized to what extent the royal party was to be shielded from us. And to what extent we women workers were to be ignored, untouchables.

After days of rain, the great morning dawned fair. The village was in fête. Bunting flapped across the streets, and banners were draped from most windows. In the harbour the boats had been given hasty coats of paint and flags fluttered bravely from their mast heads. The streets had not been widened but boxes of geraniums had been placed at strategic corners to block narrow entrances and a platform constructed where the royal person was to sit while the village dignitaries were presented. The partitions around the fish cellars had been hung with garlands, as if wilting hydrangeas could enhance the impression of bucolic charm. On the surface then all was rustic calm and innocence, underneath tensions simmered.

Before dawn the village came rumbling awake. I was used to that: the sound of matches striking in the dark to light a lamp, the creak of bed springs, the stamp of boots down the little paths, the rough, 'Alright then, boy', with which the fishermen greeted each other. Those were the normal sounds of a normal work day. Now was different. Children cried as mothers washed and clothed them, stuffing them into too-tight garments; fathers swore as they scraped at beards and tussled with ties and collars. Mothers fussed, cooked breakfast, struggled to keep children clean while they dressed themselves, most wearing the universal 'uniform' of long black skirt, high-collared blouse and small straw hat.

I confess that despite my previous misgivings Lily and I were among the early arrivals although the royal procession was not due until noon. As at St Marvell, Port Zenack's main square faced the sea and on a fine day like this it did look 'picturesque', the quay swept clear of rubbish, the nets spread on the wall to dry, the sea sparkling turquoise against the slate grey of cliffs, the seagulls dipping and swooping, their sharp cries mocking the church bells' more sober ringing. The villagers were dressed in their Sunday clothes, the cottages and gardens were neat and tidy, the village streets washed clean. And herein came the first difficulty – those village streets.

The previous rains had been heavy, Cornish rains driving out of the west. On the country lanes, mud had spilled across the surface and streams had flooded. The royal carriage soon became bogged down, giving no alternative except to walk (although how the carriage had been expected to drive down through the village is another matter. It would have stuck at the first right-angled turn.)

Walking downhill on wet streets is a skill that has to be acquired. The royal feet were used perhaps to ship decks and went forward manfully; the ladies in the party began to slip and slide; soon one half was supporting the other, a regal procession turned into a rout. Organizers who lined the way to cheer and clap came wholeheartedly to the rescue, hoisting up and tugging as if loading fish. Tempers frayed. When at last the square was reached only a miracle could have restored dignity.

The miracle of course was attempted. Little girls appeared dressed in frilly skirts with long pink sashes, their hair tied with ribbons of the same colour. They carried nosegays bound with deeper pink, which they offered shyly with bobs for curtsies, not village children, but belonging to the local officials, the ship owners, the squires. These gentlemen and their wives were already installed on the platform with the royal entourage, had made their own bows and curtsies, were preening themselves like peacocks at their offspring. Speeches followed, *a few well chosen words*. A string was pulled to reveal a plaque in honour of the occasion, to clapping and cheers. In turn, rising from his chair (purple-cushioned, borrowed from the vicarage), the royal personage, still puffing slightly from unexpected exercise, said he was delighted with everything, fishing was his hobby, fishing made a man. And how splendid were the fishing boats, built to be used by hearty sailors, the pride of the English navy. (Here he hummed and hawed.) And the fish cellar where the real work was done, a model of its kind.

He turned with his expansive smile, struck his fist against the hoarding. 'The backbone of England,' he began. With a creak and a groan the whole edifice collapsed inwards, garlands swinging madly, dust settling in white clouds. Behind the ruin the awful evidence lay heaped: the piles of refuse, the pungent casks, the kegs of salt, the rotting offal that no one had known what to do with.

While the royal party looked aghast, some ladies not quite managing to hide their retching, handkerchieves now pressed to their noses, and while the officials turned pale with mortification, among the villagers there was a gasp, a snort, a sudden burst of laughter. 'That's how real fish stinks,' someone yelled, 'don't do to cover it.' 'And how about help for we fishermen?' another shouted. 'We deserve it if the navy does.' The fisher women, plucking up courage, stood out in a group and shouted too, things like, 'Our wages bain't much', and 'Womun and chilrun first'.

In a fit of loyalty I joined them. And I will say they looked grand, 'handsome' as the Cornish say, dressed in their clean clothes, a real cluster of Cornish women, eyes sparkling indignantly, hair curling, skins in truth as soft as Cornish mist. The royal personage was clearly impressed. And given his liking for female pulchritude it's not surprising he made conciliatory gestures, turning and beckoning to the local gentlemen to answer the 'ladies' requests'. And probably because I was young and the only one holding a child, and attuned as he was to the mood of crowds and knowing how to milk a moment, he beckoned to me to step forward and, 'Speak up, my dear,' he said.

I handed Lily back to Jeb, did step forward, did speak up, saying things I'd thought about that were needed, a long speech although I tried to keep it short. I could see the local gentry were taken aback and would have shut me up if there had been a way to do so decently. The royal personage smiled, stroked his short sailor's beard, nodded to the equerries who surrounded him as if to say, take a note of that. And after he had shaken my hand and asked my name I told him, 'Guinevere Ellis,' perhaps proud as a peacock myself. And when the local papers published details, a downplaying of failure and vast trumpetings of success, my picture, albeit blurred, appeared with the royal personage who was shown holding my hand in his.

The village took this mark of favour with singular calm, nothing loath to cut pride down to size. How they enjoyed the mock servility and made sly jokes at my expense. Some-one even tried throwing fish scales at my feet in lieu of roses. I accepted all this teasing patiently. I knew my fellow workers well enough by now to realize they bore no grudge, at least not in the beginning. The company owners took a different tack; they had the most to lose, were the most at fault, wanted most to cast blame on someone else.

Whether they would have done as they threatened, closed the fish cellars down and sacked those who had 'behaved with such disloyalty' (their words) and whether the fisher women would have let them is a matter for conjecture. As people had pointed out, once the royal visitor had turned his back another fifty years could pass before he remembered his promises to us. But things don't happen in a vacuum, without a past or future. They hang together, dependent upon each other, entwined like strands of mooring rope. If the royal visitation hadn't cost so much money, if I hadn't said my say, if I hadn't had Lily to worry about, my picture would never have appeared in the paper. Sir Robert Polleven would never have noticed it. And would never have come looking for his grandchild.

He appeared in the alleyway one morning; well, 'appeared' is too grand an expression for Corset Alley, rather he had fitted himself in and was hammering at the door with the head of his riding crop until the neighbours came out to stare. I knew him at once, although I could only see the top of his head. He had taken off his hat and was holding it, and his thatch of silver-grey hair almost touched the eaves, while no doubt he looked about him with his bird-of-prey eyes, his mouth curling contemptuously. Together with his black frock coat, black boots, and fine white linen he was all of a piece, a gentleman, as out of his depth in these miserable surroundings as I had been in his more elegant one.

When he asked for me I heard the ripple of shock through the floor boards, as the little widow bowed and scraped and tried to invite him in, all the while piping up the stairs for me to come down, come down, 'some gentlemun wants 'ee.' And I felt curiosity throb through the walls as the neighbours all craned discreetly. Usual noises ceased while people strained to listen in, eavesdropping a pastime, a hobby, a besetting sin, in Corset Alley.

I picked Lily up from her cot and wrapped her in a shawl, came slowly down the stairs and went outside. Sir Robert had declined to enter, had said he would wait for me in the square. He was standing by the water's edge, back to the village, legs apart like a captain on his deck. He didn't look as I approached although he must have known I was there. 'You are Guinevere Ellis?' he asked. 'You've proof? I shan't take things on chance. And that's my son's child?'

He wasn't speaking loudly, just loud enough for me to hear, but he was enunciating clearly as if I were deaf. Or stupid.

I said, 'I've brought Lily for you to see, if you wants to. But she's mine.'

He spun round on his heel at that, looked down at us. His brows contracted. I almost expected him to raise his whip as he had once before. What stopped him was the baby, not her herself exactly, but her looks. I think he was startled by the resemblance to Julian, I think he may have seen her father's eyes in her. He didn't comment on that, said only, 'Lily?', with a curl of his lip as if I had uttered an obscenity, although whether it was the name or the sex of the child I couldn't be sure. Then, 'You don't deny that she is my son's?'

Here was a reverse of what I'd expected, he stressing the relationship, not I. I couldn't understand it; it made me nervous.

'I don't deny naught,' I told him, 'I don't ask naught. I . . .'

'Good God, girl,' he broke in, 'I'm not interested in what *you* want. But that child is the only thing of my son's left. I won't have her living here. Oh, don't protest,' as I began to do so, 'I've found out all I need to know. My grandchild, abandoned in a fishing village with a fishwife as a mother, good heavens, you can't expect my son to have wanted that?'

He was clever, Julian's father, skilfully knowing how to play on feelings. He turned his back to me, again stared out to sea. 'I can't discuss my son with you,' he said, 'I don't intend to try. Sufficient to say after his death his papers were sent to me. I found reference to you. Of course it was nothing I knew about before. I wish to know nothing now. It was my daughter, Miss Polleven,' he coughed as if reluctant even to mention her name in this place, 'she read about you and remembered.'

He didn't elaborate. I wondered almost idly what Ruth had told him. It all seemed so long ago, so very unimportant.

'I've made inquiries,' he continued, the thin veil of distaste still showing. He coughed again. 'If the child is a

Polleven, and that too must be proved,' speaking heavily, ponderously, his words a mixture of aversion, grief, and duty, 'then she should be brought up as a Polleven. My wife and I have discussed what we will do. I'm a rich man,' he added when I didn't respond, 'an extremely rich man if it comes to that. She'll be taken care of in proper fashion, adopted into a suitable household. I already have in mind a person. And so will you be taken care of,' he added hastily as if I had asked for something, 'my solicitors will see to that.'

'Lily isn't for sale,' I said.

'Hah,' he snorted. Then distinctly, so there should be no mistake on my part, 'I own many of the boats in this harbour, as I'm sure you are aware. Men work for me, as I decide. I own the major share in the fish cellars, the foreman also works for me. How will you live if you've no job, Miss Ellis? For there will be no job if you make difficulties. And if I have to, I'll go to law. There isn't a magistrate in Cornwall, or England come to that, would let a child grow up the way you've been rearing her.'

I wrapped my arms round Lily as if he were already trying to tear her away, so tightly she began to cry. I couldn't speak. The threats were worse than nightmares. 'Come now,' he was saying and his attempt to cajole was even more threatening, 'you're a sensible girl, I'm sure. It can't be easy living here. I could set you up somewhere else, wherever you want; you're young enough to start afresh. Besides, you're . . .'

He swallowed the thoughts as if he were going to say, 'You're beautiful,' just as his son might have.

I said, 'You know that Julian came looking for me once? And if he had lived he'd come again. He'd want me to keep Lily. She's all I've got.'

'Be reasonable,' he cried. 'How can a single girl, an unmarried girl, care for a child? That's denying her a chance. Isn't that what you said yourself, didn't I read those very words, "I want my daughter to have a chance."' He mimicked me. '"She's all I've got." That's pure poppycock, that's selfishness.'

He leaned forward persuasively, driving his argument home, 'And what's this I hear about another man? He may not want her. Jeb Martin may be right for you, but not for Julian's daughter. Give her to me and marry him, I'll see you taken care of.'

I almost laughed. 'Jeb wouldn't give Lily up,' I said, 'why, he loves her.'

His face drew down into a frown. We faced each other across a gulf so wide that nothing in our experience could bridge it.

'That's as may be,' he said at last, face black as thunder, lips obstinate, 'we'll see about that. You'll hear from me again. Or from my solicitors. And I shan't be so generous.'

I waited until he had untied his horse, swung himself on its back, ridden heavily up the hill, an old man, used to having his own way. I thought, it's not really Lily that he wants, Lily means nothing to him. She's something of his that he feels he owns, and the not having it eats at him. He won't rest until Lily is accounted for. Like my Mam there's nothing of feeling, only pride.

When he had gone the neighbours came prying, not as in St Marvell to drive me out, rather to help and surround me with advice. They obviously had not heard all that was said, Sir Robert had been too shrewd for that, but his looks and gestures had set them thinking. Besides, gentlemen of his worth didn't come into villages without good cause, didn't talk to village girls out of kindness. The reason they latched on to was very close to truth, the one that Sir Robert could use as weapon. 'Could close us down,' they said, 'could stop the fishing fleet. What did he say about that, maid? That's some important.'

I couldn't blame their preoccupation, fishing was their livelihood. And I couldn't tell them all his threats. On the other hand I didn't want to lie and pretend he hadn't threatened. I pushed past them and went back to Corset Alley. In the kitchen Widow Pendar rattled pots and clanked the poker. She didn't want me to leave but if there were trouble she would.

It was late when Jeb came to the entrance of the alley. He whistled as he used to do of an evening, but when I began to tiptoe out, Widow Pendar was waiting. 'Seems to me,' she said, ''ee be making free with time, fer a widow woman. I don't like it in my house.'

'Oh, hold your tongue, afore I knots it.' Jeb was standing in the doorway, towering against it, safe and reliable as a rock. He sounded angry but his eyes were twinkling. 'Come on, missus,' he urged, 'have a heart. You must be blind not to know what's going on. But if she'll have me, we'll be calling of the banns and there'll be an end of it. It's a wedding that there'll be from your house, so don't take on so.'

He brushed aside her exclamations of delight, good-naturedly endured her chatter. 'Get on now,' was all he said, 'you'm worse than any gadfly. Spread the word, there's my handsome, and leave us be. For there's something to be said.'

When she had gone, her shawl ends flying, 'What do you say, my love,' he said. 'Not as I want, but the only way I know how to stop him. Married, Lily is ours, and I can adopt her. If you agree that is, if you but tell me so.'

I looked at him. There were fine lines of tiredness under his eyes where white showed against the brown; his neck was red with sun above the white collarless shirt; he held his cloth cap in both hands, twisting it from nervousness, just as my father had done. I liked it in Jeb. But I still didn't love him, and he knew I didn't. And yet I would have to accept him, there was no way else I knew to save Lily, although it wasn't fair to use him. And when I answered him, the slow smile that spread painfully across his face almost made the saying worthwhile.

CHAPTER 9

*T*rue to his word, next Sunday Jeb had the banns called. His sister had frequently confirmed she was not a church-going woman but Jeb sometimes went to chapel of a Sunday. His love of music and his deep baritone were welcome additions to the choir for which Port Zenack was famed.

` The chapel stood halfway up the hill, a square building with a long extension fitted next to it and a bell tower on top. It was built of local stone, snugly fitted, with steps of Delabole slate reaching up to double doors. Underneath was what was called the Wesley Room after the well-known preacher. Its plain front and solid look suited the people who used it. I took a pew two rows in front of Jeb as it wouldn't have done to be sitting next to him. I could feel his presence behind me though, large and dependable, in his best suit, carefully brushed for the occasion. His red hair was flattened wet, he opened his mouth and sang: 'Praise God from whom all blessings flow.' I knew that was what he believed and that I was his blessing.

I held Lily on my lap. She seemed to recognize the importance of the moment, didn't squirm, or reach for Jeb, but chewed on toy or fist, a model child. Beside us Widow Pendar beamed, the roses in her straw hat nodding with satisfaction. Around us sat the others of that little community whom I had come to know and trust, my women friends, their fisher husbands. They too looked pleased, except perhaps some of the younger girls. As I had once suspected they had had their own designs. But I scarcely noticed them, their giggles of embarrassed surprise blending into the background of whispered congratulations and 'I told you so's'.

The minister was intoning the familiar words: Jeb Martin, bachelor, Guinevere Ellis . . . the names might have been borrowed. They had no connection with my life. For all that I owed Jeb, for all his devotion and caring, I went through the ceremony cold as stone. And that was the frightening thing, how easy it was to have no sensation left, how simple it was to become like my Mam, empty of feeling.

All week Jeb had kept watch like a bodyguard, although he wouldn't admit it. Each evening when I went to bed I'd seen him at the alley entrance. Wrapped in his fisherman's coat he'd lean against the wall until morning. He would be gone then with the boat, for the season was now well under way and I wondered that today in chapel he could stay awake. He laughed at my protests. 'You must be mistaken, 'tweren't me.' He laughed again. 'But certain sure it weren't Sir Robert.'

I'll admit all week that dread had grown, until I was afraid to leave the house, imagining Sir Robert's men might be lying in wait. And even locked indoors I had moments when I thought how, like those excise men of old, some officer of the law, some policeman, might break in to snatch Lily.

Understanding these fears, Jeb'd said more seriously, 'I don't work a Polleven boat, I ain't beholden to any Polleven. And even if he did close me out of the "Mermaid", I've still got the "Lily". The cove's mine, we'd do alright. And once you're there he'd not harm you.' For all his optimism I think he guessed Sir Robert was capable of ruining him; he just refused to admit it. A rich man has all the advantages a poor man hasn't. And as Ruth Polleven had shown me once, so had the rich man himself, how readily privileges could be claimed and bought.

Jeb had smiled with happiness, with content. But he didn't come close, didn't touch me. He'd not yet offered a kiss, hadn't dared. I wondered if the thought of it was closed to him as it was closed to me, as all that side of love was closed. Or if he too dreamed of miracles, that with marriage all would come right. I didn't share his optimism. And again it seemed so unfair to him that like my Mam I was willing to settle for a parody of love in return for security.

Outside was Sunday quiet. For once there was no wind, the village streets steamed in the heat, the sea was a purple sodden mass. The air was brazen. Inside the chapel was overcharged with the press of bodies. I think the whole of Port Zenack had turned out full force to do Jeb Martin proud. Light slanted across the wooden boards and the smell of dust tickled the nose. People shifted their feet, coughed, a child whispered and was shushed. The plain wood pews creaked as the congregation braced its collective back to listen to the sermon. The minister was a dull little man with a dull little wife and a host of appropriately dull little children but surely goodness was in his words, and trust, and homely wisdom. I thought, this is what hell is: to be offered choice unchooseable between marrying a man whom I am incapable of being wife to, and losing a daughter, becoming 'expendable' to her.

A shift in the quality of light made me turn my head. Because of the heat the wooden doors had remained open and the momentary darkening of the shadow on the threshold was as alarming as a shout. A man was framed in the doorway, outlined by a halo of light, so bright that his actual shape was indistinguishable. I was the only one who seemed aware of him, the only one who turned, the only one who got up, yet I felt his presence, or rather the disappearance of it, like a physical blow. My heart began to thud, slowly, painfully; despite the warmth I felt sweat chill as ice along the spine. And a feeling akin to outrage, I can't explain it, a feeling I'd never had before, swept over me, that even here, at this moment, in the presence of God, fate should try to re-establish its malignant hold.

I thrust Lily into the widow's arms, ignored the stifled protests from the others seated in the pew, pushed my way out to the central aisle. As determinedly I walked towards the door, oblivious to the broken-off sermon, the shocked murmurs of surprise, only having sense left to motion to Jeb to keep his place, for he would have followed me had perhaps some look on my face not prevented him. Because it wasn't only outrage I felt, it was something more, having nothing to do with anger or fear. I had gone far beyond them into some primaeval urge to take hold of whatever had been haunting me all my life and beat it down so that afterwards there would be nothing left to fear. And so perhaps I think when the die is finally cast, all creatures, human or animal, fight for survival if they must, motivated by that unexplainable sense of what is due to them.

But whatever the feeling was, and whatever motivated it, all dissipated like frost in the sun when I saw who it was that was waiting outside. And it wasn't Sir Robert Polleven.

It is perhaps unfitting that I didn't collapse on the spot, or faint from surprise or joy, or wasn't overcome with emotion, anything other than that sense of injustice, almost rage, at this final trick of fate. Not rage at Julian of course but at that fate which once more too late reversed its course. I might almost have been forgiven had I shouted, 'Why couldn't he stay dead, dead is something I've learned to manage.'

I didn't of course. I couldn't say anything.

We Cornish are great believers in the supernatural; our legends are full of headless hauntings, of ridings by night and dread warnings of disasters. A ghost at midday is harder to accept, even the ghost of the man I loved. I stood at the top of those slate steps leaning on the rail for support. He had gone down to the street below. For a moment his face turned up, as if he also was uncertain and needed reassurance. I noticed things about him almost unconsciously: that he was thinner, scarecrow-thin under the stained uniform; that the

140

tan which gave his face a superficial appearance of health seemed stretched over a skin so colourless it was less than white; that when he moved he dragged one leg, swung it awkwardly from the knee, although when he got the swing right he could move with surprising speed. As he now began to do, not as his father had done downhill towards the sea, but up, towards the open headland, the cliffs, the moors, as if he found the village too confining, as if like me he needed space to breathe.

I forced myself to go after him. I closed the door, went down the stairs, followed at a distance. I knew he must have seen me, had paused long enough to take in what he saw. And if he in turn didn't speak perhaps it was because he felt the same overwhelming sense of outrage that his return had been honed with such razor-sharp precision, had been so accurately timed, as to cause the greatest damage to the greatest number of people.

When he came to the top of the lane to fields similar to Upper End where he had met Emma at her blackberrying, he turned aside through a gateway where his horse was tied. It wasn't the grey that I remembered but a chestnut which flicked its tail at the flies and stamped nervously as I came through after him. There was no one about although the gate had been tied back with twine and deep ruts were carved in the ground by the passage of horses and wagons. He went on walking fast with a curious lopsided gait, as if he didn't know when to stop, as if he couldn't. The bushes along the hedge were strung with wisps of straw; stubble crunched underfoot. From a sheltered lower field came a familiar smell of cut wheat, and where the shocks had been stacked the ground was parched a golden brown. And always lower again, the sea lay like a strange, almost purple, cloud fading into haze, against which the sky looked pale. When he came to the last hedge he stopped, facing it, as if suddenly aware there was nowhere else to go. The stream of unspoken questions that trailed behind him were bramble-barbed. 'Why did you never write? Why did you let me leave, knowing I had misunderstood? Why did you hide from me?'

His questions were knife wounds. To each thrust there was a thrust of the knife back. 'Why did *you* lie, why did *you* leave after that first night? Why didn't *you* look for me?'

What he said was unrelated to those thoughts, an even-voiced remark, made, if not exactly to a stranger, to someone to be held at a distance, in a cool, collected way, devoid of intimacy. 'A Dutch farmer kept me hidden, you know, after I escaped from prison, three months until he could smuggle me back to the English lines. I worked on his farm to keep up pretence I was a city nephew come to learn country ways. And to recover strength.'

He made a chopping motion with his arm to encapture fields and cliffs and the purple sea. 'It didn't look like this, a Boer farm, acres and acres of bush and scrub, a landscape of dust. But every time the Boer patrols rode past I hid in a barn where grain was stored. That smelled the same.'

He didn't ask how I was, or anything about Lily, he didn't say any of the things he should have done. I could have been angry except it dawned on me that perhaps he didn't know, not the whole of it I mean, that only parts had been revealed to him and those the ones that would show me in worst light so that he should think the worst of me. And if I were to tell him all the truth then I must reveal facts about his own family that would damage it and his relationship to it, probably beyond repair. And like a scene that is so well known that everything about it is familiar, the image of our first meeting rose up out of the past with all the same connotations, the same power in miniature to do harm, the same kind of cause and effect.

It made me pause. And perhaps he felt it too. For he frowned, for a moment resembling that father I had at first thought he was, and said, 'I arrived home last night. Is it true then, what they say, that you weren't married when I came back last year? But that you will be now? That those were your banns I just heard? That it's your wedding that's being planned?'

He looked at me one keen hard look, then turned aside and stared out to sea. And the last of the unspoken questions hung unanswered and unanswerable, 'Couldn't you have waited?'

His shoulders were hunched as if to ward off another blow. I suddenly remembered what had been said of Boer prison camps, and the treatment prisoners endured. And for a moment we stood transfixed, his back to me, I behind him so that when he asked the last questions that he had to ask I hardly heard. 'And you're happy, you're in love?'

Then, 'No,' I cried, the words at last forced out of me, 'I wrote it all out for you in letters even if you've never got them. And I wasn't married, never meant to be. Except now I've had to give me word. Had to, had to.'

Tears were streaming down my face but I didn't notice until later. And when he turned with the same awkward movement as he had when walking, as if he had to struggle to keep upright, I think he was crying too. 'Listen,' he said, abruptly, 'I want you to understand. What happened before I went overseas, and then after I got there. It wasn't like I imagined at all, a war we shouldn't have been fighting in that way, in that place. The Boers were too damn good for us to begin with. And I didn't mean to leave Cornwall as I did, unfinished business, isn't it called? But after I came to St Marvell for you and thought you were lost for good, I didn't much care what happened afterwards.

'The first time, I searched for you all day, you know,' he went on in the same bleak tone. 'I came back as I said I would. I walked the moors looking for you. When you didn't come up on the tor I went to the farm, knocked at the door, waited for you to let me in. Farmer Penwith said he didn't know where you'd gone. "Cleared off," was his expression. And he told me to do the same. "No call for you and your ilk to hang about," he said, as if I were some itinerant tramp.

'Your mother, it must have been your mother, told me you'd stolen money to run away. I didn't believe her. But when my sister convinced me that you'd gone to Zenack Road Station to catch the Waterloo train, well, I had to.

'Ruth told me she had seen you there. She looked at me straight as she described what you were wearing, and how you smiled as you bought your ticket. And when she explained how you'd come to the house, she was clever enough not to hide that, and some of what you'd said (not as it really was, of course), she persuaded me that you'd really gone. At home, everything was in confusion; Ma shut up in her room, in her restrained way grieving at my leaving; father stumping around like a man possessed, trying to foist off gifts in lieu of goodbyes: guns, horses, cash, his way to buy affection. And I forced to pack and return immediately to barracks, all orders changed because of the possibility of war – there just wasn't time to sort out what had really happened.

'You must understand about my family,' he said. 'My father's not one to confide in, and my mother's not up to it. Oh, she's sweet and kind enough, incapable of wrong, incapable of anything, a mere cypher, dominated by my father. I couldn't rely on her. That left Ruth, at best a weak link, but the only one I had. Ruth promised to help. "I'll find her for you," she said, "she won't have gone far. I'll pry it out of the station master" (for she persisted in that story). She looked at me straight, put her hand in mine in a loving way like she used when she was small, spoke so feelingly, saying how sorry she was, things like that, I was sure for once she understood. "I owe you that at least," she said.'

He seemed to brood a while, then roused himself. 'It wasn't until August, my last leave before we set out for Africa that I caught glimmers of another tale.'

I remembered what he had said about his sister's lying the first time we'd met. *I don't know why she does it.* I remembered the shrug. 'Spent half my life covering for her lies,' he'd said. And I remembered the pale, elegant

144

mother, the strident father, his family as he now described them.

He was explaining about the little parlour maid. How she'd slid up and whispered that he look for me at St Marvell. Which he had done, with the result we both knew of.

He was quiet for a moment then. 'I can only imagine what it was like for you,' he said. 'It was death for me. When we got the command to charge at the relief of Mafeking I was almost glad. Even that didn't work. The grey shot out under me, my knee smashed, months in a Boer prison camp before I managed to escape, I'd plenty of time to think.'

He said, 'I never got your letters, not one. I suppose they could have been kept at headquarters, or forwarded in a bunch to Africa. In either case when I was reported dead, they'd have been sent back here with the rest of my effects. But they're not with my things, I've already looked. So either they were lost somewhere. Or father destroyed them himself.'

He said this last matter-of-factly. 'He might not have opened them at first, at least not until a few weeks ago when he knew I was alive. After that, I suspect he, or Ruth, would have read every line, if only out of curiosity. There'd have been plenty of time afterwards, to get rid of them I mean, when they heard. It took a while before I could ship home.'

He added, 'After the farmer arranged for my return I still couldn't walk right, needed a spell in hospital to get back on my feet.'

I thought, then his father knew Julian was alive when he came to get the baby. He knew, and yet he came, didn't share the news, never let on a word.

And of all the cruel things that seemed the cruellest.

I said, 'How did you know where I was today? Did your father tell you that?'

'No,' he said evenly. 'My mother did. Ruth wouldn't say a word at first,' he continued, 'although I tried to squeeze news out of her. That might have been remorse, of course;

145

she might have regretted what she'd done. We'd had a stormy parting in August after she'd pretended your "return" to St Marvell was recent and therefore unknown to her. I'd like to think she was glad to see me back and wanted to spare me grief. Myself, I doubt it. I think she was saving it for one last trick.'

His brow constricted as if with pain. 'So I tackled my mother,' he said. 'Breaking years of habit is difficult. I'd grown up protecting her from unpleasantness. You don't know the relief it was finding someone like you, someone who could face life honestly, without crumbling up. I went to her room last night and asked. When she began with her usual line: "I don't know, I don't understand, I can't cope"; when she tried to excuse Ruth, oh, things like, "After all, she's never been suited to a younger sister role" and "She's always fancied being your father's heir," the usual stuff, I knew I was on the right track. The final appeal to sympathy, "When your father's gone, she'll be dependent on your goodwill. Try to understand, Julian, be generous," left me unmoved. As did her tears when I insisted.'

I never remembered him so stern, so determined. It made him almost hard. I thought, yes, he's changed too, although the seeds of hardness were always there, the detachment, the coldness.

'I told her I wasn't interested in Ruth,' he went on, 'only in you; what had she heard, there must be something. What she finally revealed wasn't much but could have come from only one source. It's not the sort of thing my father would talk about. Finally she showed me a newspaper. "I haven't read it of course," she said, "but all the country's talking of it."'

He said, 'When I saw your picture and read the story, I knew what a fool I'd been. I was shattered, like being hit all over again. And as I left my mother's room, Ruth came in. "I warned you," she said, looking at me reproachfully as if my mother's distress were my fault, as if it were all my fault. "I told you it wouldn't work," as if she were glad that it couldn't, as if she wanted me to fail. When I began to push past her, "I told you her mother was a whore," she cried, "like mother, like daughter. And even so, you're still too late."

'"They're reading the banns today," she continued, smiling a little, that smile of triumph that used to drive me wild. "She's marrying some sort of fisherman. And all because she'd had his child."'

There was another pause. 'And if that's so,' he spoke deliberately short and loud, as if even in his thoughts he was fighting for balance, 'if, as you've just said yourself, you *have to*, then answer me two things. Whose child is that you were holding in the chapel there? And how old is it?'

I thought, oh God, he's endured enough. It's too late to try and hide. And I came up close, put out my arm to touch his. And I said, 'She's our Lily. Born early this past spring, your daughter and mine. And I'm marrying someone else to keep her safe because her grandfather, your father, wanted to take her away from me.'

Somehow he had put out his arms to steady himself, to steady me, somehow I was enveloped in them. All the months of yearning, all the sadness and waste were swept away as that ghost at last turned to flesh and blood. And questions and answers became as meaningless as chaff blowing to and fro in the harvest field.

Then we were falling together; we were lying side by side beneath the hedge, somehow I was holding him and he was holding me, the yearning and insistence part of each of us. And as I sank into his cool embrace, as I let my body shift and move of its own accord, as I too came back to life, 'God, I dreamed of this,' he was whispering at my ear, his hands busy with the buttons of my skirt, the palms rough as they slid under the waistband. I felt them inch up my back, I felt them as I had been feeling them ever since we first met, as I in turn had been imagining, all the emptiness suddenly filled, all the longing sated. And it seemed to me that there never had been a time when we

147

had not been doing this, when we had not been joined, as natural as breathing.

Afterwards, he stretched out his leg carefully, favouring it, but still kept his head buried against my breast. 'In that hell,' he was saying, 'thoughts of you kept me alive. You were all I had.'

We lay in the shadow of the hedge, its shade welcome after the heat. Overhead a lark was singing, pure liquid notes, crickets chirped. The sky was a strange misty shell against the darker sea. 'So for me,' I thought.

What we said then was for ourselves alone, a lifetime of saying, all the things we had meant to say forgotten in this torrent of new ideas, half-broken sentences, half-interrupted thoughts, overlapping, combining, echoing each other, as if thoughts like bodies can be joined. It was well into afternoon before we stirred. Then, conscious at last of what and where, he pulled himself up into a sitting position, looked out towards the west where the sky had begun to thicken into bands and ridges of cloud. 'This'll be the last of the fine days,' he said, 'there's storm in the air, can't you smell it? Lucky they've got the grain in in time. The weather's changing.'

I remembered another harvest, another storm, another time he'd spoken of farming to give me chance to recover myself, and I'd been startled by his knowledge of it, a soldier wasn't meant to be a farmer, and know about such things. As if he guessed he laughed a little and stroked my hair while I reached up to pull the fronds of grass from his. His eyes still had their hawklike intensity, that couldn't alter, but they were shining now, with happiness.

'I told you at heart I was a tiller of the soil,' he joked, 'I've come back to till. I've a little money of my own. My father can whistle in the wind; there are other places than Polleven Manor to farm. But one thing won't change. I want you with me. And Lily.'

He said, almost shyly, 'It's funny to think of having a daughter I didn't even imagine I had. I don't know much about babies, except you have to ask about their teeth. Has she any? Who does she look like? You, I hope. Does she know about me? What did you tell her about us?'

He sounded eager, inexperienced, and I suddenly felt protective as if he were much younger. I thought of all the lonely days when I had wanted protection. And I thought of Lily and her smile and her eyes like her father's, and remembered when she and I had needed him. And for the first time since leaving the chapel I thought of Jeb. Slowly I sat up too, straightening my skirts. 'Julian,' I said, even the name sounding strange as if my lips couldn't fit around the syllables, 'it seems to me you've heard all sorts of versions of my life, but not the truth of it. I've not told you it; I didn't even write you all the bad bits. Oh, nothing to do with love or love making,' as he began to interrupt, 'there's been no one else. But that article in the paper will have shown you how I lived. It was honest work, that's the most that can be said of it. Long ago I feared 'twas I that dragged you down. And so your father said. "I'll not have my grandchild's mother a fisherwife," were his words. But in that loneliness of spirit when I thought to die myself, I found friends among the fisherfolk. And two of them were the best and dearest anybody could hope for.'

And so I told him about Beth and Jeb. And how Jeb too had sworn to love and protect me and Lily, and what today, now before his friends, I had promised in return.

And when Julian cried out, 'But you promised me first,' there was nothing to answer to that either. Except the memory of the little painful smile on Jeb's face, as if he could not believe God would be so generous.

Away in the distance a bell began to toll, an odd hour for it but it made me conscious of time. I had to return to Lily. And Jeb. And Jeb would be wondering, they all would be wondering where I was. I found I was surprised, in a vague sort of way, that Jeb hadn't come looking for me already, and I was beginning to describe him to Julian, wanting to unwind some of the complications of my life, when a sudden violent noise startled us, and explained why we had been left undisturbed.

It was a cannon shot. The gun was old, had been kept on the slipway for children to play with, left over they said from some war a hundred years earlier. We could see a white puff of spray out to sea where the cannonball had dropped, and the sound was so loud that even Julian was startled as if he thought war had been newly declared. In the upper field his horse whinnied and reared, jerking at the tethering rope as once the grey horse had done.

'What's that?' he asked me, narrowing his eyes against the sun. 'It sounds like a search party . . .'

I laughed but I'd no idea what it meant either until I heard the hubbub break out from the village below, a noise that could only mean one thing, the thing they'd all been waiting for.

'It's a pilchard shoal,' I cried, starting up, trying to rub the grass stains from my dress. 'That's the huer, listen, don't you hear him?'

Down to our right, on the eastern headland, there was another great burst of shouting, 'Hevva, hevva, hevva', just as my nephews had taught me, and the blowing of trumpets and then the noise of a second cannon boom.

'Never thought to hear it again.' Julian was still frowning. 'God, that's a welcome sound; no wonder the village is going wild, good luck to them. But where does it leave us, Guinevere Ellis? You're the mother of my child, the light of my existence, my reason for being. Can't lose all that to a fishing phenomenon. Or a fisherman.'

He was exaggerating to make me laugh, or to hide anxiety. When I tried again to explain reasons, tell him I must be going, he caught me to him one last time. 'My leg won't get better, you know,' he said in that same conversational way that didn't really hide the fears underneath. 'I'm damaged goods. But I repeat I won't change. I want you, and her, the three of us. That's what I've come back for, that's the only thing that makes sense. For all that he's a fisherman and probably twice my size, I need you more than he does. Besides,' and his dark eyes held mine and wouldn't let go, 'besides, it's me you love, not him.'

And as before there was no reply to that.

He let me go reluctantly, with the promise of a meeting next day. 'Not like last time,' he said. 'Really meant, sworn to.'

The choice of that expression was intent, his oath to me, mine to him, the anxiety back full force. It was easy, that promise, eagerly given on both sides, heart meant, yet underneath surely there were doubts, old fears that lingered. I watched him mount and ride away on horseback, not so very different after all from the Julian of those months before, the laughing boy whom fate had caught and tried to tame. I thought, both he and Jeb have needs, they both love, who am I to choose which one has more right? But I had chosen, long ago, there was no turning back on that.

My feet scarcely touching ground, I ran down the streets. They were empty, as were the houses, doors and windows swinging wide, a child's toy left where it had fallen as if some unexpected catastrophe had swept everyone away. A great crowd of people was gathered above the beach, pointing out to sea, the more energetic villagers were clambering up to the headland, straini.g to look westwards. The horizon was already obscured in mist, but the heat if anything seemed more concentrated as if drawn down into the one place, accentuated by the mass of bodies.

I found my landlady at the edge of the crush, Lily still in her arms. 'Where did you get to then?' she asked. 'Warmth overcomed 'ee, I suppose. Not surprising tho', never remember it so hot.' And pushing back her hat she wiped away a trickle of sweat before handing the baby back. I stood with the other women and watched, listening with half my mind while the other half pondered the miracles of the world. They say that at the edge of the surf where the wave breaks, there is a special quality to the air as if it is charged with some ingredient, like wine. The immensity of what had happened left me equally lightheaded, as if I walked on clouds; joy overflowed in me so that I thought it must seep through my skin, and be obvious to everyone. Yet if Beth, perhaps, had been there and had asked, 'What is it?' I should have answered, 'Julian's come', as simply as if his journey had been short and he always expected back. And when the women standing near me said things like, 'A great girt shoal, three miles out, spotted off the Rumps, moving east,' and ''Tis Sunday, girl, they won't go,' and 'St Marvell fleet be waiting, have the jump on us if they can,' again I had the strangest sensation of already having heard these words in another time, and knew beforehand what the outcome was.

Over the heads of the women I could see the men. They came lumbering down the slipway for the tide was out. Some were still dressed in their suits although they had taken off their coats and rolled up their shirt sleeves. Others were more suitably clad in workmen's overalls and wading boots. All of them carried the yellow oilskins that they wore in rough weather along with their wide-brimmed fisherman's sou'westers, secured around the chin with an elastic strap. To make the women laugh a village wit leaned over the wall and shouted, 'Be 'ee set fer boiling then? Heat keep up, that shoal'll be proper cooked afore 'tis hauled.'

The fishermen didn't laugh back, conferred together in serious whispers, not joking as they usually did, arguing among themselves, gesticulating, pointing to their boats that lay on their sides like beached whales.

Gradually the jesting died away, the crowd's merrymaking spirit faltered, other rumours began to spread: 'Trawlers'll get there first; them St Marvell buggers already be setting sail'; followed by 'Feel how the heat's sucking in the wind, drawing of it like a magnet. I seen clouds like this afore.'

This last was spoken quietly by an old, old man, with withered brown face and sunken brown eyes. He had gone climbing halfway up the cliff before turning to inch back, was wheezing for breath but his voice still held traces of former authority. 'Saw a similar shoal afore too,' he said, pulling at his beard, one of the village 'ancients' like the man I'd met in St Marvell. 'Covered the water like scum. So many fish scales showered off you could see 'em floating down in sheets. Biggest damn shoal I ever seed and if we'd got 'un 'twould've been the catch of the century. But pilchards be a funny fish, one sound can startle 'em, a gun shot, a voice, a thunder roll.'

Now he had everybody's attention, even the fishermen turned to listen. 'Seed the worst gale of the century then,' he said, 'blew out of the west, in heat like this. Had to cut and run, no way to outride a wind like that 'un.' He cleared his throat and spat.

'Could be blowing up again,' he said. 'Us can do without that risk. Or do 'ee want a second St Marvell here. Then God have mercy on yer souls, say I, fer greed and cussedness.'

Without his saying so everyone knew he was speaking of the dreadful storm of many years before, the storm in which my father had drowned along with many other men from St Marvell and neighbouring ports.

There was a little silence then, as men, and women, contemplated that old disaster and the prospect of a new one. Finally one of the men on the beach who was readying his boat, running out the ropes to drag it down to the water line, shouted out what he really thought, desire to succeed heavy on him. 'Blamed if it's the truth,' he cried. 'So what? Us wasn't to blame that time. My father never cut nor runned afore any man nor storm. But if sails and spars be bad what chance then or now of holding on? I say go out while the weather lasts. With luck we could get there first. And with luck, drawn to shore, why boy, 'twould take more than a hurricane to uncouple me from them there fish.'

A hubbub broke out when he had finished speaking, men trying to talk him down, women agreeing. The crowd swayed back and forth, wild with indecision, a mob out of

153

control. Some were for pulling the boats down and launching them forthwith, others for caution, while a third group led by the most religious claimed that any fishing on Sunday was a sacrilege, punishable by God as offence to Him. I looked for Jeb, expecting him to intervene. Usually his size made him stand out among the mass of men, but he wasn't there.

'He's in the "Mermaid" and already off,' a woman whispered, guessing who I was looking for. I knew her from the fishery, a heavy woman with arms like trunks, used to heaving baskets of fish. 'Bain't proper. But there, Jeb Martin 'ain't one fer letting chapel talk stand in his road.' She looked at me sideways. 'And I hear you bain't that particular,' she went on, 'fer by my book bain't proper neither to offer to wed one man and then go courting of another all on the same day.'

She sidled away out of the press. Once more I felt my blood run cold. Foolishly I had assumed that no one had followed Julian and me, that no one had seen us. But in a village this size nothing escaped detection long. It was the speed, not the fact, that chilled; suppose Jeb had heard. Suppose he had already heard and sick with hurt was trying to escape; it wasn't like him to take risks and normally the other men would have waited for him to decide, turned to him for advice.

Wrapping Lily in my shawl as if it were already growing cold I pushed my way up the cliff, where boys were in danger of falling over the edge, leaping up and down in their eagerness. The huer was standing on the highest point. In his hands he held two paddles wrapped in white cloth which he waved about as if practising. I remembered what my nephews had said, and the gestures they had made, using the gorse twigs as a kind of semaphore: both arms crossed in front and waved on high meaning set sail, arms stretched in front and twirled about, meaning drop anchor, and various more complicated signs indicating direction and speed and such. Beneath the huer and further out to

154

sea, a number of boats bobbed up and down, waiting for the real signal to show them the *stem*, or area of sea where the shoal could best be handled.

Although the water looked millpond still there must have been a current running. You could see the swell and there was a line of white foam fretting at the edge of the rocks. The third time that day a wave of cold shivered down my spine. And I thought, there's no hurry, let them wait. But I knew they wouldn't.

CHAPTER 10

hen I went back towards the village, the men on the slipway were bustling into activity. Rollers to drag the boats over the wet sand were put in place, and the regular cry of 'All hands' went up. Usually I liked to watch how six men or so to a boat, with the younger boys of my nephews' age tagged at the end, heaved together to a regular rhythm. To the sound of their chant, 'Hoh, launch 'un, boy, bear up, bear up', the boat lurched forward in a series of jerks until it came down to the sea's edge. Little waves slapped against its prow with surprising regularity, and the boys held it steady like a restive horse. Meanwhile the men trudged resolutely to and fro up the causeway to collect their gear: sails, oars, anchors, tarpaulins and, most important of all, the neatly coiled nets used for the fish.

It was already growing dark, an early dark unlike a normal August evening, when the first boat rowed from shore to join those riding at anchor off the point. Determination in every move, the men bent to the oars with powerful strokes, the little sail at the stern loosely flapping. By then most of the women had gone home and were calling their children for their tea. The chapel-goers on their way to Evensong passed with averted eyes, the women triumphant, the men glum, their boats still firmly moored. I stood with Lily on the slipway, watching until all the boats had been launched, a little flotilla, a little Armada, off to win a victory from the sea. Silver flashes showed as here and there an oar dipped. Then all was still. Presently the twinkle of little riding lamps revealed where the fleet had hove to, the only lights in a night having neither moon nor stars, making the sky more dark and lowering by contrast.

Lily slept. Fed by Widow Pendar while I had been with Julian, she rested heavy in my arms. When I bent my head I could feel her cheek like satin and hear her breathing soft as a kitten's purr. All of her life lay before her, what she should have, what I had wished for, now justly hers. Part of me was overjoyed. But part was still apprehensive. I had Jeb to worry about, Julian had his father. My being a 'fishwife' had horrified Sir Robert before, he'd balk double now. He'd come between us if he could, he and his daughter both, for all that Julian dismissed their efforts so lightly. As for Jeb, who'd always known he was second best, who had patiently agreed to it, for whom my consent, however reluctantly given, must have seemed miraculous, this real miracle of Julian's return would destroy his hopes, would turn expectation to despair, perhaps destroy him himself . . . I couldn't bear the misery my new happiness would cause.

When I returned, the Corset was a-hum, like a bee hive. Whispers went tickling at earlobes as families sat round their tables. Each little house with its whitewashed walls and blue stone floors sprinkled with sand was as familiar as the one I lived in. As I pushed open our door my landlady jumped guiltily up from the settle where she had been resting. 'Fancy that,' she said in the artificial voice she used for strangers, "ee've come back. I thought 'ee were off again with someone else.'

I knew at once what the whispers said, what she had heard while I had been on the cliff. She didn't offer to hold Lily as she usually did. Nor did she invite me to sit down and join her at her Sunday tea although it was already laid, her grandma's teapot and blue clome cups, the lace-fringed cloth over the scoured table, the preserved apples in her best glass bowl – all prominently set out as signs of elegance. Nor did she cut me a piece of her fruit cake which summer and winter she usually baked, a little luxury that set her apart from the other Port Zenack housewives. More significantly she didn't cut a slice for herself but sat bolt upright, hands hugged across her breast as if protecting her integrity. Her brown eyes, usually gentle and mild, had grown shrewd, her bland face sharpened. Just by looking at her I could hear her thoughts. 'I took you in on trust. Oh, sure enough, I heard things about 'ee, but I didn't pay them no mind. The other women took to 'ee as well, and they'm no fools.' Like Julian's mother she might have added, ''Tweren't my business to judge. When Beth and Jeb Martin vouched fer 'ee, 'twas all I needed.'

What she did say gave her away by following that line of reasoning. ''Twere bad enough when that Sir Robert Polleven were nosing round, but they do say his son's comed back.'

She turned that unnaturally suspicious look at me again. The logical sequence, 'They say it were he you were took up with afore. And him you've just been seen with', trembled on her lips but she didn't say it. Not to spare my feelings, but her own. As a war widow I had been acceptable, someone she could identify with. That illusion gone, she was as morally lost as if set adrift in her dead husband's boat. And as vulnerable as I to gossips' barbs.

I didn't blame her for suspicion. Whatever scandal, this time I had only myself to blame. So I didn't try to explain, but went about my chores silently while the baby slept. I wanted to say to her, 'Suppose now, this moment, the door of your cottage opened and in stepped the husband you thought dead. Suppose you were my age again and he the father of a child he'd never seen. Try to imagine what you'd feel. Being married or not wouldn't matter, not if you loved like I did. Marriage'd be the last thing you'd think of.' But I knew she'd not see things like that. The only one capable of understanding would be Beth. But Beth was miles away in her home near Truro. And in this case even

158

she'd be prejudiced since she must take her brother's side. Once more a wave of sadness overcame me that in losing him I lost her too, but that also must be borne.

Perhaps something of my dilemma came through at last, for presently Widow Pendar sighed one final time, unlocked her arms resignedly and addressed me in a more normal voice. 'I bain't one to speak,' she repeated, once more her likeness to Lady Polleven clearly pronounced although it was one that never would have occurred to her. 'Never had no chilrun of me own. Come to that, never had no kin at all being an orphan reared. Lily be that dear to me, dear as any grandchile. There, I've admitted it. So do 'ee let me rock her in me arms, even if 'tis fer the last time.'

She took the baby and settled down with a sigh of pleasure. 'Then 'ee can pack yer things more easy like,' she added ingeniously, 'fer certain sure village life'll not keep 'ee now, not with better things waiting.'

In this gentle way she showed what her experience of life expected, that, given the circumstances, Julian would win. And even if he didn't, she had no place for me. But the future didn't happen simply like that. I didn't leave, not with Julian that is, nor pack, although what Lily and I owned wouldn't have filled one suitcase. I tried, but I couldn't get far forward, could only grasp the start of that future, could get no further than stepping from the chapel door and seeing Julian's upturned face. What lay ahead was too precious to be framed in thoughts, or too danger-fraught, overcast like the sky outside.

It was very hot tucked in under the roof and no air stirred through the narrow passageways. As night came on the heaviness increased as if a weight were settling on the houses, as if the village were groaning under it. Outside there was a strange calm, everyone deliberately quiet, on watch for morning. I suspected few of our neighbours slept and in the adjoining room I heard the widow shift on her straw-filled pallet, groaning slightly at each move. Even before first light, as the remainder of the fishing crews put

159

out to sea, they seemed unusually subdued, no muttered greetings, no clumping boots, walking quietly on tiptoe, barefoot. When day finally dawned, a close, heavy day, inert and still, one felt that nature was holding back, and the silence seemed overwhelming.

Close to the sea like this, one grew used to the sound of gulls. Their raucous cries dominated the village; they swooped in great squawking clusters when the fleet came in, screaming over titbits, fighting for space. The pre-dawn scratching of their feet on the roofs where they perched was as familiar as an alarm clock. Today they were silent too, all those herring gulls, those vicious black-backed gulls, those screeching black-headed gulls, gone from chimneys and causeway and cliffs.

'They'm gone inland,' Widow Pendar said as she emptied the teapot out the door, 'know where they'm better off. Dirty thieving things.' She tapped the glass of the little round barometer which hung on the wall. 'And when my poor dear husband's boat went down they did the like. We'm in fer a blow, make no mistake.'

By then everyone in the village was convinced of the same thing. And any other thought, any other gossip was submerged in this growing anxiety. Almost momentarily the barometer seemed to drop, and the air felt stagnant. The little shops closest to the water's edge prudently had already brought in their outdoor stalls where they normally kept their vegetables and fruit, had battened down the doors, as in winter months. Houseowners, following their example, now shuttered up their windows and brought their summer plants inside. The few boats still left afloat were drawn up on shore and firmly tied, staked out under the shelter of the causeway wall, while lobster pots and other gear were either stacked in great piles well out of the sea's reach, or rapidly carried away and put under cover. The nets which, when not in use, draped the edge of the walls for their owners to bark and mend were rolled up and bundled in the under-crofts; everything was arranged as if a siege were pending.

The fisheries however remained open and women in their working clothes stood chatting or knitting at the doors, prepared to rush into action when the shoal was netted and dragged inshore.

The majority of the fleet was out to sea, rocking uneasily round the western point where they had been joined by boats from St Marvell. Although the sea was still smooth its colour had changed, dulled into pewter under a wrack of dull grey clouds. There were no waves, at least none to speak of, but the edges of the cliffs continued fretted white as if a heavy swell were sucking underneath, and whereas normally the boats would have been surrounded by a mass of gulls now nothing flew. I had the feeling that I was watching the stirring of some mighty beast, some dreadful sleeping creature just about to surge awake.

Many of the villagers had trudged out beyond the nearest point round the headland where from higher ground they could look far along the western coast. The path was one I knew by heart, having walked it so often with Beth, and I was tempted to go on towards the cabin where I had once lived and where, a few days ago, I had thought to make my permanent home with Jeb. And for a moment, just a moment, the temptation was strong, to go there where I felt I belonged, set myself down among those well-known homely things in the place where Lily had been born. Instead I stayed where I was for as long as I could, straining to see the boats, straining to spot the shoal which it seemed had submerged once more, adding to the tension. So what with storms, disappearing fish, hostility against rivals (St Marvell persisting in its claims), the village remained in sober mood, although many of the confident, convinced the oily calm would lure back the fish, swore that all was not lost, as long as the weather didn't worsen.

With the turning tide the boats came in, all those that had been out since the previous morning, their crews bearded and stiff with salt, muscles strained with effort. Agog with curiosity the villagers crowded round, treating them like

161

heroes, hanging on to their every word. Hearsay passed for gospel truth, the assessment of the shoal's size consoling. 'Big enough fer all of us,' was the final verdict. 'They say 'twill be a record. Some record, boys, if it come up again. And we catch un.'

They bit into enormous 'meat and taty' pasties, gulped down their tea while they debated the numbers of the pilchards, their size and weight and the probable place of their reappearance. They might have been discussing football scores. Even older hands, who should have been more cautious, were convinced they could track the shoal, could feel its enormous mass stirring in the depths, could sense its presence.

They spoke of a catch big enough to divide with St Marvell, but, despite their generosity, they really didn't want to share it. The competition between the two villages, always fierce, now flared anew over who was to get the lion's portion. And as I listened gradually I began to understand how Port Zenack men meant to adapt age-old tactics to defeat their rivals in a situation made ever more complex by the actual presence of that 'enemy' and the threat of bad weather.

It seemed that in olden days, when seining for pilchards was common, there was always one main boat which was in charge. Known as the 'seiner' it was supposed to oversee all subsequent operations, staying on watch until the shoal was sighted and remaining at sea until the task was finished. Now since both villages by choice had reverted to this traditional method, both had selected a 'seine boat' which, like a jockey manœuvring for position, would try to outflank the other.

The seine boat's main task was to drop the huge 'seine', or net, used to encircle the shoal without frightening the fish away, after which they would draw it close. At the same time, like an admiral of a naval battle, they would direct the other boats under its command and tell them what to do. The seine itself consisted of a vast length of netting, small-meshed, attached at the upper edge to corks so it could float, the whole anchored to the bottom by massive ropes which were later used to pull the loaded net back to shore.

Meanwhile some of these other boats, called 'volyers' or 'followers', were used for subsidiary tasks, such as closing the gap when the ends of the great net were drawn together, thus preventing fish escaping. Others, known as 'tuckers,' were called upon to work inside the main seine with smaller nets which hauled up segments of the catch so that the rest of the fleet remaining outside could scoop up the fish in basketfuls.

Clearly these manœuvres required patience and dedication and great attention to detail, and since it had been years since they had last been carried out, naturally argument waxed loud and long about the best methods and correct procedures, depending to a large extent upon the state of tide and weather. Most important of all was the choice of the seine boat. For even if all agreed that the two villages would mutually share the shoal and fish it together, the actual *trapping* of it, or 'shooting the seine' as it was called, was an honour both villages desperately coveted. Both wanted to be sure the best 'skipper' in their fleet had the best chance to get it.

This was partly a practical matter, to substantiate a claim if at a later date there should be any dispute over ownership. But it was also a matter of principle. The Port Zenack fishermen had no wish to play second fiddle to St Marvell; they wanted their seine boat to have the privilege of capture. A third reason, strangely enough having nothing to do with fishing, seemed equally important. It dealt with historic record. 'May be the last time,' the village sages said, nodding their heads. ''Twould never do to let St Marvell get their fingers on it first; we'd not hear the last of it. They'd be in all the newspapers, crowing their heads off like cocks on dung hills.' Not unexpectedly, Port Zenack had entrusted Jeb with being seiner, and as skipper he and the crew of the 'Mermaid' remained at sea on duty, taking turns to sleep,

163

and having food and drink brought out to them by their comrades. St Marvell's choice had fallen on my brother.

The decision had not been so obvious there; it seemed it had been hotly contested. To everyone's surprise Ben had insisted on being nominated, for once stepping out of character and overwhelming the opposition. I myself had not heard of him for several months, not since coming to Port Zenack, had of course not seen him for over a year. I listened to the Port Zenack men discuss the weaknesses and strengths of his selection with special interest. As they spoke, I could imagine him sitting in the local pub, sticking out his jaw truculently.

'Me father were the chosen leader t'other time,' he'd say. 'First to come and last to leave. 'Tis my place by right.' He'd thump his tankard down hard on the bench and glare round challengingly. Not in drunkenness, not in maudlin self-pity this time, but in defiance. And although there were those who might have questioned his ability, none did the fitness of his claim.

They said he had stationed the 'Dolphin' close inshore in the lee of Varley Head, sat crouched over the tiller, wrapped in an old blanket, eyes bloodshot with watching, for he refused to sleep even though his crew took turns to spell him. He didn't say anything, scarcely ate or drank, just sat there, taut like bow string. 'Like he'm possessed,' the Port Zenack men reported, 'like he'm sold his soul to the devil, he'm that determined like.'

By contrast Jeb and the crew of the 'Mermaid' seemed almost relaxed, seemed light-hearted, although they too kept as careful a watch and were as ready to move into action. And if he had heard anything to my detriment, or feared for his marriage, Jeb did not let his own troubles distract him from his duty.

All morning we waited. I had remained on watch myself while Lily stayed safe indoors, although for my part I was also waiting for another reason, expecting, hoping to see Julian again, dreading a confrontation with Jeb if he should

164

return to shore. By now news of the pending catch had spread inland and many of the farming community, townspeople from as far away as Bodmin, some of the local gentry who had fishing interests, had begun to make their appearance, either on horseback across the fields or on foot from the village. It was said that a special bus had come out to bring sightseers and the great personage, reached in his London palace, had sent best wishes, hoping his earlier visit had brought 'good luck'. These new onlookers kept to themselves, ragtag stragglers having nothing to do with us, and as if in protest the fishing folk closed ranks, contemptuous of the 'landsfolk' whom they saw as intruders. Only the agents for the various ship owners bustled importantly to and fro, exhorting the ship crews to greater efforts and then presumably reporting back to the owners themselves. Again the Pollevens were noticeable by their absence.

Many of the St Marvell villagers had come to join our own, among them my niece and older nephews, although as far as I could tell their mother preferred to remain at home. The boys were over-excited, proud and apprehensive. 'Our Dad's the leader,' one boasted, while the other, too restless to stay in one place, tried to clamber down the cliffs to be nearer to the boats, and had to be hauled back by older men who smiled as they cuffed him. Only Emma looked pale and listless as if she hadn't slept and on seeing me ran into my arms and hid her head while her shoulders trembled. When I tried to comfort her, 'They'm saying my Dad'll drown,' she sobbed, 'just like my Grandpa; they'm saying that's what he really wants, not the fish. Say it ain't so, Aunt Jenny, say he'll come back.'

Before I could answer a hubbub broke out, everyone shouting and gesticulating at once, the 'huer' jumping up and down, arms going like windmills. We craned forward to the edge of the cliffs, peered down. Just visible under the grey surface was a reddish gleam, a dull copper stain that broadened and deepened as we watched, broken in places by splashes of white as if a solitary fish had leapt upwards

165

and fallen back. The two rival seine boats shot forward followed by their respective 'fleets', the rowers' backs bent with effort as each side strove to outdo the other. And as they closed upon that muddy streak the first squall of the day came upon them.

It blew out of the north like a gush from a furnace, a rush of hot air that seemed to singe before turning ice cold, a violent gust of wind as fierce as it was unexpected. There was no protection on the headland, no trees or bushes, and the force sent women's skirts flying, blew off hats, bowled small children over so that their mothers screamed in fright. The rain it brought with it slashed like silver darts. To the men in the boats below us the effect was catastrophic.

The sea, which a moment before had been quiescent, suddenly erupted into ferment, the water folding up as if pleated, the wave crests boiling white as if a million, billion fish had all surfaced at once. Two boats, caught midships by a gigantic backsurge from the rocks, were swept sideways and almost capsized as the oarsmen fought to keep balance, then the rain came down like a curtain and hid the rest.

Over the howl of the wind I tried to shout to my nephews, all the while clinging to Emma to keep her safe. Everyone had scattered, scuttling for shelter with strange crab-like movements, all protocol forgotten as gentlemen and fisherfolk fought each other for precedence and struggled together along the narrow path. We followed them, most of the St Marvell folk preferring to come back with us than risk the open cliff. When we reached Port Zenack the children were red-cheeked and breathless, drenched and thick with mud for the rain that stung their face and eyes had washed the summer dust along in a torrent. We found a village already under attack as the wind drove now full force straight in, funnelling through the cove and up the causeway as through a tunnel.

The streets were washed black, slick like ice; the gutters

full to overflowing. Windows rattled, sheeting flapped, the noise of falling tiles was like gun shots. The sea which when we left had been at low tide was already racing towards shore, not huge waves yet, they would build, but a froth of foam like a cauldron simmering. Clearly now you could see the race where the currents swept, a line of ominous bubbles circling round the bay then driving outwards. Everything was coated with mist so thick that if you licked your lips you tasted salt from the spray and salt coated doors and glass.

The two disabled boats, listing badly, had been sighted, straining round the nearest point, some of their oars smashed. We waited until they came within the reach of shore and the men had jumped out and begun to tug them up the beach towards the slip. The waves came surging after them, licking hungrily, curling round men to knee, waist, shoulder depth although the sandy bottom was flat. You could hear the beginnings of thunder as breakers hit the outer reefs and came screaming in across the sand in line after line of tumbling water.

The men were grey with fatigue. 'Big.' They were too exhausted to answer questions clearly. 'Big, sure enough, but we'll be some lucky to hold it.' They pushed help aside and stumbled wearily up the causeway towards their waiting families. But even they didn't know which of the seine boats had made first cast nor what had happened to the rest of their comrades.

The children and I crowded into Widow Pendar's cottage. Although it was sheltered it was already filled with smoke as the wind came whistling down the chimney. The children shook themselves dry like puppies and settled down with the baby, playing with her happily between drinking mugs of tea. The widow and I exchanged nervous glances as the roof creaked and beads of rain slashed across the leaded window panes.

For the rest of the day the wind gusted, but there were still moments when it died away and the sun glinted briefly

167

beneath the scudding clouds, although it more resembled a winter sun, pale and weak, than a late summer one. In these clear intervals everyone came outside, like prisoners deprived of air and exercise. It was during these intervals that we heard the news. The shoal held, and both Ben and Jeb had cast their nets side by side enclosing a large area. So far, so good. We also heard that the wind had veered and was settling out of the north west, the worst possible direction, forcing some boats to break away and head for shore while they could, making it so difficult for St Marvell boats to turn back that their crews, unable to make headway, would be obliged to run before it into Port Zenack. But the main part of the fleet still remained in place, fighting valiantly to round the point to clearer water where the loaded nets could be made fast, either to be hauled out right away, or if that proved impossible, to be contained until the storm had passed.

During the course of this uneven day when on shore everything was at sixes and sevens, the streets crowded with sightseers and fishermen from both villages, striding wearily to and fro; with the Village Institute set up as relief headquarters (where women ran with flasks of tea and cut mountains of sandwiches, emptying the village bakery), I had two visitors of my own, one longed for, one the opposite. The first was Julian. He came in the early afternoon, drenched from walking, his too tall frame stooping under the door lintel, where he paused to survey the little group inside.

Emma was lying on the hearth rug, back to the settle, the baby caught between her outspread skirts, the boys kneeling on either side trying to make Lily laugh. I knelt beside them to control their exuberance while Widow Pendar sat crocheting on the other side of the fire, a simple scene suiting a cottage setting. As the door opened to let in a rush of cold air, we all looked up at him as if, for a moment, he seemed an intruder. I thought, 'This is how we are, nothing grand or proud about us; take us as we are.'

Julian didn't say anything at first, but I am sure he felt what I was thinking. He just leaned on the doorframe letting the wet splatter, as if contemplating what he saw. Or as if bemused by it. Or as if afraid to look away in case it should disappear. As I jumped up, 'Don't move,' he said, 'don't ever move.' And as all the children stared openly at him, 'Dear God, you can't know what a sight that is.'

The moment passed. Emma smiled and cried, 'Aunt Jenny, 'tis the man on the grey horse, the one I told 'ee of.' Flustered at his arrival, her previous hostility forgotten, Widow Pendar came bustling forward, overwhelmed by his actual presence. While she tried to take his hat and coat, tried to offer hospitality, he knelt down beside his daughter and lifted her in his arms. She came willingly, as light as thistledown. As in the past I let him take the lead, remained with the other children while he sat in one corner of the settle. His gaze never moved from the baby on his lap except from time to time one quick glance around as if to reassure himself he wasn't dreaming. He never spoke, never mentioned family, father, mother, sister, except once. 'Here's all a man needs,' he said. And in one way his just being there, in quiet content, peaceful, seemed to make a charmed circle of that humble room, a safe haven, although outside the wind mounted and the sea roughened. And men battled on.

It was during the worst blow so far that my sister-in-law burst in, the door swinging open as if the wind had caught it. She must have come by the road for the coastal path was deemed impassable, and her ragged shawl and tattered dress were blown to disorder. She also paused as if to take in the peaceful scene and for a moment her expression softened as if she were thankful her children were safe. Then she scowled. 'Whatever made 'ee come here, then?' she scolded, swooping forward to drag Emma up and shaking her fist at the boys. 'Danged nuisances. I've been looking fer 'ee all day. Took me best part of two hours to walk and fetch

169

'ee. And yer father stubborn as a mule still out in the storm.'

She rounded on me. 'Suppose you're too high and mighty to bring them home, or think of bringing them,' she snapped. 'Name in the paper and such, suppose after that don't matter that yer brother be at risk out there, drowning fer all you cares.'

She spotted Julian, started when she recognized who he was, then drew back as if afraid. Or curious. It was not until the children were fitted out in my landlady's collection of old coats and boots to keep them dry that she recovered. She didn't address Julian directly, nor even look at him, but the way her gaze slid round him showed where her interest was focused. And in a curious, indirect way, although she spoke to me her conversation was aimed at him as if he were the real centre of importance. It wasn't until later that I remembered her jealousy, as if even at this moment she couldn't bear to acknowledge that I could be preferred to her, that I was the one to be loved and wanted.

'All right fer you, girl,' Charity now cried, bridling with an attempt at dignity, 'bain't we all snug like! How am I to keep even a roof over my head if my man perishes? His foolishness's yer fault too tho' I doubt if 'ee'll ever admit it. He's never got over what 'ee did to him. I told 'ee yer shame would be the death of un. As fer you.' She turned as fiercely on my landlady, who during this exchange had tried to make herself as small as possible. 'You ought to be ashamed as well, aiding and abetting as ever was. Thought better of you than that, I did, a pillar of the church, party to such goings-on.'

Julian had struggled to his feet during this speech, limped forward now, perhaps with some idea of protecting me, and perhaps with some thought of soothing Emma who had again begun to cry, and was still clinging to me while her mother tried to pry her loose. She looked past him. 'Well, there 'tis,' she pronounced, 'flaunting sin. It's killed yer brother. And 'twill kill lots more if them Polleven boats stay out like they was made do afore, with no real reason save pride to make 'em.'

Julian said evenly, 'There're no orders on my family boats, not this time. They've had no instructions from us except a general one to defer to the discretion of their skippers and the safety of the crews. So you're wrong about that, Mrs Trevarisk, isn't it? And you're wrong about me and Jenny.'

Charity gaped at him. He spoke in such an honest way, in such measured tones with such degree of sincerity it would have been impossible to doubt him. She probably had never heard a man talk like that before. Again it crossed my mind, just in this alone, how fortunate I was in comparison.

Perhaps she thought so too. Once more she bridled. Then she smiled, a curious smile and for a moment I thought of my mother. 'Well,' she said, 'if you'm a Polleven, you'm the one to come to, right, if some'at goes wrong. If yer boats go down, you'd pay up handsome-like to them that were left behind. You don't have the look of a man who'd want innocent chilrun to starve a'cause of their father's drowning. And if a woman asked you right, I bet 'ee could be generous.'

She smiled again, just as my mother had at Farmer Penwith, while Emma wept the louder and even the boys set up a howl. Julian put his arm about them. 'There's no danger,' he said, and in a louder voice to their mother, 'For God's sake be quiet.'

He might have been referring to her talk of drowning, or to her pitiful attempt at cajolery. She couldn't support either rebuff. With one last jerk she wrenched Emma free and cuffed her. 'God damn the pair of you then,' she cried, spite turning her face bitter, taking all the prettiness away and replacing it with venom. 'You done alright fer yerselves, I suppose, and the devil take the rest.' And to the boys who were trying to argue, 'Oh, stop yer sniffling and come on home. And thank yer Aunt Jenny and her lover fer making all of you orphans.'

171

The door banged shut, the children's crying was shut off, we three were left behind. And so we remained for several moments as if recovering from some intrusion into our quiet happiness.

CHAPTER 11

ulian regained his composure first. 'I'd better see what's happening,' he said, 'make sure all's accounted for, neat and tidy. No Polleven boat'll be kept out if the storm worsens, I've already had my father's word on that for what it's worth. And whatever happened before, if it happened as she said, well, that was years ago when we were children. But I'll double check.' And as Widow Pendar discreetly disappeared into the scullery with the dirty dishes, 'Don't fret, my love. The past can't harm us. There's no fault. Or if there is let me take the blame.'

He held us in his arms, me and Lily, and whispered, 'You're my family, nothing can come between us.' And clasped in his warmth I almost believed him.

By now it was growing dark, again an early winter dark not right for August. If there were boats out they must be hard pressed to last through the night. The streets were still crowded, unnaturally so, mainly with fishermen who debated with each other in low tones, discussing their chances. Many of them came from St Marvell and just as their boats now jostled ours, moored side by side as high up the causeway as they could be dragged, so their crews intermingled. Neither side had time for petty rivalry, all were concerned for safety, safety of their catch, safety of their crews. Julian moved among them. Many of them recognized him, took a moment from their own troubles to welcome him back, listened to him intently. It was hard to tell from their expression if they were relieved or disappointed, but their wives must have been pleased. I heard a few murmurs and 'God bless 'ees' from the direction of the fisheries. But Julian's assurances didn't solve their worst problems.

Most of the 'volyer' boats had returned, it being deemed too chancy to have them risk sitting out the storm. As each one struggled round the point now, greeted by cheers and sighs of thanksgiving, the sea seemed to cover them as the wind caught and hurled them forward. They came towards the causeway in bursts of foam, and even so close to shore they might have been in danger of sinking had not their companions on land plunged into the surf to help. Like marker buoys they were hauled in, the sea boiling round them as they tried to hold the boat steady, preparatory to being pulled up along the jetty wall where there would be some shelter. The returning crews were full of praise for their captains and the way they had netted the shoal, but in private, both Port Zenack men and St Marvell's made it clear whom they trusted.

'Jeb Martin's got us anchored between Varley Head and Lobber Point out of the worst of it; Jeb Martin says we'm better off where we be 'til dawn.' *Jeb Martin says, Jeb Martin does*, his name was on everyone's lips. It pained me just to hear it although I also felt proud. I noticed at once that no one looked at me deliberately when he was mentioned, out of tact I suppose, although in the normal way of things someone would have said something or made a joke to show they appreciated our relationship. I didn't dare look at Julian, although he didn't show any signs of the perturbation that I felt. But it stopped me from noticing right away what they said about my brother. It only dawned gradually that they were critical of him. 'Ben's all for lying closer in,' they said. 'Ben's that stubborn, nothing will change his mind, even tho' the rest of us argue until we'm hoarse. But if the wind shifts 'twill trap him, net and all, and all will be lost.'

All depended now on the wind. It had already reached gale force and throughout the night it mounted steadily. Inland damage to trees and flooded roads made travel dangerous. There was no possibility of leaving Port Zenack at this stage and Julian wouldn't hear of it. 'Wait until it's over,' was his advice, 'can't have Lily out in this. Nor you.' He put his arm around my shoulder. 'There's time a-plenty, sweetheart, a whole lifetime before us.'

He didn't go home either, remained all night, what was left of it, on the waterfront with many of the other men, their concern only apparent when dawn came.

It was a watery dawn, overcast and dreary. For a moment the wind seemed to drop and a glimmer of grey light showed a massive sea curdled white and running. ''Tis the eye of the storm.' The word went round as wearily the villagers struggled up, few of them having slept at all this night. Once more the Institute opened its doors and dealt out tea and biscuits. Just after seven the last of the Port Zenack boats rounded the headland, followed by others from St Marvell. They came ashore with similar difficulty, leaving only a couple of the fleet to accompany the two seine boats. But Jeb had chosen wisely. The nets had held; some of the shoal had already been hauled in, the remainder, the great thrashing mass, still netted, was still afloat.

The storm was in abeyance, but by ten all respite was over. Once more the wind changed course, gusting now from the north in great sweeps, blowing straight into the bay, swirling foam in clouds. Not long after those watchers strong enough to withstand its blast on the cliffs reported the anchored nets were dragging. 'Hev to scat 'em abroad, yeu, cut loose fer sure,' their cry went up and echoed mournfully through the village.

We waited. With the out-going tide the size of the waves neither increased nor diminished but as each wave crest broke against the headland, the force sent plumes of spray like smoke, making the safety of the remaining boats of prime importance. And as these in turn made the treacherous run back before the wind a cheer went up as if another potential victim had been snatched from a common enemy.

The last to come in was Jeb. We saw the boat's sides with its black lettering only once before a giant wave caught it and sent it reeling. It rode low in the water since it must have been full of fish and although the wind drove it headlong, the currents off the cliffs spun it in circles, the wind forcing it in one direction, the waves the other. 'There's a seaman who knows his business,' Julian said approvingly. He had been watching through his binoculars, admiring how the oarsmen managed with their oars, first on one side then the other to keep the boat steady. He stole a look at me, snapped the case shut. 'If that's your "friend", he's clever.'

With that cryptic remark he left me sheltering under the overhang where we had been standing, and throwing off his coat limped down to the causeway. Ropes had been already strung out and men were waiting to hang on to them while others, stripped to the waist, prepared to wade out into the surf to hurl the ends to the oncoming boat. I gathered up the wet folds of jacket and cradled it as he joined those on the slipway. Acting as human anchors, they tried to hold the boat against the weight of water. In the surf the lines of men slid up and down, sometimes overwhelmed by the waves, sometimes bobbing up like corks.

The beaching of the 'Mermaid' was a lengthy business. I couldn't believe that crew or helpers could withstand so much punishment. When they had finally achieved it all stood around the boat, leaning against it, straining for breath, grey with fatigue, the oarsmen almost too tired to ship their oars or clamber from their seats. In the bottom of the keel, aswirl with water and seaweed, the pilchards for which they had risked their reputations glistened round their knees, wet and shining, a fraction of that mighty catch now apparently lost for ever.

As he came up the causeway I scarcely recognized Jeb. Gaunt and drawn he seemed to have lost weight and his back was bowed. When he finally straightened he spoke through salt-cracked lips that bled even as he opened them. It seemed three giant breakers had snapped his net, no chance then of holding it. Almost snapped his boat in two as well, almost broke its back. But even half-submerged as they were, even half-sinking, he could have saved the other net and brought it in with him, except Ben Trevarisk wouldn't let him. Ben refused to budge. 'I'm well enough set where I'm at,' he was reported once more to have shouted, stubbornly ignoring his own companions' advice to heave to, ignoring his own crew's frantic warnings.

'And now I'm feared 'tis too late,' Jeb said. He shook his head, as if shaking the water from his back, as if shaking off trials and worries. He didn't look for me either, never turned his head in my direction and for that I was grateful. We needed calm to talk, he and I, peace and quiet to say what had to be said. But I knew that was an excuse on my part, cowardice that I would regret. For there was nothing I could say, nothing I could do. It was 'too late' for that as well.

It seemed Ben's stubbornness was now reaping its punishment. He was being swept too close to the reefs. 'There'll be no way of rounding 'em,' Jeb said, 'if he don't take the chance now while there's low water. Come high tide he'll be a goner.'

Above the hubbub I recognized Charity's scream. She was in the crowd then; she would have heard what Jeb said. As I tried to fight my way back to find her, Julian came struggling towards me. 'Bad news,' he said, looking grim. 'They've sent for the lifeboat out of Padstow but the telephone wires are down and there's not a chance of launching in time. And I doubt if it could help even then. We're off up to the headland. Keep indoors, my love, I'll soon be back.'

But I didn't stay indoors for long, just dragged on Widow Pendar's old oilskin coat that had been her husband's, and with her admonishments ringing in my ears set out after him.

The actual climb up to the point wasn't so bad as it had been on the climb down, the slope of the land in fact helping keep off the worst of the blow which hit full force when we got out on the headland. Some of the villagers stood in the dip with the onlookers, but most had braved the harder clamber out towards the eastern side where ropes already had been looped between the thorn bushes to serve for handholds. Clinging to them I inched along until I came to where I could look down over the edge, near to where my nephew earlier on had tried to go climbing. The 'Dolphin' was clearly visible almost under us although there was no sign of the net that had kept it there for so long. Close in, under the shadow of the cliffs, at first it seemed well positioned, out of the worst of the storm. Only gradually did I realize that it was listing and as the current now swept it, so was it being inexorably drawn towards the rocks where the waves sucked and broke with sickening regularity.

For a moment, the vastness of the scene, that great expanse of heaving water, the power of it, made one catch one's breath, made one feel one's own insignificance. Then a cry went up from the 'Dophin', repeated by those on the cliffs. Or rather, since it was difficult to hear any sound above those of wind and sea, the gestures of both seemed to reflect what everyone was saying. 'Sea anchor's broke, no way to hold her now.'

All the able-bodied men, Jeb among them, began to run, difficult in their heavy boots and clothes, their oilskins flapping as they shucked them off. Some disappeared over the edge of the cliff and began the treacherous slide down, slipping and groping along the rabbit tracks that threaded through the bracken. Their objective was a patch of beach, a thread of shingle and seaweed opening up between the rocks, a tidal patch which was only uncovered at low tide, difficult to reach in good weather, now almost impossibly wet and treacherous. Meanwhile the rest on the cliff above remained bent over a complicated apparatus attached with

178

ropes which they were trying to ready. I spotted Julian among them and gave a sigh of relief that at least he was still safe.

''Tis a breeches buoy,' one of the women explained. She hugged a shawl about her, shivering with cold. 'That's my man out there,' she added in an off-hand way as if hardly expecting anyone to listen. Compared with Charity she was calm, resigned, and Charity's continual screams upset her almost as much as her husband's precarious position. 'Proper carry on,' she said, 'no call fer it, they'm doing all they can.'

Charity herself was moaning non-stop, hand to mouth, rocking back and forth like a woman gone mad. I couldn't help remembering the off-hand way she'd reacted to Ben's distress when I'd first arrived, how she'd turned her back on him then. I pushed down the thought that her act was insincere, calculated to win pity. I wanted to go up to her myself and hold her fast and tell her to have courage, for the children's sake, and Ben's, not to give up. I didn't dare, I had no right to criticize grief. As for myself, when a second time I gathered strength to go close enough to look I could see how my brother was throwing all his weight against the oar, his broad shoulders bent with strain, as if willpower alone would fend the boat off the rocks and bring it round into the wind. I wanted to clap my hands at his courage. He never seemed to me so like his father as he did then. And like the first Ben Trevarisk, like Jeb Martin, in extremity the younger Ben showed all his inborn seamanship as he persuaded his crew into even greater efforts.

What Jeb had barely managed within the shelter of Port Zenack Bay Ben was trying in the open, and couldn't, not in the position he was in. It was only a matter of time before an oar snapped or a larger wave than the rest rolled the 'Dolphin' over as it now was forced ever closer to the rocks, almost at the sea's mercy. No one, not even Ben Trevarisk, could fight that storm, and he had left it too late as Jeb had warned. But the men had reached the beach, were stringing out the ropes and preparing themselves to pull the boat in if they could get hold of it. And on the headland, the breeches buoy was ready.

It went off with a surprising whoosh like a firework rocket and a thin line of cord snaked off through the air towards the foundering boat. The first attempt fell short, the rope caught by the wind. It was hauled back, the loading apparatus coiled for re-aiming. A giant wave, the sort they said was most dangerous, came upon the rocks, broke, surged back again and caught a second oncoming wave with a clap like thunder. Water spewed up like a fountain, trapped the 'Dolphin' at the point of collision and spun it round, sending oars flying. On their backs, the men were tossed this way and that, desperately scrabbling for balance. Before they could recover a third great wave washed over them, in that instant burying them from view under a wall of water.

Another cry went up. Women screamed, men cursed, the workers struggling with the breeches buoy worked feverishly to fire again. As the wave subsided we could see the boat drifting helplessly towards the rocks, the men still trying valiantly to stem it off until another wave hit them. But there were still six of them, two to the remaining oars, all pulling with superhuman strength. Their efforts brought little respite. Several more waves in rapid succession broke over the prow of the boat and filled it with water. The next series tossed the boat like a top against the reefs with a crack that was clearly audible, and there it lodged, half on, half off, while the waves broke over it with sickening regularity.

The breeches buoy was ready. Again it fired, again the line snaked out, this time straight to the target. A succession of other ropes and pulleys were secured, all with rapid precision yet it seemed to take hours before the first man was winched across the abyss, fitted into a pair of what looked like canvas trousers.

'That's my Jim,' the woman who had been standing next to me said. She gave a sigh, wound her shawl even closer over her head, stepped forward quietly. Only the puckering of her mouth and the restless plucking of her fingers on the edges of the shawl revealed the tension, deep and heartfelt. The man landed, was helped out, the buoy was re-wound for another firing. 'Well, Jim,' was all she said, and 'Well then, Grace,' his reply, as he struggled to his feet, while the neighbours around them said things like, 'Proper job, yeu', and 'Handsome', and 'Vitty'.

Not so Charity. While the buoy went out again and again, while the waves continued to break and the 'Dolphin' slowly settled, each pounding now causing it to shift with dreadful creaking, she herself went on moaning, covering her face and refusing to look as each man was winched to safety. Time dragged, every firing of the buoy seeming to take a century. The worst part was watching how the crew tried to fit themselves into the harness. As waves broke and receded people anxiously counted aloud, numbering heads, while the men inside the boat clung on with all their might.

'They'll leave Ben to last,' Charity cried. Accusingly, she rounded on her neighbours. 'No matter he'm a father several times over, with wife and chilrun to support, no matter that them that's with him be younger. There's no fairness in this world. They'd no call to give in to him and let him take charge in the first place.'

Her cry was universal, a cry from all womanhood, all those whose men leave them for danger and death. Yet she shouldn't have made it, not with some of her husband's crew lying there drenched, stretched out on that wet grass like drowned rats, not with her husband's friends working like madmen themselves to wind and send those whizzing ropes that tangled and snarled now at each attempt, causing more delay.

The boat was obviously breaking up. Each pounding jar caused it to settle further down over those jagged points, sending shudders stem to stern. Between waves that now swept right over it, the remaining men clinging to gunwales and thwarts gave feeble thumbs-up signs to show that they

181

were alright. There were only three left. But the tide was almost at the turn. With the incoming seas they would be submerged. We began to reckon hours. Time against tide, it would be close, minutes between life and death.

We all knew that, and so did the men in the 'Dolphin'. So did Charity. Once more she flailed out at those around her, calling those who had escaped cowards to have deserted her husband. They never replied, although they or their wives could have said with truth, "Twas his choice, we begged him not to.' Nor did they say with equal truth, 'Ben be skipper of that boat, he chose that too, he's just doing what any skipper ought.' Only one boy, the last saved, dark hair plastered to his skull, still heaving from the water he had swallowed, leaned on his elbow to look at her and muttered through bruised lips, 'He's a proper fellow.' While his two friends, who were scarcely in better shape, nevertheless insisted on taking their turn at the winch, the more anxious to help since they knew what it was like to be on board.

Only two more to go. And for the moment the wind had eased, although the seas ran as heavy. Those men on the little strip of beach were clustered near the edge where a spit of rocks separated them from the wreck on the other side. If they could get ropes somehow around that narrow point they would be within helping distance. 'They've got to swim that line round,' Julian said. Unbeknownst he had come up beside me. He didn't mention my being there, stared down thoughtfully. 'How many of them can swim?'

I could have told him. Fishermen work the sea, not play in it. Few fishermen have time to learn the art of swimming. Like many men who have dangerous jobs they seldom took precautions, were fatalistic about their chances. Although Julian never explained the reason for his question I knew what he was thinking and, like Charity, I felt my heart sicken. Yet I didn't try to stop him. God forgive me, but I couldn't make myself open my mouth and scream as Charity did although every nerve in my body wanted to.

The breeches buoy was jammed, spray almost hid the men in the boat, the wind was driving the tide in faster than usual. The end was inevitable. One final crash, the sides of the boat seemed to slide asunder. Like knife through butter a gap appeared, widened, disintegrated into froth and spray. Planking tore loose, was driven under, floated up. I saw the name plate 'Dolphin' borne away on an outgoing current. But the two men left had survived, were still clinging to the sides of the boat, fighting for purchase, until another wave smothered them. When it receded only one man was left bobbing about, his head small as an apple, a human reduced to the size of a black dot in a swirl of white.

It was Ben. He had anchored himself firmly about a piece of plank, was riding it clear of the rocks, trying even in that violence to head out into clearer water. He must know the cliffs well, would have remembered that little strip of shingle, would be making for it as the only possible refuge. Of his companion there was no trace, the sea had swallowed him as absolutely as it had swallowed that enormous shoal, never to be seen again.

A third shout went up. Even the men who had been operating the breeches buoy left their labours and made their way to the cliff's edge to look down. I turned aside. I didn't have to look to know what was happening. It didn't take cries and comments to tell me what I had already guessed. I closed my eyes. In my mind I watched Julian's painful progress down the cliff, his leg giving under him. But he could swim. And in the water a lame leg would not necessarily be a hindrance. 'Murderers, both of you.' I heard Charity's accusation. 'The past can't harm us.' I heard Julian's response but her charge would have stuck, would have meant something to him.

Nor did I need the woman who finally revealed the last piece of information I'd already guessed – how he and Jeb Martin were both stripping down, as if, even in this, neither would let the other out-match him. And so it was when Ben's wife and Julian's father finally bore down on me I already knew how the two men I had set against each other were united in their plan to rescue my brother and felt the blame of it before they heaped it on me.

I'll never know and have never asked what made both men risk their lives like that, what masculine sense of competition. Or was it more than that, simply their natural decency of nature, their desire to help a fellow being, that set them apart from other men? I don't even like to think that Ben's being my brother made any difference, although both Charity and Sir Robert seemed to take that for granted. And I didn't want to know, and would never ask what either said to the other as they plunged into that sea together. But knowing them I suspect they said nothing at all except what had to be said briefly and succinctly concerning their common venture. Not so their relatives safe on land.

It wasn't clear how long Sir Robert Polleven had been standing on the cliffs or if anyone else had noticed him. Certainly Julian hadn't. Or if he had he'd utterly ignored his father. Wrapped in a great cape, his head capped, leaning on a great hawthorn staff, in one sense Sir Robert might have been hard to miss, yet since all the onlookers were similarly clad, perhaps he was difficult to distinguish among those who still thronged the scene, many of them avid with curiosity. Certainly Charity had spotted him and was intent not to let him escape, turning all her spite on him, making him her scapegoat. I almost felt sorry for him – in Charity he'd met his match.

I suppose too it seems unbelievably narrow-minded, petty to the point of ridicule, that in the midst of all this danger, Charity should still be obsessed with her own wrongs, as my potential father-in-law was with pride. He came stalking me, seething with indignation. Hot on his heels, Charity pursued him, at her most vindictive.

'Ask her,' she shouted, pausing, hands on hips, her eyes sparkling with animosity. 'Ask anyone.' Her gesture took in the whole of the spectators on the cliff. 'They'll tell you her part in it. And tell you your fault too, if it be news to 'ee, how much in the past you owes me and my husband.'

Sir Robert ignored her outburst. 'They say my son's gone down there,' he cried, waving his stick. 'They say you sent him.' He ground the point into the turf as if grinding it into someone. 'I suppose you think it's worth his life, encouraging him to gamble it away for this, this creature.'

Charity screamed, 'I just explained, 'tis her brother.'

'For God's sake be quiet,' Sir Robert told her just as his son had done. And to me, in a voice that showed panic rising, 'Couldn't you have stopped him? Wasn't it enough to alienate him from his family, cut his mother to the quick, destroy my hopes? What can you expect to get out of it, you must be mad.'

'That's a truth,' Charity said. She stopped her screaming, speaking quietly so the words hissed like darts, but loud enough so that everyone should hear them. 'That's my sister-in-law all over, me lord, I saw it in an instant, playing one off against t'other, all fer fun. She's got them on a string, Ben, Jeb, yer son, why, yer son never stood a chance. And fer what?'

She stepped back. 'I'll tell 'ee fer what,' she said, even at that moment her jealousy rampant. 'All fer vanity. All to show the rest of us what she's got that we haven't. And now my husband's drowned dead because of her. So don't you complain. If yer son's drowned dead too 'tis only time you knew what suffering is.'

Once I would have argued with them, once I would have contradicted to take away the misery of their accusations. Now I didn't. Grief takes some people like that, turns them vicious. Let them wear out their anguish where they found it. Instead I shuffled off the oilskins, knotted up my skirts, crept over the edge of the cliff myself and began the long descent. One thought only was in my mind, that whatever happened I wanted to be close enough to bear my part. And so I in turn crawled along those narrow tracks that snaked back and forth across the cliff face, bracing myself against it when the wind blew, clutching at stalks of bracken and heather to inch forward, digging my nails into dirt that sprayed like mud, scrabbling for footholds with the heels of my boots. One prayer sounded in my head like an echo. God be merciful to all of us.

On the beach there was a pause, the men apparently still in two minds, some for trying again to scale the cliff face, others for swimming to take advantage of the lull. Julian had already tied a rope around his waist. Clad only in trousers and shirt he began to edge into the sea, diving headlong through the first breakers only to be swept back by the force of the water. Jeb had followed him. For a moment the two of them stood side by side in the surf, one tall but of slighter build, hampered perhaps by his war wound yet used to the water; the other older by a few years but still young, a giant of a man, powerful and determined. In that instant of time did Jeb glance at Julian and wonder what it was that I saw in him; did Julian do the same in reverse?

The second time they started out in unison, each harnessed with a rope which could be used to drag them back if they got into difficulties. Together they dived through the waves that crested high over their heads, making slow and painful progress. Despite all their strength, each time they had to dive deeper and stay under longer, were swept back further by the next wave's backwash. Yet they were making progress. They too attempted to stay well out into the centre to avoid being dragged upon the spit of rocks. Poised halfway down, blown by the wind against the cliff, clinging to it above that intervening spit of reef, I had a bird's eye view of both sides, my brother floundering still among the rocks yet between waves making valiant efforts to thrust himself clear into open water, the two swimmers sometimes lost to view completely, then reappearing side by side, Jeb's red hair clearly visible beside Julian's brown.

Afterwards they said it was the squall of wind, a sudden vicious squall that caught me unprotected on the cliff face, which had the momentary effect of flattening the tops of the worst of the waves. Or perhaps it was the burst of rain that accompanied it, stinging like hail so that I almost relinquished a handhold to protect my face. Whatever it was, for a few moments the waves' fury abated giving all three men the chance they needed. My brother, kicking strongly as only a man with prodigious strength and a prodigious will to live, broke free of the rocks on his side of the reef and emerged into the open, far enough to see where Julian and Jeb were edging towards him. He turned his plank towards them, they swam to meet him. Another burst of rain hid all three and another squall of wind threatened to tear me from my perch. Unable to go back, forced to go on, I again crept downward. Perhaps it was just as well that I couldn't see where I was going, for part of the time my feet seemed to be sliding over vacant space. Half-buried under roots and debris that went slithering from my grasp, I reached the end of the cliff in a slide of stone, floundering for footholds on the seaweed and algae that lined the underlayers.

No one paid any attention. All eyes were strained out to sea where a grey pall seemed to have covered the surface, a pall of mist and spray as the wind veered again. Out of it the three men appeared for a moment, all clinging now to the plank which they seemed to have fastened somehow with ropes for it was the planking that was being pulled in-shore. A final wave, topping them by twenty feet or more, rose out of the sea bed, smothering them, tearing the plank from their grasp and tossing it like matchwood. The wave hurtled towards the beach, a line of water, forcing the men there to give ground as it tossed them like ninepins, making them flail for footing. There was a rush of shingle, a mighty heave as if the whole of the beach was being lifted towards the base of the cliff where I was standing, then a swishing sound as it drained back again coating everything, beach, rocks, cliff base, with foam.

The men on the beach had been knocked over but they hadn't lost their hold on the ropes; they clung to them grimly, their friends' lives depending on them. As the water went down they staggered up, began to heave again, those towards the back looping the coils at their feet as the rope slid through their fingers, as if in some game of tug of war. Before the next wave could hit them three bodies came snaking out of the surf, like fish hooked on a fishing line.

CHAPTER 12

People were already following me down the cliff, risking the climb out of wish to help – or out of curiosity. I heard a woman scream, '"Tis terribule, they'm dead, all drown dead.' Her voice went echoing up the rocks, wild as a curlew's, full of liquid melancholy, to be taken up, expanded into one long wail. 'Terribule, terribule,' the cry was full of disbelief. I disbelieved too. Yet for a moment the men crowded round those three shapes seemed like gods deciding on a sacrifice, and as newcomers scrabbled past, angling for an oracle, I remained anchored where I was, arms unconsciously stretched out in supplication.

Now they were dragging the dark shapes further up the beach out of the way of the incoming waves. The tide was properly on the turn and they had to work fast so as not to be cut off. Like athletes shifting weights, they bent over, stretched, bent over again, unhooking lines, cutting off clothes. There was a shouting, a gesticulating for onlookers to move aside, then a silence. That silence was of the sort that cannot be diverted. It either takes years away, or adds to them, makes the world stand still or spins it into chaos, brings light out of darkness or makes darkness complete. But usually only one or the other, never both at once. Except this time.

A cheer broke out, a clapping of hands, another cry, muted by the wind, as first one shape and a second stirred,

189

coughed or retched, sat up or rather was propped up, was fed brandy, slapped on the back, congratulated. The third shape never stirred although men still were bent over it, trying desperately to force air back into its lungs, trying somehow to staunch the gash that streaked its head redder than the red of its hair.

I stayed long enough to see the two brought back to life, to know the third was dead, to watch stretcher bearers, loaded with blankets and flasks, lower stretchers sideways on ropes, to let all the bustle of rescue crowd in upon that little strip. I made no move to join them. That was no place for me. Julian was safe, my brother safe, that was light in darkness. But Jeb was not, and there came chaos.

My legs were heavy as lead as I turned to climb back and without help I would have fallen. Fortunately it seemed that at every ledge someone was waiting to go down, willing to pull me up, like a conveyor belt. The higher I went the louder the rejoicing. Two spared. That was the general shout of relief, two saved. I thought, 'tisn't so. 'Tis only a substitution. One for the price of one. I wanted to cry out against the disproportion of the exchange. The blame laid to my charge became overwhelming and my rejection of the dead man, without explanation, without even attempt or chance to explain, caused more guilt than either Charity or Sir Robert Polleven could dream up.

At the cliff top were more eager hands, more crowding forward, more pressing for news. ''Tis true then,' was the constant cry, 'they got Ben out, by God 'tis some proper job.' They hadn't taken in the fact yet of those other deaths, of Ben's crewmate, and Jeb, but in time they would. They had to. A fishing world is harsh, no room for sentiment. In lives that are a constant battle all is compromise, a struggle assessed in practical ways between profit and loss: first count the gain, then the loss, in human terms as well as fish. But afterwards, there would be mourning time in plenty for both drowned men; Jeb would be remembered. And when he was, the story of his devotion would be woven in, a loyalty so strong that he should risk his life for my brother. And in so doing should also save the man who supplanted him. True or not, that was what would be told of him. And as the legend spread so would that devotion highlight my treachery, that even as our banns were called, even on the brink of marriage, I should have left him for Julian Polleven.

Charity was surrounded by a group of well-wishers who goodnaturedly forgave her earlier insults. She was quiet at last. She had sunk down on the rainsoaked grass, her head buried in her knees, the picture of Grief personified. As she rocked to and fro her excess emotion seemed tasteless. Once more the thought crossed my mind that had Ben drowned she would have assumed the same pose, her grief having nothing to do with him or her children. But then again, who was I to judge what she felt? My thankfulness for Ben was for him himself; his sons and daughter should have their father back. I passed by Charity without a sign. And I would have passed Sir Robert too if he hadn't stopped me.

'Julian's alive?' he asked, even as others nearby were reassuring him of that fact. 'He's safe out of danger? Not harmed in any way?'

He grasped at my arm to support himself, stuttering a little as if even framing questions was difficult. He had taken off his cap and thrown aside his cloak with the obvious intention of going down the cliffs himself and stood there in his rain-stained clothes, immaculate cravat awry, hair streaked in grey strands as if he had been restrained only with greatest difficulty. In that short space of time his face had become lined and drawn; the possibility of his son's drowning had aged him. Only his eyes, like his son's, remained alert, fixed on mine to draw truth out.

We stared at each other for a moment while round him details continued to pour in, in actual fact not at all as I had imagined. The two rescued men had refused to be carried back, were already beginning to flex their limbs, to stand up, move about, wrapped in blankets. 'Tough as steel,' someone boasted.

But Jeb Martin had been equally strong, perhaps stronger. Weakness had not caused that piece of decking to fly up and strike his head, breaking his neck with the same blow; that was bad luck. Or so the story spread. Jeb Martin was already dead when Julian had dragged both him and Ben to shore, it was Julian who had rescued him and Ben; Julian who was the hero of the hour, Sir Robert should be proud. I felt my own heart swell with pride until I read Sir Robert's look.

'I don't care whether my son be coward or hero,' that look said, 'he's survived. And whether he lives or not you shan't have him. He won't marry you, not as long as I'm alive to prevent it.'

Suddenly, all the events of the last few days, even to the impossibility of Jeb's death, diminished under that unyielding animosity, like the mounting of one of those waves. And all the joy which Julian's safety should have brought, which Sir Robert and I should have shared, was destroyed by that Polleven stubbornness.

I nodded to Sir Robert to show I understood although in truth no word was exchanged between us, just one nod, a gesture very like that between the first saved man and his quiet wife, no other needed. But whereas their understanding had been born of trust, a lifetime of it, ours was based on possession, a possessiveness so raw and cruel it brooked no interference.

I thrust aside the helping hands, calmly reached for the borrowed oilskins which had not blown away although they were too wet to put on. Carrying them under my arm I made my way through the assembled villagers who parted quietly. They never said a word to me, either out of respect, or out of sympathy. But when I had pulled myself around the headland along the strung-out ropes I heard talk break out with even deeper humming.

I paused then, my outward calm deceptive. Underneath my thoughts were aswirl. True, even after Julian's return I still had had fears of the father. But events had moved so rapidly, his hatred seemed almost irrelevant in the midst of all the drama. Of course I wanted Julian back, of course I loved him. For the first time it occurred to me that happiness still could come with too high a price. And Sir Robert meant to exact it. That was the dreadful part. And everywhere I looked, every step I took, I was surrounded by other reminders of part of that price.

Below me was Port Zenack Bay where Jeb used to moor the 'Mermaid'; beyond it, the causeway where we used to walk and the village streets where he had remained on guard. I seemed to hear his whistle above the wind, I tensed for the sound of his quick stride. And it seemed wrong, wicked almost, that all that energy should be lost without a chance to ask forgiveness, in loneliness, not even his sister there to mourn him, in sacrifice, there was that word again, in sacrifice for a relationship which Sir Robert Polleven never meant to happen.

In Port Zenack chapel two days ago I had geared myself against Sir Robert. Believing him outside the door, I would have attacked like a tiger. My effort had been superfluous since it hadn't been him after all. For the first time I remembered Ruth Polleven's boast: 'No one does us harm while the Polleven dragons are on guard.' They were all out in force, those dragons; even when death threatened they didn't let down their guard.

When I reached the village I found chaos. Sand and grit were strewn across the cobbles, and in the corners of the fishery debris was packed, broken lobster pots, crab buoys, enough planks of wood to keep us in fires for a winter. The beached boats behind the wall were half-filled with water in which odds and ends of seaweed floated, and great puddles too wide to jump stood among the paving stones. I splashed through them and went towards Corset Alley, where the wind kept up its battering on the chimneys, stepping over shattered tiles and pots as if on a pebbled beach.

Our little cottage was relatively calm although still smell-ing of smoke. Widow Pendar sat at the table with Lily, spooning porridge into her mouth. She must already have heard the news in that way of villagers, and her instinctive good nature now revealed itself in her greeting, fussing at me to come indoors and sit by the fire. 'Dang thing do blow some'at fierce,' she scolded, rattling the poker through the bars, giving voice to her concern by her mild use of epithet.

She didn't mention the wreck or its consequences, she never spoke of Jeb nor Julian, but the way she waggled her finger and said, 'Yer best skirt and blouse be hanging on the hook upstairs, I ironed 'em fer 'ee,' suggested a kind of proprietary interest that she'd not shown before. It would have amused me once, and the way she smiled, an arch smile suggesting she knew who my dressing up was for, and added, 'So get off them wet things, 'ee'll catch yer death.'

This example of village practicality was the last straw. I knew it didn't mean she had forgotten what drowning was, after all her own husband had drowned; it didn't mean she had forgotten Jeb, whom she had dearly loved, or that he was to be cast aside like an empty sack no one had use for, but it felt like it. Off with the old, on with the new . . . with clothes as well as men.

I had started to climb the stairs but halfway up I paused. The narrow stairway set in the wall seemed as steep as those cliffs, the flickering firelight in the grate as treacherous. I felt sweat break out, as if I wasn't soaked already, water streaming from my clothes and dripping upon the carpet. I thought, this is how my Mam felt when she heard of my father's drowning. She must have stood like this, paralysed with grief before coming to her momentous decision. I was little, a couple of years older than Lily when my mother inflicted her terrible hurt. The harm that followed had been irreparable.

Now I had always claimed I had no knowledge of what

she did, it was before my remembering. But I must have known. It seemed to me as I stood there I became party to her thoughts as I never had before. It was as if a curtain which hid that past had been drawn aside, as if when she had hurried me away from that parting with her son, I had heard her pour out her soul in an agony of confession.

'I don't do anything out of selfishness, 'tisn't meself I'm trying to spare, tho' they will accuse me of it. 'Tis to prevent further hurt, my darling.'

And bending down she must have seized me by both shoulders as she had often done in Penwith Farm. 'I wish no harm, do you hear me, I mean no harm to anyone.'

And it seemed to me that only now after all these years I could really understand what she felt, and that like her I now faced a similar choice. And if I didn't choose properly, if I didn't act in the right way, my own child would suffer as Ben and I had done.

I drag you down. I thought, 'I'll not have it so.'

So I turned on the stairs, took up the baby from the kind old woman. 'If Julian Polleven comes looking fer me,' I told her, 'say I've gone home.' And without paying any attention to her protests, I went out of the door and began to walk up the hill, bending almost double in places where the wind came sweeping round unprotected corners.

I knew she tried to run after me, her apron blowing wildly, her voice trailing in feeble protest. I went too fast and she was soon left behind.

The higher up we went the fiercer the wind, although at first the interlocked houses sheltered us from the worst of it and I had enough sense left to wrap the child inside a ,coat to keep her warm. Despite wind and cold I went on walking. I had a mission to perform; as once before it kept me going.

Afterwards they said that we were lucky not to have been swept away by floods, or hit by falling trees or cables, that we traversed dangers like the Israelites crossing the Red Sea. I was strong in those days, used to walking even through a storm, and Lily was used to being carried, so we made good time. When we came to the crossroads that led towards Beth and Jeb's hut, I hesitated but I didn't go down. The hut would remain empty, the sides cave in, soon no one would remember its existence, and the little boat which carried Lily's name would rot away. And all that Christian goodness, those loving spirits would be lost to me as I to them. That too was a price that must be paid. I thought again of Beth, far off, in her Truro home, still oblivious to all that had happened, and once more I held her in my prayers before going on.

The road inland was more sheltered and we made better time although evening was already closing in, a second unusually dark evening for that time of year with no let-up of wind or rain. Away from the coast like this you could still smell the sea and sometimes in the trees hear the sound of it like a distant moaning. I knew the way by heart. Even in my dreams I knew the way.

When we reached the churchyard I paused by the old gravestone, searching out the names from that long-ago shipwreck. I wiped the moss from the top and made space for three more names, for three men who needed a fitting memorial, although the third being unknown to me must wait for recognition. I picked up a flint from the path and scratched in the two names I did know, one long dead, one new, so that Ben Trevarisk the elder and Jeb Martin should receive the acknowledgement they deserved.

Lily had begun to whimper so I stayed a while in the church porch, trying to hush her as the wet dripped from the yew bushes and the grey light turned to dusk. I remember beginning to sing to her, some song I didn't know I knew, a lullaby retrieved also from some forgotten memory. It occurred to me that I had sat there once before when I had felt defeated. I didn't feel defeat today, only a sense of purpose. And it also occurred to me that perhaps I had sat here like this with my mother, perhaps she had rested here with me in her arms when she first left St Marvell and

196

came south looking for shelter and a new life. And as now Lily and I sat huddled together under that stone archway which had been old when the Normans first came to this part of England the plan which had brought me here from Widow Pendar's house formed and hardened, as perhaps my mother's had done.

When, worn out, Lily slept again, I crossed over the road, reached for the key from its former hiding place and opened the gate. On top of the posts the strange mythical beasts stared over my head.

The trees that lined the drive were more overgrown than ever, their branches almost meeting, the driveway itself more pitted and worn as if in the intervening year it had not been used at all. I followed it round until I came to where the bushes ended and I had stood watching the Polleven family on the terrace steps. They were empty too of course and the windows closed but a light shone out from an upstairs room and a door banged somewhere in the rear of the house as if the wind had caught it.

In my nightmares that house never changed, with its broad, bland façade and its imposing appearance, although today it showed signs of storm, the terrace covered with water, the drive littered with branches and leaves torn from the trees. But the meadows stretched away complacently, the river still curved and flowed, year in, year out, through centuries of privilege. Again I thought, who am I to challenge it?

I went up the steps that I had climbed in another age and rang the bell. As then so now I must have seemed a gypsy, drenched and bedraggled. When the little maid, surely it was the same one or her double, opened the door a crack I put out my arm and pushed so hard she let me in.

I'd often wondered what the interior was like; God forgive me, sometimes half-ashamedly I'd let myself imagine what luxury was. I couldn't take in the space, the spread of carpets, the ornate furnishings, paintings, flowers, lights, all those

197

trappings with which the rich and powerful surround themselves. The maid must have started to scream, hand to mouth as if terrified, but perhaps she made no noise, perhaps she recognized me and didn't like to protest; perhaps as before she wanted to help. I stepped resolutely forward and said in a voice that carried, 'Tell Lady Polleven Guinevere Ellis has brought her grandchild.'

I'm not sure Lady Polleven would have remembered me from that long-ago evening either, nor did I look like the dim photograph in the paper she had tried to hide. And I would not have recognized her, quite different from that pale, elegant mother in the blue dress who had leaned on her daughter's arm. Her eyes were red with crying and her fair hair had straggled loose, she looked as unkempt as I did. 'Who is it?' she was crying over the balustrade. She hurried across the landing, feeling for a foothold and clinging to the rail as if afraid of falling. 'Is that you, Julian?'

She sounded so pitiful that like her son I felt a twinge of regret. I could see what he meant by indecision; it was written in every move which took her from the shelter of her room. She must have gone into seclusion there since his return, perhaps since he forced her to tell him where I was. For a moment I faltered, indecisive myself. Not so my daughter. The lights and noise jarred her awake. She began to wail loudly, making no secret of her presence.

'Who is it?' Lady Polleven's voice sharpened. She leaned over, peering down into the semi-darkness of the hall. 'What's that noise?' And then, 'Whose child is it?' she asked in the same tone that Julian had used.

As she now descended the staircase, slow step by step, I drew her out of hiding, I forced her into collusion with my plan, trusting now in my own instincts, and hers. *She's sweet and kind, incapable of wrong.* I thought, yes, and she adores her son. That's something he didn't count on. She'll not have wrong done to him. So I unwound the baby who cried the louder at the indignity, and when Lady Polleven reached the hall, I held her out.

198

She didn't look her best either, my beautiful Lily, red-faced and furious, her fists flailing and her eyes, those lovely Polleven eyes, filled with tears. I could see Lady Polleven was taken aback then, as she looked and listened, fascinated, captivated, smitten, all her dormant loving taking over. 'Don't stand there,' she cried, and to the little maid, 'Quick, heat milk, bring water and fresh towels.'

She hurried before me into a panelled room where the curtains were drawn to shut out the encroaching twilight. Matches were set to the fire, lights came on, chairs were drawn up. Before I could measure success coat and shoes were removed, towels brought to dry hair and face, tea served in china cups. Wrapped in fresh linen and propped on a sofa between brocaded pillows, Lily drank from a bottle and wriggled her toes. Her grandmother and I sat on either side and adored. And when I was sure adoration had done its work, and Lady Polleven had no resistance left, 'Now,' I said, 'how to manage when the men return.'

I had already told her all she needed to know of Julian's bravery, and thinking of the danger she had smiled as she wept. So did I, both of us taking comfort in the other. When she now said, 'His father's with him still, but Ruth's off with friends,' I knew she was weakening. And when she added, 'His bark's worse than his bite, you know,' her echo of her son's words put her on my side.

For a second we sat in silence, listening to the splutter of the fire, and the gurgling of a baby who, whether we wished it or not, had become a pawn in the coming battle. The sudden quiet was off-putting after so many hours of storm, instinctively one almost wanted to shout it down. She said, 'They'll be here soon. Someone brought a message. Sir Robert's car is to fetch them; Julian's too lame to walk.'

She didn't add, 'He's kept his father waiting while he went for you,' but I guessed that was what had happened. And if he had seen Widow Pendar she would have told him what I'd said.

We sat on in silence. When car wheels crunched up under

the windows and doors slammed, Lady Polleven half got up. The door bell pealed, the curtains shifted, rain splattered again on the coals.

'What the devil are you doing?' Sir Robert peered in the half-opened door and looked crossly at his wife. He was testy: waiting about in the wet had not improved his temper. 'Julian's gone upstairs to change. He's . . .'

His voice broke off, he advanced one hasty stride. Then coldly, 'What's she doing here?'

He ignored his wife, her instinctive strangled protest nothing new, stopped again and peered over the edge of the sofa. Like his son in Widow Pendar's cottage, he was silenced by the picture of domesticity.

Behind him Julian said, 'That's Lily.'

He was leaning on his father's stick, his limp very pronounced. He sounded tired and his face was lined like his father's, scored down one side where shingle and rocks had scraped. But his eyes shone. 'That's my daughter,' he now said, 'and her mother, Guinevere. Guinevere whom I'm going to marry and live with happily ever after.'

He smiled at me, and stretched out his hand. I took it. It felt good, warm and strong and confident, although the palm was cut and callused. 'Come out of the storm,' he said.

After a while he added, 'You know Guinevere, I think.' Beneath the casual tone his own pride showed. Recognize her, it said. And the note of warning, be careful if you don't.

I got up, dragged myself up for I was suddenly more tired than I remembered, as if the wet and cold had stiffened in my bones. 'You wanted Lily,' I said to Sir Robert. 'So I've brought her to you. But she belongs to all of us. There's no need to have her for your own, we all can share. And there's no need either to think I'll take your son away. 'Tisn't taking away that's wanted, 'tis putting together.'

'That's my Jenny,' Julian said. He smiled again, touched my hair to smooth it down. 'And speaking of putting together, that's what I need myself.' He felt his face along the jaw and grimaced. Then, suddenly more serious, he turned to me as if we were alone. 'I have a message for you too, sweetheart,' he said, his eyes dark. 'It will grieve you but it must be said. "Tell her I wish her well," that was Jeb's message. Nothing else, but it should do.'

He added softly now, 'It's no more than what I wished when I first misunderstood you were married. I can tell you it was meant. I was proud to know him,' he said simply. 'Without his help I'd have been done for. I'd never have got off the beach. Coming in was a nothing compared with that.'

He smiled his open generous smile. 'He couldn't give us anything we needed more, Jenny, that was his blessing.'

He turned back to his parents. 'Now give us yours,' he said.

Sir Robert Polleven drew himself up. Despite the wet he still looked imposing, hair slicked back into place, a handsome man. Beside him his wife was reduced to insignificance, incapable of anything. But she spoke first.

'My dear Julian,' Lady Polleven's voice was low but it carried, 'my dear son, I prayed for your return, even when they said you had been killed. And all afternoon I've been praying. And here you are back safe and sound. A hero, that's what they call you.' And as Julian made a small deprecating gesture, 'You deserve some reward, more than we've given you so far. Whatever you want for yourself I want for you. As for Guinevere . . .' She turned, Julian's name for me sounding strange, making me something that I wasn't. She put out her hand. The skin was soft and smooth, a lady's hand that had never worked for anything. She wouldn't know what work was, would have no idea how the fisher women in Port Zenack lived and yet if asked would have wished them no harm. 'As for Guinevere,' she said, 'you've had a hard homecoming too.'

It was probably the longest speech she had made in years as her husband's startled look showed. I don't know if it influenced him more than it did his son, for Julian suddenly went up to his mother and hugged her, but it must have had some effect. And perhaps those anxious lonely moments on the cliffs and the suspense had undermined his resistance more than he knew. I don't mean he capitulated at once, he'd not do that, nor even that he accepted me, and welcome would be out of the question. But he loved his son. Faced with his wife's resistance and Julian's resolution he must have felt he had little choice. And perhaps some part of him knew just what wrong he had contemplated, and how painful the consequence. I guess at these things. Then, all he said was, 'It's too late to talk tonight,' adding, in grudging tones to be sure, 'Since you're all so determined I wash my hands of you. Now get some dry clothes on so we can eat.'

When he was gone, 'He'll come round,' Julian said confidently. 'Don't worry, my love, it's going to be alright.'

That's a simple expression too for all that it has to carry, reason, result, that whole interlinking of cause and effect.

Perhaps he guessed what I was thinking for again he smiled. 'I told you we've a lifetime on our side,' he whispered. We had.

I don't say either it was always easy, or that bridges can be built overnight. We didn't live at Polleven Manor and until Ruth herself married, our visits there were always constrained. But Lady Polleven was a frequent visitor to our own small farm, beloved by her grandchildren, especially by Lily with whom she always had some special bond. And as we prospered even Sir Robert showed more appreciation of our way of life, enhanced by the birth of a second child, a second Robert, for him to spoil. He liked the idea of an heir to shower gifts on. In my own family, Ben's gratitude was all that it should have been, even Charity's hostility could not diminish that. When, with Julian's help, Ben finally acquired the boat he'd always dreamed of, he and his sons' future was secured. And after we were settled on our farm, Emma often visited us, gradually her stay becoming permanent.

In a real sense she became another daughter, more secure in our house than in her own. Emma Trevarisk and Lily Polleven grew up like sisters, a relationship which, just as Emma had once explained, became acceptable to all parties 'since the marriage', (an expression which in time reverted to a family joke, all the pain it had once caused forgotten).

I never saw Beth Martin again and all attempts to keep in touch failed. Julian once tried to meet her, but even that was unsuccessful, although he would not say how or why. I knew only that her marriage to Mark Chote produced children and she was happy in her new life. Nor did I ever take my children back to see my mother, nor did we go to Penwith Farm, although after Farmer Penwith's death she did inherit it as she had dreamed, and lived alone, a prosperous widow. She came once or twice to that little inn where we were meant to have had our Christmas meeting. 'She's like 'ee, Jenny,' she said once of Lily, 'her soul's in her eyes. And like 'ee she'll hold on tight, pity any man she's after.'

Lily laughed and tossed her hair, of an age to scorn boys, but the older Emma looked thoughtful. Julian put an arm about them both and looked at me over their heads. 'Can't spare either of my daughters,' he said, 'can't spare their mother either.'

I knew what he was remembering. For that first night, after we had endured a formidable meal in the formal dining room, I wrapped in one of Ruth's dresses which proved too large, and Lily bedded down on cushions by my feet, and after I was shown to a bedroom, huge and elegant, big as Widow Pendar's whole house, there was a tapping at the door. It was Lady Polleven.

'I hope you will be comfortable,' she said, her voice formal too, the perfect hostess, offering me anything I wanted.

'Thanks, mother,' Julian's voice came from behind her, full of mischief. 'I'll take care of that.'

He waited until she had withdrawn, then came inside and barred the door. He was still dressed in rough clothes for he hadn't changed for 'dinner' as they called it, a nightmare meal of strange foods and wines, and he still was limping. Now he sat down on the edge of the bed, and began to unlace his boots.

'She'd better get used to it,' he told me, 'mother, I mean. When the telephone's back in order and the road's clear we'll find someone to marry us, but until then I've no time to waste.'

His arm came round my waist, he drew me down beside him. 'Can't spare you for a moment,' he said.

In her makeshift cot Lily murmured, shifted, was still. Outside the thick walls, the wind soughed. All night long Julian and I lay together, that was our true homecoming.